MAGGIE SHAYNE

EMBRACE THE TWILIGHT

MIRA®

ISBN 0-7394-3205-2

EMBRACE THE TWILIGHT

Copyright © 2003 by Margaret Benson.

Printed in U.S.A.

To Christine Norris, just because.

1

The *gorgio* dropped three pieces of silver into the woman's palm. It was a beautiful palm, a beautiful hand, Will noticed as she closed it into a fist. Dark and slender, but strong, not fragile looking, as slender hands tended to be. She wore rings on every finger, and gold and silver bangles on her wrists, which made tinkling music every time she moved.

"Thank you," she told the pale-skinned man. "When the predictions come true, tell your friends. And be sure they ask for Sarafina when they come."

He backed away, nodding, thanking her profusely, but never turning his back on her all the way out. As soon as his feet touched the ground outside her wagon-tent, he crossed himself and ran away.

The *gorgios* might deny it, Sarafina thought, but they were every bit as superstitious as the Gypsies. Will thought it was odd that he could hear what she was thinking as well as what she said aloud. It was almost as if he had retreated into *her* mind to escape the pain, instead of his own.

But he was distracted from the odd notion by her smile. She smiled slowly, and it transformed her face from dark and sullen and exotic to something of

sheer, glowing beauty. He loved her. Everything
about her, from her smooth olive-bronze skin to the
masses of raven hair curling wildly over her back and
shoulders. He loved her lips, how full they were, how
ripe. He loved her eyes, gleaming onyx gemstones,
set very wide beneath heavy brows most women
would pluck down to nothing.

She tucked the coins into the heavy drawstring
pouch that dangled from one of the colorful sashes at
her waist. "Ten already this week," she whispered,
as she leaned over the table to drop a black silk scarf
over the crystal globe that held court in its center.
The "table" was an upturned wooden crate covered
in more silk scarves, as was the chair. The chair on
the other side of the table, the one for the customers,
was also a crate, but an undressed one. She wasn't
about to have one of *them* sitting on her silk.

Andre. She was thinking of Andre now.

It gave Will a bitter pang to realize it, to feel the
little leap of her heart when she thought of the man,
but he stayed with her all the same, like a shadow
hidden within her own. She left the tent, her strong,
bare feet padding down the fold-up steps of the
wagon, then pressing onto the cool brown earth as
she crossed the camp. Will loved tagging along when
she went outside, because the camp was such a fas-
cinating sight; concentric circles of painted wagons
and tents, and odd combinations of the two. Bells and
prisms hung from most of them. At the center was a
communal fire, though many smaller ones burned

here and there. The center was where people met.
There was often music, dancing. The women in their
brightly colored skirts, with their countless scarves
trailing them like comet tails as they whirled. The
men with their tight-fitting trousers, and red and gold
vests. The musicians with their violins and tambou-
rines and pipes.

They were a beautiful, vibrant people, these Gypsies. He didn't know *where* they were. He was un-
certain *when* they were. Not that it mattered, since
they were mere figments of his imagination.

Too vivid, too detailed, to be real.

Many greeted Sarafina as she passed. The younger
ones bowed respectfully, while the elders looked upon
her as an equal. She was spectacular, walking with
her head high and her hips swaying, proud of who
she was.

She was a gifted seer, and she used that gift to
bring wealth to the tribe. That earned her the honor
and respect of the group, just as it did her far less
worthy sister. But Will worried about the woman.
Lately, she'd been feeling poorly, and her gifts of
prophecy refused to tell her why.

The fire in the center of the camp jumped and
danced, yellow-orange flames spreading a pool of
light in the midst of the pitch-black ocean of night.
The wood smoke smelled good, warm and tangy and
familiar. Many of the people had gathered around the
fire that night, listening as the old ones told tales.
Stories of adventures and the misdeeds of their youth

brought gasps and then laughter from those gathered around to hear.

Sarafina loved these people. They were her family, and family was all that mattered to her. And they loved her in return. Except, of course, for her sister. Katerina was her own blood, but she had hated her sister from the moment Sarafina had drawn her first breath. Sarafina liked to pretend the feeling was mutual.

It wasn't. Her sister's hatred ate at her like a cancer.

Katerina's *vardo* stood on the opposite side of the camp from Sarafina's, as was always the case wherever the tribe made camp. As Sarafina approached it, leaving the light of the fire far behind, a dark form emerged from the wagon, turned and hurried away into the shadows. A man, Will thought, but he was gone before giving either of them more than a brief glance.

Sarafina stepped up and reached for the door flap, and the bells attached to it tinkled as she drew it open and stepped inside.

Her sister looked up at her with an expectant smile that turned to a grimace the moment she saw who it was. They were so different, the two of them. Katerina's black hair was long and perfectly straight. Her eyes were small, close set and round. They looked like cold pebbles. Shark's eyes.

"Did you think your lover had returned, Katerina?" Sarafina asked with an edge in her voice. "So sorry to disappoint you."

"You've done nothing but disappoint me from the day our mother died giving birth to you, little sister. Why begin apologizing for it now?"

The words stung. Will could feel Sarafina's pain as acutely as she herself felt it. But her heart had toughened and formed calluses over the years, thanks to her sister's constant attacks. It didn't hurt as much as it would have once.

Smiling, Fina lifted her coin pouch in her palm, bouncing it slightly so the coins inside jangled. "Ten *gorgios* have come to see me this week. *Ten*, Katerina. Twice as many as have sought *you* out for divination."

Her sister shrugged. "Your wagon is nearer the road than mine."

"They ask for me by name," Sarafina countered. "They come to me because I am the most skilled seer in this camp, and because word of my abilities has spread throughout the town. I'll have still more of them crossing my palm with silver next week. And I predict *you'll* have even fewer."

"Bah! By the week after that, when not one of your false predictions has come to pass, they'll see that your only talent lies in deception, and they'll begin seeking my counsel instead." Katerina tossed her hair. "We both know the truth. Not only am I the more gifted diviner, I am the rightful *Shuvani* of this tribe, Sarafina."

Will cringed inwardly when he heard that, knowing there was not much that could make Sarafina angrier.

No one got away with calling her gift into question, much less questioning her status as one of the tribe's two wise women. Most tribes had only one. There was no question that this tribe would have had only one, as well, had Sarafina been firstborn.

"Thanks to your false predictions, the whites will likely brand all Gypsies liars and cheats," Katerina went on. "And we'll be forced to move on, because of you, yet again."

"My predictions are *not* lies! I am a far better seer than you, and you know it."

"Not so great a seer, I think. Or you would know the identity of the man who just left my *vardo*."

The words were a blow that knocked the very breath out of Sarafina's chest. She looked around her sister's tented wagon, even as Will whispered to her to be calm, to resist rising to her sister's bait. But he knew she couldn't hear him. She never could.

The sleeping pallet was untidy, the blankets upon it rumpled and askew. The table in the corner, not a crate like Sarafina's, but a real table that had belonged to their mother, held no crystal, no cards, but a blazing oil lamp, two tin cups and a wine jug lying, uncorked, on its side.

Katerina's soft laughter brought her sister's head around fast.

"He's far too good for you, you know. But he knows now that a real woman desires him."

"Are you saying it was Andre I saw creeping away from here as I approached?"

Will thought that if Katerina valued her life, she would deny it.

"Of course it was Andre. He's the handsomest, the strongest, the wealthiest man in the camp. I couldn't very well let *you* have him."

"*Bi lacho* bitch!" Fina shrieked the words even as she lunged forward. She brought her hand across her sister's face, nails slashing her cheek.

Katerina didn't even pause to give note to the pain. She lurched forward, eyes blazing, arms flailing. The two collided, tumbled to the floor and rolled in a tangle of skirts and scarves, ring bedecked hands and bangled arms. They hit the table, and it tipped over. The oil lamp shattered, and the oil spread in a pool of blue flame. Panic rose in Will's chest as they pummeled and bit and clawed each other, both of them shrieking.

Will tried to shout a warning. He focused everything in him on Sarafina and on shouting one word. *Fire!*

Sarafina shoved her sister off her in one mighty thrust, looking around as if she'd heard something. Will realized, though, that a crowd had gathered outside the tent, probably drawn by the commotion of the fight. They were shouting at her, too. He had no way of knowing which voice she had heard. It didn't matter—not now. He saw her face change as she realized the entire wagon was ablaze.

"Look what you've done!" Katerina screamed. "We'll burn alive because of you!"

Sarafina looked for a way out, but the fire was licking at the sides of the tent all around them. Then, suddenly, someone plunged in through the flames. A form, swathed in blankets. He dropped his makeshift cloak. It was Andre, his dark eyes blazing.

"Wrap yourselves in blankets," he ordered. "Quickly!"

Both women hastened to obey, as Andre grabbed the water vessel from near Katerina's bed and doused them with it. Then he retrieved his own blanket from the floor. "Run, right through here," he said, pointing. "You must run as fast as you can. If you hesitate, you will die." He gathered Katerina in his left arm, Sarafina in his right. Will braced himself, all but holding his breath. "Now!" Andre shouted.

Sarafina closed her eyes and plunged into the wall of fire. There was searing heat on her face and on her feet, but only briefly. An instant of torture, and then she was falling to the cool earth.

She landed hard. Wrestling free of the dampened blanket, she sat up, the fire blazing behind her. Will was nearly limp with relief that she was all right.

Most of the tribe surrounded her, looking down at her and her sister, who had landed close beside her, in stark disapproval as the flames lit their soot-streaked faces. Will knew that Sarafina's dignity was deeply wounded, as was, perhaps, her standing with the tribe.

"It was all her!" Katerina shouted, scrambling to her feet. "She accused me of trying to steal her man

and attacked me. By the Gods, all I have is gone!''
she cried, waving a helpless arm at the leaping flames.

People gasped, muttered, shook their heads in pity
as Katerina's tent and her every possession burned to
cinders before their eyes.

"She lies," Sarafina said. "It was she who began
this. I only finished it."

Andre bent to help her to her feet, pausing a moment to study her face, then pulling her close to him.
His arms went around her, holding her intimately,
tightly. Will writhed with jealousy.

"Oh, Sarafina, tell me you don't believe that I
could be tempted to another. It's you I love. You I'll
take as wife. No one else."

Sarafina stared at him, and she suddenly understood
that her sister had lied to her. Katerina was only trying
to plant seeds of doubt that would grow to destroy
the love she and Andre shared, she told herself. *Someone* had crept away from Katerina's *vardo* tonight,
but it hadn't been Andre.

Will shook his head slowly, whispering in his
mind, in *her* mind, "Oh, Sarafina, don't be such a
fool."

Sarafina glared at her sister in triumph, but then
she went still at the look Katerina returned. It was
cold, steely and deadly.

Before she could begin to understand what that
look might mean, there was a horrifying scream that
rent the night from somewhere beyond the camp.

Everyone went stiff and still for one brief moment, as if the sound had turned them all to stone.

"No. For the love of *Devel,* not again," someone whispered. Will thought it was Gervaise, the reigning chieftain of the tribe. He didn't know what Gervaise meant and wondered if he was about to find out.

But before he could learn anything further, he was shocked out of the fantasy by the sensation of his lungs slowly filling with ice water.

A hand clasped him by his hair and jerked his head out of the tub of frigid water. Will dragged in a desperate, hungry breath, before that hand shoved his head into the tub again, holding him under.

His hands were bound together behind his back, his legs bound at the ankles. His body screamed with pain, pain he had managed to escape only moments before. But all that dulled beside the stabbing need in his lungs as they spasmed in search of air. Small red explosions danced behind his tightly closed eyes. He was going to pass out, and then he would drown.

The hand jerked him out of the water again, and even as Will sucked in greedy, noisy breaths, slammed him down into a small, ladder-back chair.

Water ran from his hair and face, soaking his ragged, filthy shirt.

A bearded man wearing a spotless white headdress lifted Will's chin and stared down at him, then spoke to one of the guards, using one of the tribal dialects in which Will was fluent, though he had managed to keep that fact from them...thus far.

"He has returned to his body. You may resume the torture now."

"Why should we waste our time? He will only leave again when the pain becomes too much for him. How does he do it? Where does he go?"

The first man shrugged, crossing the floor of the cave to where a fire had been burning earlier. It was now a bed of glowing coals. They'd placed long iron rods in the embers, and it was one of these the man pulled out, using a piece of fabric as a makeshift pot holder. The hotter end was neon-orange and reminded Will of the beer sign hanging in his favorite bar back home.

"Now, Colonel Stone," the man said, speaking heavily accented English. "You will tell me what I wish to know."

"I've told you already," he said softly, though it hurt like hell to talk, because of his split, swollen lips and the dryness of his throat. "There are no American spies in your training camps."

There were, actually. There were thirteen, to be exact, and Will knew who they were, what names they were using and what camps they had infiltrated. They would have received word of his capture by now. They would remember their training, and they would know exactly what to do, where to go, when to meet there for extraction. It would take them another forty-eight hours to get out of harm's way, he thought.

Judging the passage of time was tricky, given the circumstances.

He had to hold out until the men were safely out of the country.

"If there are no spies, then how do the Americans always seem to know our plans?"

Will didn't shrug. The movement would have hurt too much. "Technology?"

The man laid the cherry-red end of the iron flat across Will's chest. The pain was beyond bearing, and he tipped his head back and grated his teeth against it, while the smell of his own burning flesh choked him.

Even when the rod was lifted away, the pain remained. Burning, scorching pain deep inside him. He closed his eyes, tried to find that place inside his mind where he'd been hiding before. That place where the pain couldn't reach him. He saw the woman, standing far in the distant reaches of his subconscious. Sarafina, the dark, exotic fantasy woman who lived out her tales in his mind so vividly that she swept him away from the torture, the pain.

He'd stumbled upon her quite by accident, when they had beaten him nearly unconscious. He'd been hovering on the edge of oblivion when he'd seen her in his mind's eye. Just her eyes, glowing black eyes. He found himself focusing on those eyes, getting caught in them, sinking slowly into their black-water depths, into darkness. He'd felt himself sinking deeper, and as he did, the pain vanished. Once it fell away behind him, he emerged on the other side, in some other place and time, as a silent, invisible observer of the woman's life.

Ever since that first time, he'd found he could use the pain to find that place again. The trick was to just give himself over to the agony, not to fight it, but to embrace it. And then he would close his eyes and search for hers. All he had to do was find her eyes, stare into them, and he would sink again into her world, where the pain couldn't reach him.

She was pure fantasy, as was her story. He knew that. But she was also his salvation. And the salvation of those thirteen Americans who would be tortured to death unless he kept their names secret.

So he closed his eyes as they placed the hot brands on his skin. He relaxed his jaw and tried not to fight the pain. He let the pain drive him closer to her, closer, until she turned and faced him. Her eyes opened wide as he fixed his upon them and rushed willingly into their cool black depths. Then he was completely immersed, having left his body far, far behind. He swam, every stroke taking him farther. And he wondered if one of these times his captors would do him the favor of simply killing him, so that he could remain in that other place. But would it remain, opening, welcoming him inside? His own custom-imagined heaven? Or would it vanish as his brain cells slowly died?

At this point, he wasn't certain he cared.

2

For only a moment, Sarafina felt an alien presence in her mind. As if someone else, someone unseen, were watching her. Watching *over* her.

Many times she had felt this unknown presence. Many times. She sensed him—and yes, she knew he was male, though how she knew, she could not have said. He *felt* male. He was protective of her. He filled her with warmth and a sensation of security. As if there were one all-powerful spirit in the entire world, and its only job was to take care of her. Love her. Watch over her.

She thought of him as her guardian. Her guide. And each time he came, she thought she came a bit closer to being able to see him, speak to him, touch him. She'd heard him this time—very briefly, but clearly.

She tried to focus on her beloved spirit, but he seemed to withdraw. Fina sighed in stark disappointment before shaking away the feeling, and hurrying to join the others, who were already racing into the woods, toward the sound of the horrible screams. Like her, most of them knew already what they would find.

She was the fastest runner, despite her ill health of late. More than that, she knew exactly where to go.

How she knew, she could not have said. Some dark instinct led her, and she didn't question it. She was a gifted diviner and a *Shuvani*. Knowing things she oughtn't know was a part of that. So she quickly caught up to the tribe, then broke off from them, veering through the woods at an angle that led her unerringly to the spot.

She came upon the two of them moments before anyone else. Melina, an old woman, a cousin of Sarafina's dead mother, crouched on the ground, her body bent over that of her teenage daughter, Belinda. A torch lay on the ground beside them, its flame struggling to survive. Sarafina picked it up to better see the old woman rocking and weeping, and the young one lying so utterly still. By the light of the torch, Belinda's slender arms and her face were as white as snow, and her eyes were open wide but already bore the unmistakable glaze of death.

Placing a hand on Melina's shuddering back, Sarafina said, "Come, rise up away from her. She is gone from this world now."

Sobbing, the woman straightened her back, lifted her head and wailed in anguish as tears streamed over her weathered face. "My Belinda is dead, killed by a demon!"

"Come." The others were arriving now, drawn by her cries, many of them bearing torches of their own. Sarafina helped the old woman to her feet, hugged her close and looked over her quivering shoulder, down at Belinda. She had been more than a cousin.

She had been a friend. Lifting her torch higher, Sarafina let her gaze skim the girl's pale throat, until she saw what she had known she would see. Two small wounds, scarlet ribbons of blood trailing from each of them.

Something deep inside her stirred, as if waking from a long slumber. She couldn't take her eyes from the wounds, and involuntarily, she licked her lips.

"It's happened again," a man said. It was Andre, standing near her. Katerina was right beside him, watching her sister with narrow eyes. Had she noticed Sarafina's odd reaction to the scent of fresh blood?

She forced herself not to look at the body again, nor at the two wounds in its throat. But the scent of the kill made her nostrils flare and her stomach clench into a hungry knot. Sickening. She detested her body for reacting this way yet again.

And just like the other times, she could sense the creature that had done this. It was near, she realized suddenly, and she shot her glance toward the edges of the gathered group, where small children with huge, frightened eyes clung to their mothers' skirts.

"Get the children away from here," she whispered, pointing at the little ones.

The most respected man in the tribe, the Chieftain, Gervaise, looked at her, crooking a dark brow. "Sarafina?"

"It's here," she told him, her voice dropping to a bare whisper. "It is still here, I tell you. Gervaise, get the children away."

There was no hesitation. Gervaise gave a nod, and nearly everyone obeyed, turning to hurry back toward camp, all of them gathering the children close as they went. Several of the young men remained, including Andre. Katerina stayed, as well.

"Set guards around the camp," Gervaise said to the young men who stood awaiting his word. "Put others to work building the coffin. Two of you, go fetch weapons and come back here. This spot shall be guarded until dawn." The men rushed off to obey.

"How did you know?" Katerina whispered.

Sarafina trembled at the tone of her sister's voice. She *had* noticed. She'd noticed Sarafina being the first to arrive, and she'd noticed her reaction to the sight of the demon's kill—neither one for the first time. "How did you *not* know?" Sarafina asked her. "You're supposed to be a seer, like me."

"Unlike you, I have no bond to demons."

"Do not accuse me, sister. You know nothing of this."

"It's the same as the other times," Andre said, rising slowly from Belinda's body. He'd examined the wounds, all without touching the corpse. Then he glanced at the weeping old mother. "I am so very sorry, Melina."

"The demon has found us again. We must bury her quickly and move on," someone said.

"What good will it do?" Katerina asked. "It will only pursue us, find us again, just as it has ever since our tribe was cursed by the birth of my dear little sister.''

Melina gasped, and Gervaise frowned deeply. Andre put his hand on Katerina's shoulder. ''This is not the time—''

''You all must know it's true! The first time this demon took one of our people was the summer Sarafina was born. I've studied on this, consulted the spirits. Every sign, every omen, tells me she is somehow bound to the creature that stalks us. She's the reason it plagues us so.''

''That's madness!'' Sarafina shouted. She looked at the faces around her, the speculation in them as they studied her.

''You knew it was near,'' Katerina said. ''You *always* seem to know.''

''I am a seer.''

''It attacks only by night. You, more and more, are becoming a creature of the night yourself. Up until all hours, sleeping long into the day.'' Her gaze swept the others. ''You've all seen it.''

Melina nodded her head in agreement. ''It's true.''

''I sleep when I'm sleepy,'' Sarafina said softly. ''That does not mean I am in league with this creature.''

Katerina looked around her, perhaps saw the doubt of her accusations in some of those faces, and shrugged. ''If it isn't you the demon follows so persistently, then I say we should put it to the test.''

Frowning, Sarafina searched her sister's face, her eyes, for some clue what she was up to. "Test?"

"Leave us. Leave the tribe. Stay behind this time while the rest of us move on. If the demon follows again, even without you among us, that will be proof of your innocence."

Andre stepped forward, putting a protective arm around Sarafina's shoulders. "I won't permit it, Katerina."

"Nor will I," said Gervaise. He studied Sarafina's face, leaning heavily on his staff, his back bowed and his once jet hair long since gone to silver. "We are all frightened and aggrieved at the loss of Belinda. But turning against one another is not the answer. We must not let this evil divide us."

Now everyone present was nodding, including the two young men who had returned from the camp with rifles. Everyone except for Katerina.

Gervaise fixed his stern gaze on the two sisters. "You two will prepare Belinda for burial."

Katerina paled visibly. Sarafina felt her own blood run cold at the prospect and blurted, "Surely you can hire a pair of *gorgios*—"

"You two will do it."

"With respect, Gervaise," Katerina said, "my home and all my possessions have burned in a fire caused by my sister's carelessness. I must see to it that I have shelter tonight."

Gervaise crooked a brow and rubbed his chin in thought. He truly was the wisest man in the village, but he was unused to having his commands questioned. "You, Katerina, will share your sister's shelter and her possessions. It is high time the two of you learned the meaning of family." Then he glanced at Belinda, and his voice softened to a mere whisper. "Do neither of you understand the role you play? Your mother is dead, and, since last summer, your grandmother, too. You are the seers. And you are the *Shuvani*."

Melina shook her head. "I said from the start, they are too young to be the tribe's wise women."

"They are all we have." Gervaise patted her gently before refocusing on the two sisters. "Now do your duty to Belinda. She lies dead while you fuss and fight. Do not shame us." He glanced at them. "Belinda is trapped between the worlds. You know what must be done?"

"I know," Sarafina said softly. She glanced at her sister. "Gather sticks," she said. "We'll need a small fire."

Gervaise set the young men a few paces away on either side, close enough to guard the women while they worked over the body, but far enough away to give them the privacy that was necessary for the rite. Katerina had taken Melina back to camp, to set her to work gathering the clothes with which Belinda would be buried. While she was gone, Sarafina arranged twigs and sticks carefully on the ground beside her cousin, but not too close.

Katerina returned, three bundles of dried herbs in her hands. She handed her sister a bit of each. "Are we ready to begin?" she asked.

Sarafina nodded, and lowered her torch to the pile of twigs and sticks. It caught on the first try, a very good omen. The flames spread rapidly. Fina jammed the torch into a notch in a nearby tree.

"First the thyme," she said, and they each tossed a handful of the herb into the fire.

"Next the sage," Katerina whispered. "And last the rosemary."

They cast the remaining herbs into the fire in the correct order, then began to walk backward and countersunwise around it as fragrant drafts of smoke billowed to the heavens. "Belinda Rosemerta Prastika," they whispered together. They walked round the fire, round the body, and increased their pace, chanting the name of their cousin over and over, a little louder each time. Seven times around the fire they went, and Sarafina felt the power they raised growing stronger all the while. At the end of the seventh time around, they stopped, each at the same instant, faced the body and lifted their hands.

Sarafina felt the energy—and, she hoped, her cousin's spirit with it—shoot forth from the circle they had trod, straight into the heavens.

Letting their bodies relax, they stood still and silent, each in her own thoughts.

Sarafina closed her eyes and sighing, lowered herself to the ground.

"The ritual is the job of the *Shuvani*," Katerina said. "One of honor. And we have done it well. Preparing the body is not."

Handling a dead body was a despised task among the tribe. When their own grandmother had passed, she had been bathed and dressed in her finest clothes even while she lay dying. No Gypsy wanted to touch the dead.

"Perhaps Gervaise wishes to teach us the lesson of humility," Sarafina suggested. "Quiet, now. Melina returns."

Melina carried a bundle of clothing, a pail of water scented with herbs and oils, and a soft cloth. She glanced at the small fire that had been left to burn itself out but said nothing. She had lived a long time and had no doubt seen the fire before. She knew better than to ask its meaning. The death rites were secret, known only to the *Shuvani*, passed from grandmother to granddaughter. Sarafina and her sister had learned them from their grandmother, as they had so many other things.

Melina knelt, watching in silence, waiting for the two of them to do the job they had been given. Sarafina thought in that moment, that even her hardhearted sister felt moved.

So they knelt, and they gently undressed the shell that had been Belinda. They washed the young woman carefully, even though every touch made chills race up Sarafina's spine. Belinda was not yet cold, but cool to the touch. She tried to keep the cloth between her palm and Belinda's flesh, but sometimes it slipped.

When the washing was finished, the two women unrolled and unfolded the red fabric Melina had brought; then they laid it out beside Belinda. Sarafina rolled the dead woman up onto one side, because she knew that while touching the corpse chilled her to her very marrow, her sister simply could not bring herself to do it. So she rolled poor Belinda, and Katerina tucked the cloth beneath her as far as she could manage. Then Fina lowered the body gently onto the cloth and rolled it up onto its other side, so Katerina could pull the fabric through.

They did a good job of it, Sarafina thought. The body rested almost perfectly centered on the open bolt of scarlet cloth.

Sarafina laid a small bit of fabric, cut in the shape of a perfect circle, upon Belinda's chest. Then, she took one side of the cloth, and her sister took the other, and they wrapped Belinda in it as carefully as they would have wrapped a baby, leaving only her head and her bare feet uncovered.

"I intended to use that bolt of cloth to make a dress for her," Melina whispered. "Now it becomes her shroud." She unfolded the clothing she had brought, turning the blouse and skirt inside out before refolding them carefully and stacking them beside her daughter's body.

The little fire had died to smoking remains by the

time they had finished. Katerina leaned over the water pail to scrub her hands.

"There should be more light," Melina whispered. "We mustn't let her lie in the dark this way."

"My work here is done," Katerina said, straightening and wiping her hands on her skirts. "I'm returning to camp. I'll send someone back with lanterns."

Melina only nodded, not even watching her go. When the sounds of her footsteps died away, she glanced at Sarafina. "You may as well go, too. I'll watch over her until morning."

"I'm staying with you," Sarafina replied. "I won't leave you alone."

Melina lifted her head, met Fina's eyes, and for a moment seemed to be searching them. Almost as if she were not entirely comfortable staying alone with her. It was dark in the hardwood forest. Oaks and elms towered around them, and the ground was thick with ferns and weeds. Only that single torch spilled a circle of pale light around the two of them, and it was burning low. The night was silent, eerily so.

Then Melina glanced past her, at a sound from one of the young men who stood guard, and she seemed to relax a bit. Sarafina sat down on the ground beside the slender body wrapped in red cloth and wondered why anyone, even a demon, would want to murder her cousin so cruelly.

I didn't kill her, I set her free, and deep down you know it's true.

Sarafina's head rose with a snap at the clear sound of a man's voice. A man she knew full well was *not* her beloved spirit. "Who is that?"

Melina paused in her rocking. "What are you talking about?"

"That voice. Didn't you hear it?" She got to her feet, brushing the twigs from her skirts and staring at the woods around her, every sense on full alert, her very skin prickling and aware. There was laughter then, deep, ringing laughter. "There," she whispered. "Don't you hear that?"

"I hear nothing, Sarafina," the old woman said. She got up, as well, backing a few steps away from the younger girl. "Perhaps...you should go back to camp."

"No. It's out here. I can't leave you alone."

That's right. I'm here. But you know deep down it's not the old woman I want. It's you, Sarafina. It's always been you. Leave this band of traitors and come to me.

"No!" she cried, pressing her hands to her ears. "Leave me alone! Leave me alone!" She turned to run away, but collided instantly with a hard chest and looked up and into Andre's concerned eyes. Sobbing, she clung to him, burying her face against his chest.

But she stiffened when she heard the voice of her sister. "What is going on?"

Blinking, Sarafina lifted her head from Andre and looked around until she spotted her sister standing a few feet away, aglow in light. She sniffed and hoped none of the tears remained on her cheeks. "I thought you were staying in camp."

"I decided to help Andre bring the lanterns." She glanced down at the glowing lanterns she carried, one in each hand.

Pulling away from Andre, Sarafina saw that he, too, carried lanterns. She understood then why his arms hadn't come around her hard and fast as they usually did.

"What's wrong?" he asked.

"Nothing. Nothing, I—I'm afraid, that's all."

"Take her back to camp, Andre," Melina said. "Take her and go. Katerina will sit vigil with me until sunrise."

"But I can stay. I'm fine," Sarafina said.

The old woman only shook her head, even as Andre set his lanterns down on the ground and put an arm around Sarafina, gently leading her away.

Sarafina knew perfectly well that old Melina was going to tell her sister everything that had happened. It would only be more ammunition for Katerina to use against her. She wouldn't be happy until she was the sole *Shuvani* of the tribe. She knew Sarafina, though younger, was better, stronger, more talented— and she couldn't stand it.

Andre helped her back to her *vardo,* and she climbed inside, tired to her very bones. It would be dawn soon. And yet she couldn't go to sleep, not just yet.

"Would you like me to stay with you, watch over you while you sleep?" he asked.

Sarafina shook her head. "No. I want...I want to be alone." She didn't, not really. She wanted to feel the reassuring presence of her guide, her angel. She wanted to hear his voice again—clearly enough so she could listen while he explained all this to her. What was happening to her? To her life? To her tribe? And why?

"Something frightened you out there tonight, Fina. Won't you tell me what it was?"

Again she shook her head. "Everyone is afraid of...whatever sort of creature killed poor Belinda. And the others before her. Why should I be different?"

"I don't know. It seemed like...more than just fear."

"Now you sound like my sister. I suppose you suspect me of being in league with demons, as well?"

"Of course not." He stroked her hair lovingly. "Get some sleep, Fina. You don't look well."

"I will. Good night, Andre."

He leaned close, kissed her mouth briefly, then turned and left her alone. Sarafina didn't go to bed. She closed her tent flap carefully and went to the small table in the center of her home. Her hands trembled as she unwound the silk from around the crystal ball. When it was uncovered, she sat down before it, in the darkness, and gazed into its depths. She let her mind go still, let her vision slip out of focus, let her eyelids grow heavy. She had never tried to summon her spirit this way before. But suddenly she was moved to try. "Come to me, my beloved. Come to me, for I need your wisdom now. Tell me, what is my destiny?" she asked. "If it is true I am linked to some demon, how may I break the curse?"

The crystal clouded and then the cloud vanished, and instead she saw a person take shape before her. A man. He was darkly handsome, though not a Rom. His hair was wet, dripping, and his shirt was torn open to reveal a ghastly scar on his chest.

As she stared at this vision, wondering at it, he lifted his head and looked right into her eyes. He looked at her—through her. And she knew him. "I have seen you before," she whispered. "Who are you?" But even as she asked, she knew the answer. This man was her guide, her spirit, the voice who spoke to her, the presence who walked with her. But why was he wet, and so battered? Was he the ghost of some martyr who had died for his cause?

He only kept staring, clinging to her eyes as if by sheer will. There were men around him, men in foreign robes and headdresses, and they were hurting him. Branding his flesh with hot irons.

Sarafina's heart twisted in her chest, her palms pressing to either side of the crystal as if she could make the torture stop, but the man never flinched. His eyes held hers through the glass.

Then the crystal clouded over again, and he was gone.

Fina sat back, breathless and sick to her stomach. He was not the demon who hunted among her tribe. She knew that without much thought at all. He was her spirit. Her spirit had a face now. But why was he so tormented? He hadn't, during those moments when they had held each other's eyes in the crystal, seemed like a spirit at all. He had seemed like an ordinary man. Though not from this place, nor perhaps, her mind whispered to her, from this time.

3

"Why do we keep him alive? If there were any spies among us, they fled when the Americans declared victory and pulled their troops out of our lands. It is impossible to know who they were, when we have so many men missing, so many dead and left behind in the desert."

The conversation was spoken in yet another dialect, one Will knew, though not as well as some. He was able to make out the words. That the U.S. had pulled out did not surprise him. This had never been meant to be a sustained operation, like the one in Afghanistan. This leg of Operation Enduring Freedom was a simple, short, potent lesson with clear parameters. Infiltrate terrorist cells, then, guided by spies on the inside, launch strikes on their training camps and then get the hell out. It had worked. The cells had been decimated, the survivors scattered, the leadership cut off. This band who'd captured him had unfortunately spotted him as he made his way to the extraction point. He had been within sight of the chopper when he'd realized they were on his tail, and he'd had no choice but to take cover and open fire, holding them off long enough for the chopper full of American soldiers to get clear.

"I say we put a bullet between his eyes and leave him for the vultures."

Fine, he thought. Just do it and get it the hell over with. How long had he been here, now? Weeks? Longer? It was impossible to be sure. The goddamn broken foot and ribs ached so badly he couldn't sleep, and whatever freaking bug he'd picked up had him so weak he spent most of his time lying in the corner, shivering—at least when he wasn't hunched over in the opposite corner throwing up.

He had expected U.S. forces to come after him. Apparently he was presumed dead or they would have by now. Of course he was presumed dead. He hadn't talked. None of the men who had infiltrated the other terrorist cells in the area had been identified. They'd had time to get out. The U.S. would assume he had died a hell of a lot more readily than they would assume he'd withstood weeks of torture without uttering a single name.

The voice of the man who wore the silk turban and diamond pinky ring, apparent right-hand man to the leader of this small pack of jackals, came next. "We will shoot him when Ahkmed says we shoot him. Here." There was a rattle, as if of paper. "Have him hold this and take his photograph."

"You intend to ransom him?" one of the underlings asked.

"They took our men to their Bay of Guantanamo

as prisoners. Perhaps we can use the colonel to get some of them back.''

''Over my dead fucking body,'' he muttered. He would have shouted it, but his throat was so raw that muttering was the best he could manage.

The lock of his kennel scraped open, and two men whose faces had become familiar stepped inside. He stayed where he was, huddled in the corner of a metal box that had once been part of a cargo truck. It was his own room within the caves where they were hiding out, though not deeply enough to benefit from the one plus of cave life: a constant temperature. This place was oven hot by day, freezing cold by night. His furniture included a large tin can he used for a toilet and a pitcher of stagnant water he supposed they expected him to drink. Most days it was tough to tell which smelled worse, though when you got thirsty enough the smell of the water didn't make a hell of a lot of difference.

When the light spilled in from the open door, it blinded him, and he covered his eyes with his hands.

''Come out, pig. We are to photograph you.''

He lifted his head, squinting at them and made his way forward. Every step on the broken foot was sheer agony, but he had learned cruelly what happened when he hesitated or disobeyed.

They pulled him out when he got close enough so they could grip his arms. He was struggling to see. The caves were lit by floodlights, powered by a generator he could hear running somewhere in the distance. Probably near the entrance.

They slung him into a chair. One held a rifle on him, while the other shoved a newspaper into his hands. He glanced down at it. Jesus, it was in English.

"You hold this up so the date is showing while we take a photo."

He lifted his gaze to meet the speaker's dark brown eyes. "This says the Americans have left the country. Are you trying to give them a reason to come back and kill you all?"

"You should shut up and do as you are told, Colonel Stone. We will trade you for our prisoners. This is your only hope of leaving here alive."

He shook his head slowly and decided to use this to his advantage. His wounds were infected. He needed to clean them. "They won't even recognize me like this," he said, running a hand over his unshaven face. "And if they do, they'll be so angry at what you've done to me that they'll just renew the bombing."

The two men blinked and stared at each other. "He could be right. Do you think we should clean him up first?" one asked in his native tongue.

"I...let us ask Ahkmed."

The two of them turned and left him there, alone, in that section of the caves. Granted, there were no weapons in sight, and he couldn't try to escape, since there was only one way out of this section, and they had taken it. But still...

He got to up onto his one good foot and hopped over to the table, where a pitcher of water and a partially eaten loaf of bread were sitting, ignored. Picking up the pitcher, he sniffed it, found the water cleaner than any he'd had in days and drank deeply. He shoved a large piece of the bread into his mouth, chewed, then washed it down with more of the water.

And then he noticed the knife. It was blunt edged, not meant to cut anything. But he took it all the same, along with the rest of the bread, and he hopped across the room to his box, tossing both deep into the shadows inside.

He got back to his chair just as the men returned. One of them carried a large basin of water. The other had a stack of clothes in his hands, a razor and a bar of soap on top.

"Ahkmed says you are to wash up and shave. Then put on these clothes."

The basin was set in front of him. "Make good use of the water, Colonel. You'll get no more."

He nodded, glad they'd taken the bait. Without getting up, he peeled off his torn, bloody shirt. He took the bar of soap, which was the ugly brown-yellow hue of homemade stuff, hard as a rock and, he thought, probably strong enough to burn out his eyes. There was a washrag, too, and he made use of it. God, it felt good to wash some of the filth away.

The men stood back, guns at the ready, watching him. He cleaned the burns and cuts on his chest and arms, even though the soap felt like battery acid when it touched them. Lye soap, it had to be. Jesus.

"It is your face that needs cleaning, Stone. Get on with it."

Nodding, he cleansed all wounds he could reach on his back, fearing he'd missed more than he'd hit, and finally rinsed the cloth in the water and washed his face. Next, he leaned over the water basin, dipping his entire head into it and then scrubbing the soap over his wet hair, dipping it again to rinse. Finally he lifted the razor to his face, but paused when he glimpsed his reflection in the basin of water. The beard was coming in nicely. It would be excellent camouflage if he ever got out of here.

He set the razor down again. "I would like to keep the beard, if I may."

They looked at each other, then at him. "You are an American. You're not worthy to wear a beard. Take it off."

Sighing, he didn't see the value in arguing the point. He shaved the beard with the dull razor, scraping his face raw in the process.

"Now put on the clothes," one of the men ordered.

He braced his hands on the table to push himself up onto his feet, though he kept his weight on the good one. Then he balanced there as he managed to get his pants undone and off. The shorts went, too. He didn't have a single qualm about baring himself, because it meant being relatively clean for the first time in a month. He snatched up the soapy washrag and washed his lower body before they had time to object.

The water was filthy by now, and littered with whiskers floating in the soapscum. It was still valuable to him.

"The clothes, Colonel Stone!"

"Yeah, yeah." He managed to pick up the basin of dirty water and set it on the floor near his chair, as if he were moving it to make room for the clothes.

One of the men set the stack of clothes in the now-empty spot, in between splashes of water. Will cringed when he realized the clothes placed before him were the uniform of an American soldier. Regular Army, by the looks. Not green, but desert camo.

He pulled on the pants. No shorts had been provided. "Where did you get this?"

"Shut up and put it on."

Will shut up and put it on. But first he sat down in the chair, bent to quickly roll up the pant leg and lowered his wounded foot into the basin of water. There was enough of the lye soap floating in it to disinfect the open sores, and the water was ice-cold, so it couldn't hurt the swelling. As he sat, surreptitiously soaking his foot under the table, he pulled on the tank-style undershirt and the long-sleeved sand-colored outer shirt. He buttoned it up slowly, stalling for time, looking at the chest for any sign of the uniform's origins. All the patches and insignia had been torn away, leaving darker spots where they had been.

"I guess I'm ready." He pushed his hand through his wet hair, finger-combing it.

The two nodded, brought the newspaper to him.

He held it in his hands obediently as they took his photo with a Polaroid One-Step camera that seemed completely out of place here.

Then they examined the resulting photo while it developed, finally nodding in approval. One left the room, presumably to show the photo to Ahkmed, The Brainless One, while the other stayed to watch him. So far neither had noticed his aching foot, soaking in the water under the table, or, if they had, they didn't care.

Will's left foot throbbed constantly. It was an interesting mix of colors—purple, black and blue. A little green here and there around the edges of the purple. It was swollen to twice its size and shaped rather oddly.

One of their methods of questioning him had been to place the foot in a vise and tighten it each time they repeated the question.

It hadn't worked. He didn't take much credit for courage in the face of torture. Frankly, part of his motivation in keeping silent had been knowing he would be shot in the head the minute he gave them the information they wanted so badly. Part of it had been the knowledge that other men, some good friends of his among them, would die if he talked. But the rest had come from anger. They'd pissed him off. He would be damned before he helped their cause.

"Ahkmed says the photo is good," said the one who had left, as he came back into the room. "Come, back to your cell now."

Nodding, he took his feet out of the basin, rising on one leg, turning to begin the hobble back.

One of the men muttered to the other in their own language, "By the wings of Allah, the foot has worsened."

"Let it rot and fall off. He's an American."

The first looked more worried, though. Will deliberately stumbled, and the man with the microscopic trace of decency came beside him to help him to the metal box. Leaning close, Will whispered, "I will tell my people who was kind to me and who was cruel when they make the trade, so that when they come back here again, they'll know who to kill and who to spare."

The man glanced behind them nervously, but his comrade hadn't heard. He had remained several yards away. As he helped Will into the box that was his cell, the younger one said, "Take this." He handed Will the white sash that had been wrapped around his waist. "Use it to bandage your foot."

"Thank you."

The man nodded, quickly closing the metal door. Will braced his back against the door as the man pulled the chain as tight as he could and snapped the padlock through it. He waited until his captor had walked away to let off the pressure, then he turned and saw that the chain was lax. He could push the door open a couple of inches.

And that, he thought, was all he needed.

That night, the illness that had been growing steadily worse seemed to hit its peak. He fought it as the fever heated his blood and his body shook with chills. He had to wait them out, stay awake until they all slept, hours from now.

But in the end, the fever took control. He fell into a fitful, painful sleep, and he was there again; in the forest near that Gypsy village, following the bright flashes of a woman's colored skirts as she ran through the dark woods.

It took him a moment to get oriented. But he finally realized where he was, what he was doing. It was a shock that his foot didn't throb when he stepped on it, until he remembered that this place wasn't real. He wasn't certain why he was following the woman through the forest, but he knew it was important. Somewhere deep inside, he ached to see her again.

The beauty finally stood still in a small copse of trees, looking around her, as if searching for someone. As if she knew he was coming.

But when he drew nearer, Will realized it was not Sarafina he'd been following but her sister, Katerina.

She had a stench about her that shocked him, but only until he saw the necklace of garlic cloves she wore. That explained the smell. He wasn't sure how to explain the fact that she wore it. What the hell was she doing in the forest, in the dead of night like this? Meeting Andre, he would bet, although the garlic was a baffling touch.

Then he remembered his last, pain-induced visit. There had been a murder. He'd been in and out, but he'd witnessed some of what had happened. He supposed his imagination was about to add a touch of Universal Monster Classics to the mix.

"Come out, show yourself!" she called suddenly. "I know you're near. I have something you want!"

He was startled at first, wondering if she were speaking to him.

"Come, I haven't much time. I'm supposed to be sitting vigil at the side of your latest victim."

So Sarafina's sister had not remained at the grave of Belinda as she had said she would. She had begged off with some excuse and instead had wandered into the forest. In search of Belinda's murderer?

Fingering a pouch at her side, she wandered a few more steps. "Creature! Vampire! Come, make yourself known. You've nothing to fear from me."

Will sensed something, some dark presence, behind her. He tried to shout a warning, but of course the woman couldn't hear him. A man emerged from the shadows—or at least, he looked like a man, a very large man who was exceedingly pale and moved without making a sound. He crept quietly up behind Katerina, leaned close and whispered in her ear, *"I've* nothing to fear from *you?* Do you want to be my next meal, Gypsy girl?''

She jumped at the first words he spoke, whirling to face him, one hand pressing to her chest.

''By the Gods, you reek of garlic,'' the vampire said, grimacing in a way that provided the merest glimpse of his elongated incisors. Then the grimace turned into a smile. ''You're amusing to me. Garlic is indeed a powerful root. It can clear a room of negative energy, purify a human body, and banish demons and malicious spirits. That you expect it to keep you safe from me means that you equate me with those things. Poisons, impurity, demons. Is that what you think I am?''

She held up her little pouch, backing away a few steps. ''Keep your distance, vampire!'' she shouted, shaking the pouch at him like a weapon.

The vampire sniffed the air, then shook his head. ''Wolf's bane? Well, that might work, were you dealing with a lycanthrope. But you are not.''

''I called you here to talk. Only to talk.''

''Then you are a fool. I don't *talk* to mortals, I *feed* on them. I am going to drain you dry in a moment, and there is not one thing you can do to prevent it.''

Will saw the fear in her face, in her eyes, and he knew the man—the vampire, if that were what he was—saw it, too. He seemed pleased by it. But Katerina tried to hide it, lifted her chin and forced herself to speak. ''I can give you Sarafina,'' she said.

''No!'' Will shouted the word but who would hear?

The vampire went very still, frowning at her. She had his full attention now. "She is my sister," she said. "And I know she is the reason you follow our band and prey on us."

The vampire rolled his eyes, smiling. "You know nothing, mortal. I take only those who need killing. And I follow only to protect."

"To protect her?" she asked. "Nonsense, you want to kill her, as you did Belinda."

He said nothing, but he licked his lips, and his gaze returned to her throat.

"The others are beginning to question Sarafina's link to you now," Katerina said, speaking quickly, one hand pressing to her throat, as if it were a protective collar. "They've seen her behavior. She isn't well. Something...weakens her."

"It is always the way," the vampire whispered.

Will frowned. What on earth was that supposed to mean?

"What are you talking about?" Katerina asked, echoing Will's own thoughts.

"Nothing. Tell me, why would you hand your own sister over to a creature you believe would kill her?"

She shrugged. "That's none of your concern."

"I watch your tribe, Katerina," he said. And she gasped, surprised, perhaps, that he knew her name. "I know about you and the man—Andre. And I know your burning jealousy. It blackens your soul and clings to you like a foul stench, more powerful, even, than the garlic you thought would repel me."

She jerked backward as if he had struck her a blow, but she caught herself quickly. "Do you want her or not?"

"I want her," he said. "But I want her alive and unharmed."

She nodded. "There is a cave, that way, with a tiny stream at the far back. Do you know it?"

God, not another cave, Will thought. He'd had his fill of them.

The vampire nodded. "I know it."

"She will be there waiting for you tomorrow night. Midnight." Katerina started to turn away.

The vampire stopped her, a massive, pale hand clasping her arm.

She went stiff. "If you kill me, you won't have her. Your chance will be gone."

"I'll have her either way," he said. "On my terms, and in my time. So tell me now, how will you do it?"

She blinked in fear. "Nothing harmful, I promise you. Only a sleeping powder. I'll put it into her evening meal tomorrow. By midnight its effects will begin to wear off. She will be awake and alert for you to use as you wish."

He released her quickly and wiped his hand on his trousers. "You are a poor excuse for a sister, Katerina. I will likely kill you after this is done, despite the fact that I imagine your blood will taste bitter as bile."

"I shall not be an easy target, vampire," she told him.

"No doubt your garlic and wolf's bane will be a challenge for me. Go on. Go back to your pathetic band before I decide to do mortal man a favor by killing you now."

Something, some urgent sense, told Will he had to withdraw from this place in the depths of his mind. But he didn't want to obey. He had to see this through. He found himself following Katerina as she hurried back through the forest. Eventually she slowed her pace, and he soon saw why.

The old woman sat there still, her head bowed low, as she rocked slightly beside the still, waxen body of her daughter.

The words of the vampire floated through Will's mind again. "I take only those who need killing."

What had the young Belinda done that made her "need killing," according to that creature's twisted logic?

Katerina stepped quietly out of the trees and settled herself on the ground. The other woman gave no sign of even noticing that she had been gone.

Will drew his focus away from them. Where was Sarafina? He had to find her, to warn her—somehow.

He looked around him but couldn't tell which way to go. Finally he simply put her image in his mind, thought of her face, her eyes, the sound of her laughter, which had kept him alive for weeks now. Through torture, starvation, the very darkest nights of his soul, she had been there. He had always been able to find her. Surely he could find her now.

He thought of her, saw clearly her face, her eyes... and suddenly he was there. Instantly, magically, he was standing inside her wagon tent, looking down at her as she slept.

Beautiful. He wanted so badly to touch her. Trembling, he reached out his hand to stroke her hair, but his hand wasn't solid. Or maybe she was the one who was made of something unreal. But whatever the reason, his hand moved through her. He couldn't touch her. He tried to speak to her, both aloud and with his mind, but neither method stirred any reaction in the sleeping woman.

God, he was tired. More tired than he could remember ever being. And cold, shivering with cold. He knew he should go, that something urgent was awaiting him back in the real world. But he couldn't bring himself to leave her, not when she was in danger this way. He had to stay with her. He had to warn her that her sister was going to drug her food and hand her over to that monster in the forest.

Gently, Will lay down beside her on the sleeping pallet. It didn't move in response to his weight. The blanket didn't move. He lay so close to her that parts of his body melded with parts of hers, but he couldn't feel her. He moved closer, until his body occupied the same space hers did. He was inside her and around her at once.

In her mind, dreams spun. She dreamed of staring into her crystal ball and seeing...him.

She was staring into his eyes and he into hers.

"I'm here," he whispered to her, putting all the force he could behind the words. "Don't trust your sister. Don't trust her. She'll betray you. Listen to me. Hear me, Sarafina."

Sighing, the beautiful woman let his image fade and sank more deeply into sleep. But as soon as she fell into slumber, she saw him again. Inside her mind, inside her dreams.

He was lying beside her in her humble bed of straw-stuffed cloth. She met his eyes there, and she smiled. "I knew you would come."

"I've been with you here the whole time." He whispered the words, never imagining she would hear, but she did.

"I know," she said. "I felt you with me."

"You mustn't trust your sister," he told her. "She's plotting against you."

She shook her head slowly. "She is jealous and cruel. But she is my sister. She wouldn't do me any harm."

"I think she would."

The pain that trembled through her was almost unbearable—he felt it. But she pushed it away and said instead, "Kiss me, spirit."

So he did. He kissed her, and her dream blossomed and grew. His voice no longer mattered. His warnings were forgotten as he let himself surrender to the dream—her dream or his, he was no longer certain. It no longer mattered.

He touched her freely, intimately. He explored her body, every scent and taste and sound she made was so real—and the answering sensations in him were real, too. Physical and visceral, and yet tender and deep. He made love to her there in her *vardo,* and she clung to him and told him he was her secret love— the only one she knew for certain would never leave her.

And then, holding him in her warm embrace, she sank into sleep. Almost against his will, he sank into her, and he slept, too.

4

When he woke, the first thought in Will's mind was that Sarafina was no longer asleep in her bed. She was gone. He was alone.

But then reality set in. He wasn't in the mystical world his mind had created as an escape for him. No, he was in real time. There was pain here, throbbing, burning pain, and bone-chilling cold. He was locked inside a metal box, in a dark cave, in the middle of hostile terrain.

Part of his mind, the fevered part that had confused his dream with something real, wanted to return to the fantasyland of the Gypsies. But most of him was aware that he couldn't do that, not now. He didn't know where the hell his mind was getting the stories it wove for him. They seemed so real it was difficult to believe they were not. But they couldn't be.

He was soaked in sweat. He understood what that suggested. The fever he'd been fighting must have peaked while he'd been sleeping. Normally he didn't dream about Sarafina and her band of Gypsies. He escaped to that realm only under torture.

Hell, his fever, combined with the pain in his foot, must have felt like torture of a sort to have instigated a dream so vivid. And it had added its own new twists, hadn't it? Now he was seeing vampires and making love to a figment of his imagination.

He moved slowly, carefully, testing his body, stretching his arms, his back, working out the kinks. Then he went still as he remembered what he'd been doing when he'd fallen asleep: waiting for his captors to fall asleep first. Because once they had, he had to make an attempt to get the hell out of here.

It might very well be his only chance. He knew damned well the terrorists' newest ploy wasn't going to work. The U.S. government would be happy to learn he was alive when they got that photo, but that didn't mean they would be foolish enough to release a pile of terrorists in exchange for the life of one soldier. Especially one like him, with no family, no ties. Hell, the general public back in the good ol' U.S. of A. would probably never even know about his existence. That was part of the reason he had been chosen for this mission, and he'd known that going in. He had nothing to lose.

He crept to the door, pushed it open as far as it would go, listened with every cell in his body and squinted into the darkness.

The room appeared to be empty, though it was so damned dark it was impossible to be sure. It was dead silent. The entire cave seemed soundless tonight.

He located the bread knife he'd stolen earlier by crawling around his box on all fours until his fingers touched it in the darkness and closed around it. Returning to the chained door, he forced his hand out through the narrow opening. The chain that held the door was looped through a short iron bar on the outside of the door. Two bolts held that bar in place, and they had grooved heads, like screws. Will managed to insert the blunt tip of the knife into the groove, and he twisted it, while holding the nut on the inside with his fingers. It didn't turn easily. When it finally did, the nut turned with it, so he held it more tightly. So tightly that when he finally did get the bolt to turn, the nut scraped the skin off his fingers. It was old, rusty, but he worked on it until he freed it up. In about twenty minutes it was loose enough to remove.

His fingers throbbed, his throat burned, and he was so dizzy he could barely stand, but he'd gone too far to stop now. He set to work on the second bolt.

An hour later, the chain was free. He pocketed his scrap of bread and his lifesaving bread knife, and pushed the door open, cringing at the slight creak of its hinges. He looked around but saw only darkness, broken up by darker shapes, none of them human. Carefully he climbed out of his prison, then closed the door. Taking the bolts from his pockets, he held the bar in place and thrust the bolts back through the holes. By all appearances, his prison was unchanged. Until they tried to open the door to bring him out again—something they might not do for a span of days if they were true to form—they wouldn't know he had escaped.

He'd wrapped his injured foot thickly in the white

makeshift bandage, so it was at least cushioned. He had no choice but to put weight on it as he made his way slowly, silently, across the uneven stone floor. He knew approximately where the opening was that led to other parts of the cave. There was only one, so it wasn't a matter of making a choice. He found it, went through it, but had no clue where to go from there. He couldn't see a damn thing. He only knew he wasn't far from the entrance—if he'd been deep in the earth the temperature would have held to a moderate level, never varying much higher or lower. And that hadn't been the case.

He was still for a long moment, wishing silently for a clue—and then he heard something: a whispering, moaning sound. The wind? Yes, it was the wind! God, please, he thought, guide me out of this hell. Slowly he moved toward the sound. Every once in a while he would meet a stone wall. Each time that happened, he had to feel his way along the wall, inching sideways until it fell away, and he could again make forward progress.

Finally he saw light, flickering in the distance, illuminating a ragged opening in the cave. He rushed toward it, despite the screaming pain every step ignited in his foot, hope surging in his chest for the first time since he'd escaped the box. But when he reached that opening, he stopped dead, even stopped breathing.

The light came from a small fire in the center of a large room. Around the sides of the room, a dozen or more men lay sleeping, breathing deeply, some of them snoring every once in a while. And just beyond them there was another break, through which he could see stars twinkling in the night sky.

Freedom.

He could smell it, taste it in the air. God, he was so close. Will swallowed hard. Everything in him screamed at him to run for that door, for freedom, but he knew better. He had to think, to use his fever-fogged brain to get himself out of here alive. Licking his parched lips, he looked around at the men on the floor. Most wore robes, others were covered in blankets. But here and there he saw men wearing uniforms. American uniforms. He guessed they had probably taken them from the handful of U.S. troops they'd managed to take out by ambush during the height of the conflict.

Crouching low, Will unwrapped the white cloth from his foot, trying not to make a sound as he did. Then he wrapped it around his head instead, turban-style. He wished to God they hadn't made him shave. To conceal his beardless chin, he let one end of the turban hang down, then drew it up, just under his chin and tucked it in on the other side.

Finally he moved forward. His foot exploded in agony with each step—even more now, without its protective wrap, than before. But he kept going, gritting his teeth and not making a sound. He moved among the sleeping soldiers, made it past the fire, reached the opening.

One of the soldiers muttered in his sleep and rolled over, and Will went so still he thought his muscles would pull away from his bones.

He waited, waited for a shout, a challenge, the back of his neck tingling in anticipation. But nothing came.

Finally, his heart still pounding, he moved forward again. He stepped through the opening. The fresh night air hit his face, and he sucked it in gratefully as he continued limping, laterally now, away from the cave. Finally he had to pause, to try to get his bearings.

He was high on a mountain, and he had no idea which way would lead him to freedom. There were no roads out here, no landmarks. Certainly no lights shining from below to guide the way.

He was thirty yards from the cave, on a stone ledge that dropped off steeply, when a man's voice reached him from behind, speaking in one of the tribal dialects. "Where are you going in the middle of the night? Is something wrong?"

He froze. He didn't turn. He swallowed his fear, told himself not to blow it, not now, not when he was this close. He replied in the man's own tongue. "Did you not hear the gunfire?" he asked. "It was coming from this way." He pointed ahead of him, toward the edge, and downward.

"Gunfire?"

"Yes, I'm sure of it. Maybe the Americans have come back."

The other man sucked in a breath of alarm. Then

he said, "But it cannot be the Americans. The border is east of here, not west. And they could only come from that way." He sighed. "I should wake Ahkmed."

"Wait," Will said. "I see something. Down there. Look!"

The man came hurrying closer and ran right past Will to stand in front of him, peering off into the distance, down over the steep precipice into utter darkness. "Where? I don't see anything."

In one smooth, silent motion Will stepped forward, clapped a hand to the man's mouth, put the other to the back of his head and jerked it roughly, fiercely, to the side. The man's neck snapped with a sickening crack, and his body went limp. Lowering him to the ground, Will bent over him, gripped his shoulders, and dragged him into the cover of some nearby boulders.

As quickly as he could, Will stripped the body of everything on it, which included a rifle, some ammo, a large curving blade with a sheath and the robes of the man's tribe. Will put the robes on over the clothes he wore. He intended to use the man's shoes, as well, American-issue Army boots, but they were far too small. His injured foot wouldn't have fit into any shoe, even had it been a few sizes too large, anyway. He did take the socks, putting them both on his good foot. Then he rewrapped his injured one in swaths of the dead man's turban before peering out from the sheltering rocks, sitting very still, looking and listening.

No sounds reached him from the cave. He dragged the body to the edge and tossed it over the side. It fell in near silence, except for the dull, distant thud when it hit bottom. Then Will began making his way down the mountain, heading in the direction he surmised, from the other man's comments, was east.

When he reached the bottom, he just walked. He used the rifle as a staff, and walked despite the pain of his foot and the raging fever. He wondered if it would be better to make use of the large blade, leave the foot behind before it killed him. But he was afraid to stop long enough to do it and worried that he would never get going again if he did.

So he walked. The sun rose, and with its first touch, it burned away the night's cold. He welcomed its warmth for a short time; then he cursed it, as it blazed relentlessly down on him. The mountain was far behind him. He'd made his way from it, down into the desert, and the farther he walked, the hotter it became. He was dehydrated already from lack of water, illness and fever. The way the sun blasted him now, he thought he would soon be reduced to a man-shaped pile of dust. But the sun did serve one useful purpose. It allowed him to gauge his direction.

At least it did until it was directly overhead and he was frying like bacon in a pan. He tried to keep moving, keep on course, just plodding, putting one foot in front of the other. He had no idea how long he managed to keep going, or how much distance he had covered, when he finally fell facedown in the sand.

He lay there, clinging to consciousness with everything in him, knowing that if he passed out there, he would die there. The vultures would pick his bones clean. He tried to get up, and, failing that, he tried to crawl.

And then he passed out.

When he opened his eyes, he was lying beside Sarafina, watching as she stirred slowly awake. She looked pale, Will thought. Her face tight, there were dark rings beneath her beautiful eyes.

She sat up, looking around her, frowning at the beam of sunlight that slanted through an open spot in the tent flap. She got up and went to it, pushed it open and peered at the sky. "Already so late. The day is nearly done, and I've slept it away yet again."

Sighing, lowering her head and the flap at the same time, she turned, reaching for the dress she'd left hanging from a nail in the wall, then thinking better of it, and taking, instead, the green velvet robe and pulling it on over the white nightgown she wore. She thought of the nightgown as a shift. It was more like an elaborate slip, with lots of lace and embroidery.

She smoothed her untamable curls with her hands, glancing back at the bed just once and smiling gently as she remembered her dream of the night before. "My beloved spirit," she whispered. "I wonder if he'll come to me again tonight."

"I'm here. I'm here right now," Will told her, but she didn't hear him. She only turned again, parted the tent flap, stepping outside this time, down the folding steps of her wagon, until her bare feet touched the ground. Will floated along, as if attached to her somehow. She was looking around the camp, noting the smoldering, charred remains of yet another wagon-tent and frowning as Andre came up to her. Will bristled. He hated the man.

"Fina, we've been so worried. Are you better now?"

She frowned at him. "Better?"

"We could only assume you were ill. Why else would you sleep the entire day?"

She shrugged. "I was up very late tending to Belinda. I was only tired. I'm not ill."

She would have walked on, but he caught her chin, lifting her face to his as if he would kiss her, but instead he only studied her closely. "You do not look well, Sarafina. I think you are ill and only denying it."

"I wouldn't lie to you, Andre." She moved closer, as if to press her mouth to his, but he turned away quickly.

Will saw the flash of pain in Sarafina's eyes, even as Andre said, "Just in case, love. I wouldn't wish to share this illness with you."

"I told you, I'm not ill!" She stepped quickly, moving past him, toward the fire that burned and danced in the middle of the encampment. "What of

Belinda?'' she asked the man who caught up and fell into step beside her.

"We buried her this morning, with most of her possessions. We burned the rest with her wagon. I wanted to wake you, but Gervaise commanded we let you rest. He, too, believes you to be ill.''

"I keep telling you, I'm fine. What of Melina? How is she this evening?''

Andre shook his head slowly. "She's in mourning. We did manage to get her to eat some dinner, but very little. Speaking of which..." He picked up his pace, hurrying ahead of her to the fire and fetching a cloth-covered bowl that rested on a rock beside the flames. Bringing it back to Sarafina, he motioned her to take a seat on a nearby log, and when she did, he set the very warm bowl in her lap. "You should eat. You haven't had a thing since last evening's meal, and you look pale and faint.''

She smiled up at him. Her eyes were warm with gratitude, and when she smiled like that, really meaning it, she was the most beautiful creature Will had ever seen. It took too little to make her beam like the sun. Just the slightest consideration from this unworthy man she thought she loved and she became luminous.

She looked at the stew, and her stomach rumbled in hunger as she removed the cloth and picked up the spoon. "Oh, Andre, it was so thoughtful of you to save this for me. Thank you.'' She took a bite, then another.

"It wasn't me, though it ought to have been."

"No?" She ate more. Her appetite seemed ravenous.

"Hmm, perhaps I should keep my counsel and let you give the credit to me." He smiled at her, stroked her hair as she scooped bite after bite into her mouth. "Actually it was your sister who saved the stew for you."

Sarafina stopped with the spoon halfway to her mouth. Will felt his heart jump in his chest. "My sister?"

"Gervaise has commanded she make peace with you," Andre said. "I think she wishes to try."

Sarafina stared down into the bowl. Only a small bit of gravy and a potato wedge remained. She dropped the spoon she was holding. "My sister means me harm," she said softly.

Andre frowned at her. "Nonsense."

"No, it's true. I was told—I was warned not to trust her."

"Warned? By whom?"

"I don't know...a spirit. He...it came to me last night, and it told me not to trust her. That she would betray me." She blinked her eyes slowly.

Oh, God, the stew, Will thought.

"She put something into the food, Andre. I feel... so..."

She got to her feet, pressing a hand to her head, stumbling. Andre was beside her immediately, holding her shoulders to support her. Frightened, she lifted her head, looking around the camp. "Where is everyone? Why is the camp so empty?"

"They went to hunt the vampire," Andre explained. "I stayed behind to take care of you."

"You alone?" she whispered, collapsing against him, but still staring up, trustingly, into his eyes.

"No. I—and your sister." He smiled gently at her, stroked her hair away from her face. "Foolish Sarafina. It's Katerina I love. It's always been her. Now she'll have all that belonged to you, including your status in the tribe. She alone will be *Shuvani*. The most respected woman in the clan. And as her husband, I will be chief when Gervaise is gone."

"You...love Katerina?"

"I was going to marry you only to ensure my status. Everyone knows you're more gifted than she. Wealthier, more talented."

"But—"

"We'll comfort one another in our grief for a time. It will seem only natural when we come together."

"But, Andre, I love you."

"Go to sleep, Sarafina. May you never wake again."

Will's rage against the man rose up inside him, but it was an impotent force. He couldn't direct it. He couldn't harm the man, though he howled and cursed him, even swung his fists at him. There was nothing—*nothing*—he could do to save Sarafina.

She slumped backward, and Andre scooped her up into his arms. Then Katerina came forward from the lengthening shadows, smiling. She picked up an unlit torch, and ignited it from the central fire. ''This way,'' she said. ''Bring her.''

Will followed. God, he had to stop this somehow. But how? What could he do? Sarafina had seen him, heard his warnings. Even taken them to heart, though she'd tried to deny it. He knew that now. But she hadn't known about Andre's betrayal. If only he could have warned her about that. And now he was helpless, able to do nothing more than watch as Andre carried her deeper into the forest and, finally, through the mouth of a small cave.

Will did not want to go inside that cave. Everything in him rebelled against the notion. He vaguely re-membered having only just escaped a cave, a larger one, but a cave all the same.

Still, he bucked up and followed them in. Deeper and deeper they went, until he heard a trickle of water and saw the flicker of Katerina's torchlight in the dis-tance. As they rounded a curve, he saw an under-ground stream, meandering through the depths of this underworld.

''There, on that boulder,'' Katerina said. ''Lay her there.''

Andre did so.

Katerina thrust the torch into a chink in the wall, then leaned over her sister, tugging the green velvet robe off her, nearly tumbling Sarafina's limp body to the floor in the process. ''This was our mother's robe. How the little whelp ever got her hands on it is beyond me.'' She took the robe away, dropping it to the floor, only to bend over Sarafina again. This time chains rang in the silence, echoing from the stone walls. They seemed to be embedded in the very granite, and Katerina affixed their manacled ends around her sister's wrists, then stepped aside to let Andre insert the bolts that would hold them closed. Fina's arms were held apart. She would be unable to reach one wrist with the other hand to free it.

Scooping up the green robe like a prize, Katerina gave one last look at her sister, drugged and helpless. ''Burn in hell with your demon friend,'' she whispered. Then she spat on her and ran from the cave, with her lapdog, Andre, right behind her.

Will stood over the beautiful Sarafina, tears burning in his eyes. He tried to free her, but his hands moved through the chains. He tried to rouse her, to speak to her, but she was unmovable. He tried everything he knew to help her, and he failed.

Sometime later—Will had no idea how long, and he wondered if he had again drifted with her into sleep—she opened her eyes. She blinked in the torch-lit darkness and tried to take stock. Her back was arched over the boulder, her head lower than her chest. She was chilled to the marrow, but she lifted her head and tried to see in the darkness. Will experienced every thought, every feeling, that she did. She heard the trickle of water that echoed endlessly. She tried to sit up, and only then did she feel the tug and hear the clatter of the chains at her wrists.

Fear jolted her fully awake, and she tugged at the chains but only succeeded in hurting her wrists.

"I'm sorry," Will told her. "I'm here. I'm with you. I won't leave you, but I'm afraid I can't help you. I'm so sorry."

She went very still, as if listening. "My spirit? My beloved spirit, are you here?"

"I'm here!" he shouted.

"You have to help me. Spirit, help me!"

He felt tears burning in his eyes as he whispered, "I can't. I'm sorry, I can't."

Suddenly she realized there was a dark presence standing over her. A shadow had emerged from the very darkness, keeping well away from the light painted by the torch a few yards away.

She gasped as a hand, cold and hard, came to her face, fingertips tracing the line of her jaw even as she turned her head aside.

"Your sister has betrayed you, Sarafina. But I never will," a voice said.

Will knew that voice. The vampire.

"Who are you? What do you want of me?"

"I mean you no harm. In fact, I come to save you."

Liar, Will thought.

"Then loose these chains from my wrists and help me find my way back to my family."

"Not just yet. First, there are things you must know. I will free you when you've heard them all."

"Free me now, and I'll stay and listen."

"You'll bolt."

She almost began to cry. Will could feel the tears brimming in her eyes, the fear bubbling in her chest. But he could also feel the supreme control she exercised over those things. She thought she could fool the beast, pretend not to fear it and gain some kind of an advantage. "At least grant me some light," she said, forcing her voice not to tremble, "so that I can see you."

The vampire grunted, then moved around her, until he stood in the pool of light. She looked at him, and so did Will.

He was big, oversize really. Heavy, but not fat. His build reminded Will of that of a professional wrestler. He was exceedingly pale, but with eyes and hair as dark as those of a Rom. He looked back at Sarafina, and she realized at last that she wore very little. Only her white shift.

"Tell me these secrets of yours and then let me go," she commanded, but her voice was shaking in spite of her efforts not to let it. His size alone was enough to terrify anyone.

The vampire nodded. "First I will tell you what you already know. You grow weaker all the time. You have spells of dizziness. Sometimes you faint. You sleep more and more, especially by day. And you are often cold, no matter how warm the sun may be or how many blankets you wrap around you."

She blinked in surprise. "How do you know these things?" she asked. "How *can* you know them?"

"Because it is always the way with The Chosen."

"The Chosen?"

"That is what we call those few, rare mortals who share some inexplicable bond with us. Only they can become as we are. We always know them, watch over them, protect them if we can. That is why I've followed your band. To protect you, because you are one of The Chosen."

She blinked very slowly. "What are you, exactly?"

"My name is Bartrone," he said. "I am a vampire."

She moved reflexively, and Will knew she would have made some protective magical sign if she could have moved her arms. But all she managed was a spasmlike tug on the chains.

"Please, do not be afraid. You're dying, Sarafina. Your mortal life is slipping away. The symptoms you've been feeling are proof enough of that. The Chosen always die young. You can let it go on and die alone, or you can let me share my gift with you and become what I am. Become...my friend and companion."

No, Will thought. *Never!*

"No. No, you're a demon, a killer. You murder the innocent. I'll never be like you!"

"Hardly innocent," Bartrone said softly. "Your precious Belinda had grown tired of caring for her aging mother. She was poisoning her."

Sarafina went very still there in the darkness. "P-poisoning?"

"Had you not noticed the old woman's health beginning to fail?"

"Yes, but..."

"I've only removed the dregs from your band, Sarafina. Those who dearly needed killing, though I should have seen your sister for what she was and taken her long ago. I'm sorry I allowed her to betray you this way."

"What way?"

He lowered his head. "Please—do not pretend you don't know. You know about her and Andre. You must know."

She looked away from him, tears pooling in her eyes as her mind replayed her final conversation with the man she'd thought she would wed. Will ached for her.

"He planned to marry you only because you were the wealthier of the two, and because he knew your gifts far surpassed those of your sister. Yet by night, he and Katerina slip into the forest, where they copulate on the ground or standing up against the trees, or on hands and knees, like animals. I've watched them. I've seen it all."

"You lie," she whispered, though she could barely speak. Will knew she believed every word the monster said.

"It doesn't matter. You can't go back there."

"I can. I must. Let me go." Again she jerked and tugged at the chains.

The vampire leaned over her, stared into her eyes

as he lowered his body atop hers and clasped her wrists with his hands. "You can't go back. My life has become unbearably lonely. You'll only die, Sarafina, unless you accept the gift. And I'm afraid I have no inclination to give you a choice in the matter."

Releasing her hands, he cupped her face, turned her head to one side and moved her hair out of the way. Will attacked him, but his blows were like air. Holding her that way, the vampire pressed his mouth to Sarafina's throat, and bit down hard, without mercy. His fangs stabbed deep into her neck—Will felt the pain she felt—and then the creature suckled her there, drinking her very lifeblood as she slowly faded into him.

She felt as if she were hovering outside her body. Looking down at the monster feeding so hungrily at her throat. Then she shifted her gaze to Will's, and he realized she could see him. She was panting, her chest rising and falling, and his was, too, as the two of them gazed down at the vampire feeding from the woman. It was erotic and exquisite and arousing. It shouldn't have been. It should have been horrifying, but somehow, it wasn't.

Then the creature lifted his head away, staring down at her still, pale face.

Has he killed me, then? Sarafina directed the question to Will, looking right at him as she spoke. *Are you the spirit who has come for me, to take me to the other side?*

I'm not a spirit, he told her. *I'm real. I'm a man, and I love you.*

She looked down at her body from the place where she hovered. Her eyes were wide and vacant. Her skin was whiter than it had ever been. *I will never love anyone again. Anyway, it doesn't matter now. I think I am dead*

The vampire drew a dagger from a sheath at his side and pressed the very tip of the blade to his own throat. Sarafina watched, amazed at the action, and mesmerized when he drew it away and ruby-red welled up in the puncture wound.

The vampire bent again, cradling her lifeless head, pressing her mouth to his neck.

Suddenly Sarafina was sucked back into her body in one rapid flash that ended with the impact of a fist to the heart. She tasted the first droplet on her tongue, and every nerve ending came to quivering, hungering life. Will felt it. He felt it all. She closed her lips around the wound and sucked the blood from it, feeling stronger with every swallow.

Finally the vampire held Sarafina's forehead with his palm and jerked himself away from her hungry mouth.

"Now," he whispered, breathless, panting, his eyes ablaze, "you rest, here with me. Later, you can visit your clan and see them with clear eyes for the first time."

She looked at the cave around her. "It looks different. I can see every color dancing in the flames of the torch! And I can hear it. The flames have a song all their own.''

''Everything is different now,'' Bartrone said. ''You are immortal. You need never die.''

''You sound different, too, and you look—by *Devel,* my senses are heightened to a thousand times what they were before. It's almost unbearable.''

''You'll grow used to it in time. You'll have plenty of time. But now you must rest. And when you wake, you will be stronger, and I will explain things to you. You're like me, now, Sarafina. You're a vampire.''

''I'm...a vampire....''

''Now sleep,'' he whispered. ''Sleep.''

She slept.

5

Will opened his eyes, and the white sun was gleaming down into them, blinding him, so he closed them again. He tried to sit up.

"Easy, easy now, pal. Don't move too much all at once."

The voice was young, and male, and...and *American?*

He tried opening his eyes again, just a little. As his vision cleared, he realized the blazing white light overhead was coming from a fluorescent bulb, not the desert sun. And the sand underneath him was a mattress, covered with white sheets that smelled of disinfectant. And the robes he wore were only a hospital gown and bedcovers.

The young man was standing beside the bed. He had dirty-blond hair twisted into dreadlocks, and an eyebrow ring. But he wore the scrubs of a hospital staffer, and the tag pinned to his chest read Danny Miller, R.N.

Will tried to talk but only rasped, so he cleared his throat and tried again. "Where am I?"

"Dude, look around. You're in a hospital." The kid pushed a button that raised Will's upper body, then he picked up a plastic cup with a straw through the top and held the straw to Will's lips.

Will drank. The ice water felt good going down his parched throat. He noted the IV bags dangling from a pole beside the bed, noticed the tubes leading to his wrists, glanced down at his foot, but it was covered by blankets. Hell, how bad was it? He couldn't feel much in any of his limbs just yet.

"What hospital?" he asked at length, trying to move the foot but feeling no response.

"Bethesda."

Will closed his eyes, so intensely relieved it was almost painful. He was home. He was in the States.

"The doctor will be in any second now. Look, I'm supposed to let some other guys know when you wake up. You up to talking to some people after the doc gives you the okay?"

"Depends on who it is. Although I'm afraid I can guess."

"Military. Lots of hardware on their chests."

Will nodded. They'd want to debrief him. It was S.O.P. "Yeah, whatever. First, though, I'd like to know about my foot."

The kid reached down to pull the covers away, revealing the well-bandaged foot. "You've still got it. That's good news, right?"

"That depends. Do I get to keep it?"

"Looks like. The doc will be able to tell you more."

"The doc" did tell him more. He told him the foot

would never be one hundred percent, that he was going to have to bear up to some intense physical therapy, and that he would have a limp for the rest of his life. He would walk, but never run. He would need to use a cane.

He did not accept that prognosis.

He spent the next month in the hospital. The PT was painful, but it was a far cry from the other tortures he'd endured. During that time he was debriefed by the military and declared an American hero by the press. He received a huge cash settlement for the damage done to his foot, and that was in addition to his pension. He was showered in accolades, awarded the medal of honor and a purple heart, and retired with honors, all before he ever got out of the hospital.

He didn't *want* to retire. He didn't want the damn money or the medals or the press. But with the foot the way it was, he didn't have much choice in the matter. So he took the cards he was dealt, and he endured the PT, and he got his ass out of the wheelchair and walked through the hospital corridors at night with the help of a cane, because he couldn't fucking sleep anyway.

Especially that last night—his final night in the hospital. He'd been there a month, and they would be sending him home the next morning. "Home" was a word that meant nothing to Will. He'd been a soldier for so long, he didn't have a home. He had nowhere to go. Nothing to do, really. Money? He had plenty of that, the one thing that had never mattered to him.

He felt as if his life had been gutted. And when he tallied the things he had lost, there was one, foolish, ridiculous item that always topped the list. He'd lost his fantasy. That Gypsy camp in some faraway time and place where he used to escape the pain, and the beautiful woman who had inhabited it. He often found himself wondering about her, just as if she were real. "What ever became of Sarafina?" he would ask himself, before his common sense would kick in to remind him that she was a figment of his imagination, a tool created by his mind to enable him to cope with the torture and imprisonment.

He'd tried like hell to conjure her image to mind during the physical therapy sessions, but apparently they hadn't been painful enough to invoke her. He couldn't find that place in his mind anymore, the one where he used to retreat to be with her. And though he knew she wasn't real, he worried about her, what had happened to her, how she had adjusted to the change.

Hell, when he thought about it, maybe there was a reason his mind had conjured the beautiful Gypsy girl and her tragic tale for him. Maybe he'd known, somehow, deep down, how drastically his own life was about to change, and maybe he'd created her so it wouldn't seem quite as bad in comparison. Sure, he'd lost a lot. Full use of the foot, his career in Special Forces, his entire life's work. But she'd lost more. She'd lost her lover, her family, her tribe—and then her humanity when she'd been transformed into something else. He wondered how she had dealt with that, if becoming a dark creature had changed who she was inside. Had she become evil just because it was expected of her, or was the change purely physical, like the change in him was?

He thought of these things as he limped along the quiet hospital corridors at 3:00 a.m. There were only a handful of nurses on duty at that hour, and they tended to cluster in the break room around the TV, sipping coffee and chatting. At the prescribed intervals they would emerge to check on patients and administer meds. One nurse would emerge every half hour or so to prowl the wing, ensuring that all the patients were all right, and of course they came out if the phone rang, or a patient buzzed, or a monitor sounded an alarm.

He liked the nights. They were the only time he could be alone to walk unassisted and unhindered. The nurses knew how painful it was for him to step on the foot, even now that it was healing. So they tended to cheer for him with every inch he gained, as if he were a toddler taking his first steps. He hated it, though he knew they were only trying to encourage him. He far preferred privacy during torture, he decided.

The walking cane was hospital issue: stainless steel, with a rubber-coated crook at the top and a tripod with brown rubber tips at the bottom. He would definitely find something better when he got out of here.

That last night, he was traversing an empty stretch of hallway, where no one was at work. The hospital lab was in this section, but it was all but abandoned at this hour. A few people came and went, but none from his wing and none who questioned him. It was his favorite place for night walking.

Wearing an expression that said he knew exactly what he was doing was all it took to keep everyone off his back. No patients roomed in this section, so nurses weren't milling around. His own wouldn't be in to check on him for an hour yet, and if they did happen to peek through the door in the meantime, they would see the blanket-covered shape of a man lying sound asleep with his back to them. Because that was what Will wanted them to see.

God, his skills were going to be utterly wasted in retirement.

There was a sound, a rattling sound, that did not belong. It brought Will's head up slowly and set his juices flowing. It had not been a loud noise or an alarming one—just an out of place one. And it came from behind the door on his left, from a room that was completely dark beyond the mesh-lined safety glass.

That told him two things very clearly. Someone was in there, and they were not supposed to be.

It was too much to resist. Will glanced up and down the hallway, saw no one, and quietly put his hand on the doorknob, then turned it. It was unlocked and gave easily. Pushing the door open, he slipped inside, noting how much more effort it took now to move soundlessly. He used to be able to slide through shadows like a panther. Now his gait was uneven and slow, and he had the damn cane to deal with, keeping one hand constantly unavailable.

The front section of the room was empty, but he sensed someone in the rear. He really had no reason to go any farther. Common sense told him to notify security and back off. But he didn't. He hadn't seen any action in so long that he was aching to know just how good he could be in this state. How effective. Could he handle something as mundane as an employee stealing a little medication for recreational use?

That wasn't what he found, though.

What he found was a man who seemed about to leap out the open window. His back was toward Will. He wore a black cotton shirt and dark blue jeans, and one foot was already up on the sill, hands braced on both sides, a sack slung over his shoulder by a long strap.

"Don't jump," Will said quickly. "There's no need. I'm not security, I'm a patient."

The man stilled, then slowly set his foot down on the floor again and turned to face Will.

Will studied him, frowning as a creeping familiarity rinsed through his mind. The man's skin was pale, but not in an unhealthy way. It was luminescent, like a pearl. His eyes, too, held a strange glow, an undeniable power. It was invisible, but palpable. There was something else about him, too. Something that marked him as "different" to Will's trained mind, but he couldn't for the life of him define how. Just that this man was not like others.

And then it hit him. It was the same sort of perception he'd had of Bartrone, the vampire in the fantasy.

The man's eyes widened just a little as he studied Will in return. But he quickly schooled his features. Will could see him trying to hide the startled expression, though he didn't know what had startled the man.

"You look familiar to me. Where have I seen you before?" the man asked.

Will shrugged, then glanced at the bag hanging at the man's side. "So what are you stealing? Drugs?"

"I have no use for drugs. What happened to your foot?"

"It was injured. How come you're using the window instead of the door?"

"I...opened it for the fresh air. Why are you wandering around the hospital in the dead of night?"

"Couldn't sleep."

The man's mouth pulled a little at one side, as if he were fighting a smile. "You're very good at answering questions without saying a thing."

"So are you. So what's in the bag?"

The man only shook his head and glanced toward the window once more. Will looked around the room now that his eyes were adjusting to the darkness. He saw the refrigerator, the label on the front, the Red Cross logo. "This is where they store the blood." He said it very softly, but the man heard him.

He nodded. "That it is." He got up on the window-sill again, then he paused, turning back. "*Time Magazine*," he said.

"What?"

"That's where I've seen you before. You were on the cover of last week's *Time Magazine*. I read the article, too."

"That's really nice, but it doesn't explain why you're stealing blood from a hospital at 3:00 a.m., pal."

"Oh, let it go already. You guessed what I was the moment you looked at me, though how you knew, I cannot say. Who is this 'Bartrone' you thought I resembled?"

"A figment of my imagination." Will stopped there, lifted his gaze. "I never said that out loud."

"Of course you didn't. I'm a vampire. I read your mind."

"Oh yeah? Prove it. What am I thinking right now?"

The other man stared at him, frowned hard. "I don't know. You're blocking."

"I'm blocking?" Will repeated.

"Perhaps subconsciously, but yes. You have a very strong will, don't you?"

Will shrugged. "If you can't read me now, how could you before?"

"How would I know? You're the one who let your guard down, let your thoughts slip out." He shrugged. "Perhaps you were startled."

Will rolled his eyes and moved closer, using the cane to help him bear the weight, though every step shot bolts of pain through his body. When he got close enough he reached out, tugged the side of the bag open and glanced inside. Plastic bags filled with blood.

"You really are stealing blood."

The other man nodded. "It's better than the alternative."

"You mean killing for it?"

"I meant starvation. I would no more kill an innocent than you would."

Will shook his head. "This isn't real. There are no such things as vampires."

"Then how did you know what I was the moment you looked at me?"

Lowering his head, Will said, "I don't know."

There was a pause. "The article said you withstood weeks of torture and never broke. It said your silence saved the lives of countless American soldiers."

Will shrugged.

"It said you walked twenty miles through the desert when you escaped." He glanced down at the foot. "As painful as that is even now, I can't imagine how you managed that."

Will shrugged again, shook his head. "Yeah, okay,

you really read the article. What do you want, an autograph?''

The vampire smiled. "I have to go." He turned again to the window.

"No, wait. I need to talk to you. I have questions—"

"Questions I cannot answer, my friend. Even for an exceptional mortal like you. I'm sorry." He turned to face out the window again, then quickly ducked back inside and to the left of the glass. "Hell, I've been seen. There's a crowd below, looking up here and pointing."

Will glanced toward the door at the sound of running feet. "Someone's coming. Tell me, vampire, are you a man of your word?"

"I am."

"Then give it. I cover your ass now, you answer my questions later. Agreed?"

The doorknob turned, and the vampire glanced that way, then out the window again. "Questions about what?"

"A vampiress named Sarafina."

"Why?"

Will swallowed hard. "I need to know if she's real. That's all. Do you agree or not?"

"All right," the vampire said quickly. "I agree."

The door was opening as Will glanced around the room and spotted a folding screen. "Over there, behind the screen," he whispered.

The vampire moved so quickly he was but a blur

of darkness. If Will had had any doubts—and he had—they were gone now. Nothing human could move with such a burst of speed. Nothing *he* knew about, anyway. "I never got your name," Will whispered.

"Jameson Bryant," the vampire hissed back.

"Willem Stone," Will replied.

"Good to meet you." There was a touch of irony in the vampire's tone.

"Same here—I think."

Three orderlies burst into the room, flicked on the light and paused to stare at Will, as he stood near the open window. He lowered his head, painted a look of anguish on his face.

"Listen, don't jump," one of them said. "It's no answer. You know that."

"Jesus, it's that Stone guy," another muttered. "Mr. Stone, you're a hero—"

"It's Colonel Stone," he muttered. "Or it was."

"It still is, man. Colonel Stone, U.S. Army Special Forces, and a fucking national icon. God, if you go out like this, then they win, don't you see that?"

"Yeah, that's right," said the other guy. "Man, don't tell us you survived all that crap just to give up now."

"Colonel Stone, sir, I just got out of the Army. I was over there. Let me tell you something, you did us proud. You cash out now, it's gonna crush all those soldiers who see you as a hero."

Will turned slowly, looking at them, even while

swinging one leg over the windowsill. "Just stay where you are, okay? I have to think."

The men stopped their forward progress. "Come on, come on back in here. You can think in here as good as anywhere else."

The door opened again, and a woman stepped in. She was mid-fifties, fit, kept her hair colored, but the smokers'-wrinkles in her face gave her age away. "Mr. Stone, I'm Amelia Ashby. I'm a psychiatrist here."

A psychiatrist was just what he needed, he thought, considering he'd just been conversing with a vampire. Shit. He almost laughed, but that would have blown the suicidal depression skit right out of the water.

"Tell me what you're feeling. Please, I only want to help you."

He pursed his lips, sighed, wondered if this was going to end up lengthening his stay, when he'd so been looking forward to getting the hell out of here tomorrow. He drew his leg inside, stood on the floor, closed the window, and grabbed his cane. "I'm not going to jump, all right? I was just...out walking the halls."

"Good. Very good. And you came in here be-cause...?"

"My leg got to aching. I was looking for a place to sit down for a while."

"I see," she said slowly, coming closer now.

To stop her from reaching the point where she might catch a glimpse of Jameson-the-blood-thief,

Will met her halfway. "Look, I'm ready to go back to my room now, all right?"

"That's fine. Do you mind if I walk with you?" She took his good arm, walked with him back toward the door.

"Sure. Whatever."

One of the orderlies opened the door. Another slapped him on the shoulder as he passed. "You hang in there, man. We need more like you, Colonel Stone."

The former soldier sent him a snappy salute.

They all followed Will and the shrink into the hallway, and then the orderlies dispersed, one of them pausing to relock the door before taking off.

Dr. Ashby walked slowly. "You're in a lot of pain, aren't you?"

"The leg? Ah, it's not so bad."

"Bad enough that it had you considering suicide."

"What, you think I'd kill myself over a little pain? I can handle pain, Dr. Ashby."

She nodded, smiled a little self-deprecatingly. "I guess I should have known that, considering. Physical pain certainly wouldn't drive a man like you to such an extreme decision."

"It wasn't a decision. More like a passing thought."

"So you didn't really plan to jump from that window tonight?"

"No. I opened it. I even stood there a while, contemplating the notion. But I never would have jumped.''

''Because you realized that you have too much to live for?'' she asked.

''Because I realized it's not a high enough window to ensure a quick end. I may have a high tolerance for pain, Dr. Ashby, but I'm not a masochist. If I'd been seriously thinking of jumping, I'd have taken the elevator on up to the top floor—better yet, the roof.''

She blinked at him. ''I'm not sure if I should find that reassuring or troubling.''

''Reassuring,'' he promised. ''I swear.''

6

Somehow—he wasn't sure how—Will convinced them to let him leave the hospital on schedule. Though he was now expected to follow up by keeping an appointment Dr. Ashby had set up for him with a New York therapist. Therapy he *didn't* need. Didn't even believe in it. You were either sane or you weren't.

He was. If his little red caboose were capable of chugging around the bend, it would have been long gone by now. He was perfectly sane.

Except, of course, for the visions. But hell, under torture, the mind did what it had to in order to survive. If that meant creating a fantasyland with beautiful Gypsies and dangerous vampires, then fine. Those little flights to La-La Land were not signs of instability. Hell, they were probably the only things that had kept his crackers from crumbling.

Of course, that didn't explain the vampire who'd shown up in the hospital lab last night. Nor the fact that Will had...kind of liked the guy.

Making snap judgments about people was not unusual for him. He'd been trained for years to size a person up in a glance, so that wasn't an issue. The

issue was that he'd believed the guy to be a vampire.
A real one. At least until he'd gotten up the next
morning to examine the theory in the full light of day
and realized how ridiculous it was. Maybe it was easier to believe in fantasies when you were creeping
around a shadowy lab in the dead of night. Besides,
he'd been through the mill, and they'd been keeping
him pretty drugged-up to boot. Far more than he
liked.

That must have been it. He'd probably imagined
the entire thing. Hell, it was a wonder he wasn't suf-
fering far worse side effects after his weeks of torture,
mangled foot and near-death in the desert. His brain
had been baked, his body dehydrated, his senses de-
prived. Top all that off with a little morphine and you
had a hallucination just waiting to happen.

The nurse pushed his wheelchair up to the double
doors, which parted automatically. He took his first
breath of fresh air in weeks, even if it was tinged with
exhaust fumes. It was spring. God, how he loved the
spring.

There was a taxi waiting at the curb. He glanced
up at the smiling nurse. "I can take it from here,
hon."

"I don't doubt it."

He got upright, his weight on the good foot. The
nurse pulled the chair out from behind him, then
handed him his cane and the plastic bag filled with
his belongings. The few that were here, anyway. He
didn't own much, or hadn't until he'd come home.

Uncle Sam had secured an apartment for him in the city of his choice, which was New York. They'd furnished it and told him there would be a car waiting in the parking garage when he arrived. His worldly possessions, most of which fit easily into a large Army-issue duffel bag, had already been sent on ahead of him.

He muttered his destination to the driver as he got into the back seat, then settled in for the ride to the airport.

It was a short, easy flight. The landing, though, was a bit of a surprise. When he limped off the plane, keeping to one side so the other passengers could rush past him in their hurry to the gate, he had no idea what was awaiting him in LaGuardia's main terminal. In fact, when he first glimpsed the press, the cameras, the people waving their tiny flags and holding up their signs, he wondered what celebrity had been on that airplane with him.

Then a reporter said, "Welcome to New York, Colonel Stone! How does it feel to be back home?"

The microphone hovered in front of his face, and he thought about laughing out loud. This wasn't home. Home was a camouflage-colored tent or sometimes a hole in the ground. It was men in fatigues carrying automatic rifles, and bad food and warm water, and anti-nerve-gas injections. It wasn't this.

But aloud, he only said, "Great. It feels great. I'm glad to be back."

"Colonel, how is your leg?" another one shouted, shouldering her way to the front of the pack.

"Foot, not leg," he corrected. "It's as good as can be expected, I suppose."

"What's your reaction to the news that earlier today a daisy-cutter was dropped on the caves where you were held?"

"I hadn't heard." He wondered if any of the men who'd held him were stupid enough to have remained in the same place this long and doubted it. "They get anybody?"

"A pile of them. They're still sorting through the remains."

He swallowed his reaction to that and wondered who'd been killed for the sake of avenging the latest American hero. He stopped answering questions, shouldered his way through the mob, not without effort, but they didn't give up until he got into a cab outside the airport.

It was only as the cab pulled away that he saw her. She was getting into a long black limousine. She wore dark glasses and real fur, and her hair was wild and loose. Her pale, pale skin, like alabaster, was almost luminous in the dusky light of sundown. Her legs were endless, her nails as red as her lips.

"Stop the car," he told the driver. "Stop!"

The cabdriver hit the brakes, jerking the wheel to one side. But it was too late. She was in the car, drawing one long leg in after her and closing the door. Then the limo lurched into motion and took her away.

He squinted at the plate number, but the sun reflected off the rear window, and he couldn't see through its glare. Then he just sat there staring after her for the longest time.

"You wanna sit here all day or what?" the driver asked.

Will snapped his attention back to where it belonged. "No. Just...drive."

Again the cab was in motion. But Will knew, he knew deep down, that he had just seen Sarafina. His beautiful fantasy. And then he wondered if maybe he should take Dr. Ashby's advice to heart and get some therapy.

It had been two months—two months that he'd been trying to banish thoughts of his make-believe woman from his mind, but he'd only become more and more desperate to see her again.

Well, today, dammit, he would. If it were possible to find her again, find that place again, then he would. He stopped taking his pain meds, walked excessively and left his cane at home. By the end of the day, Will's foot was screaming in unmitigated agony. He was damp with sweat, his entire body shaking with pain by the time he got back to the Manhattan condo his dear Uncle Sam had bought and paid for.

He went straight to the bedroom. The drapes were drawn, no lights on, and it was well past sundown. Now. Maybe now.

He fell onto the bed, closed his eyes and drew his

mind as far away from the pain as he could. He'd been determined to let her go, to just get on with his life. But she haunted him. Her eyes. Her smile. Her hair.

Part of him was afraid that he might get trapped in his own fantasy—become so enmeshed that he spent the rest of his life in a mental ward somewhere, living only in his mind. But the craving for her, the need, only grew stronger. He had to see her again. And so he tried, just as he had tried a thousand times before.

Nothing. Nothing. *Dammit to hell!*

Eyes still closed, he reached out for the cane that leaned against the headboard, where he always kept it. His hand closed around the cool shellac-coated oak, and he brought the cane around fast and hard, smashing it into his bad foot.

Pain ripped a scream from his chest. He dropped the cane to the floor as fireworks went off in his brain. Mentally he skittered into the darkest corner of his mind and cowered there, where the pain couldn't reach.

And then he found her. He saw her eyes, gleaming in the darkness, and then he fell into them, into her world, or her past, or whatever the hell this place was.

Sarafina.

She was sitting in a room, lit only by the glow coming from the dying fire in the hearth. It startled Will at first, that he could see the room so clearly in such dim light. The antique furniture looked new, and the oriental rug that covered the hardwood floor showed its vibrant reds and yellows as brightly as it would by full daylight. But then he reminded himself that he was seeing her, and everything around her, as she would. And she, apparently, could see quite clearly in the dark.

She felt stronger, more alive, than she ever had during his previous visits. But there was a hardness about her now that he'd never sensed before. He remembered her anguish on learning of her lover's betrayal, and that of her own sister, and he thought that might account for the change.

She sat in a velvet-covered chair, with a small, round three-legged table beside her. She wore full, flowing skirts of jewel-blue, a turquoise-colored satin blouse that bared her pale shoulders. Jewels dangled from her neck and her ears, and decorated every scarlet-tipped finger as she absently shuffled a deck of cards. Tiny silk slippers covered her feet. Her hair was long and loose, curling wildly around her shoulders.

"Sarafina, I'm here," he whispered. "Can you feel me?"

Sarafina frowned, a tiny furrow appearing between her full, dark brows. She turned her head to look about the room but saw only the man who had transformed her that night in the cave so long ago. Bartrone.

He sat in a chair much like hers, only larger, and placed closer to the fire. He didn't seem vibrant or alive, as she did. He seemed...tired. Exceedingly tired.

"Did you hear something just now?" she asked him.

He didn't answer but remained as he was, his shoulders slightly slumped, gaze turned inward as if he were deep in thought.

"Bartrone?"

His head came up slowly. "Yes?"

"Did you hear anything just now?" He only stared blankly, and Sarafina finally shook her head in frustration. "No, of course you didn't. You barely hear *me*. What is wrong with you, Bartrone?"

He shrugged. "Do you know how old I am, my Gypsy love? Have I told you, in all the years you've been my companion?"

All the years? God, Will wondered just how many years it had been at this point.

She blinked slowly, searching her mind. "You... no. I don't believe you have. Though I've asked many times."

He sighed, seemed to think a long while before answering. "You've heard of Babylon?"

Sarafina sat up a little straighter, widening her eyes. "How could I not, with all the books you've made me read, all the lessons you've insisted I complete?"

"Immortality spent in ignorance is wasted."

"So you've been telling me these past fifty years."

Fifty years? That long? But she didn't look so much as a day older!

Bartrone nodded, drew a breath. "I was born there."

She blinked slowly. "In Babylon?"

"The year of my birth, by the modern calendar, would have been seven hundred and one, before the Common Era." He lifted his gaze to hers slowly. "I am more than two thousand years old, my precious Sarafina. And I have come to understand that, in truth, there is no such thing as immortality."

She stopped shuffling the cards, a larger deck than the modern ones Will had seen, and simply held them in her now-still hands. "That's ridiculous, my darling. You yourself are the proof of it."

"I'm afraid I am the opposite of that." He lowered his head. "I'm tired, Sarafina. Tired of never seeing the sunlight. Of killing in order to live."

"Is it your conscience that's troubling you, then?" She got to her feet and went to him, leaning over his chair and running a hand through his long, dark hair. "You kill only those who need killing, my love. How many times have you explained this to me? That we must kill in order to survive, but that we must never harm an innocent? Goodness knows there are criminals enough to sustain us. Abusers of children. Murderers."

He nodded. "We are natural predators, like the lion or the shark. But unlike them, we have a conscience and, I believe—though many others do not—a soul." He heaved another heavy sigh. "It is unnatural for a human to live forever, Sarafina."

"We're not humans. We're vampires. It couldn't be more natural to us."

"We're humans. We were born humans. This... this condition of ours is no more than an aberration. A curse, perhaps."

She wanted to lash out at him for those words. Will felt the anger rise up in her. But she banked it, held it in check. And he realized suddenly all the things this man—this monster—had been to her over the years. A teacher, a mentor, a protector and guide, a companion and friend. She loved him—not passionately, but deeply.

"You've never believed these things before, Bartrone. You taught me to embrace my preternatural strength and power. To relish this life and all it offers."

"I know, child, I know. But with age, comes wisdom. And a new knowledge has settled on my heart these past few months."

"Wisdom, is it?" she snapped, nearing the edge of her temper. "Or perhaps a simple case of melancholia?"

He drew a long, slow breath. "I'm sorry I brought you into this life, Sarafina." Lifting his hand, he touched her face. "I need you to forgive me."

Sarafina drew away from the cool touch of his palm on her cheek. "Forgive you? Bartrone, you saved me from certain death. Already I was weakening with the symptoms of the illness. And had it not killed me, my faithless sister surely would have. She and my betrothed—plotting against me all along. You showed me the truth. You gave me the power to outlive them all. So don't ask me to forgive you. I can only thank you for the gift you gave to me.''

He smiled slowly, though the sadness he'd been describing still shadowed his eyes. ''So alive. Such a fiery thing you've become. Maybe for you it will be different. By God, I hope so, Sarafina. But for me...it's over.''

She stared at him, her entire body having gone still. ''What do you mean?''

''I've taught you well. You'll be fine on your own.''

''On my own? Bartrone, you are making very little sense. Perhaps you need to feed, or rest.''

''I've fed for the last time, Fina.'' He glanced at the clock on the mantel, as its pendulum swung slowly back and forth. ''It's nearly dawn. I intend to see the sunrise today.''

''Don't be foolish. You can't. You mustn't even try.'' She dropped the deck of cards as if she had completely forgotten them. Letting them fall and scatter upon the carpet, she took his hand, drew him to his feet. ''Come to bed, love. You'll feel so much differently when you wake tonight. We'll do something fabulous. We'll take a trip, that's what we'll do. We can travel into the desert lands, and you can tell me about Babylon. What it was truly like to live there. You see? There is still much you have to teach me.''

As she spoke, she drew him across the room,

through a doorway that led down into the basement. She looked back as she did, toward the cards that had fallen upon the floor. For just a moment, she stilled, her gaze riveted to the two cards that had fallen face-up. One depicted the pathway between heaven and earth as a beautiful woman with her feet in the one and her head in the other. The second card showed the reaper in a black cloak, wielding a scythe.

She wrenched her gaze from the cards, her mind shouting a vehement denial. It meant nothing, she told herself, and she drew Bartrone on.

He followed without argument, nodding and muttering, "All right, my love. All right, I'll come with you."

Will could feel the fear in Sarafina's heart. Fear of being alone, it was nearly paralyzing in its power. She was trembling, close to tears at the thought of it.

She drew Bartrone into the basement, through a hidden doorway, into a pitch-black room with a dirt floor. Will gasped in surprise when she lifted part of the floor upward, and he realized it was a hinged trap-door, only made to look like the rest of the floor. Another set of stairs was below, spiraling downward into the belly of the earth itself.

"I have had word from my spies," Bartrone said. "Your wretched sister is old now. Her husband died young, fulfilling the first part of the curse you placed upon them. The second part has now come to pass."

She moved only a few steps down, staring back up at him.

"A child has been born, a great-great-grandson to your sister. His name is Dante, and he is one of The Chosen."

Her heart quickened. "I have family again?" she whispered.

He nodded. "His blood is like ours. He is one of the few who can become one of us. But he is still a suckling babe. Think carefully about what you do with this information, Sarafina. Allow the child to grow to manhood, and remember what I've told you—that this life we live is as much a curse as a gift. Think on that before you decide whether to bring him with you into darkness."

Blinking, she shook her head. "The only alternative is to watch him weaken and die in the prime of his youth, Bartrone."

"That may be his preference. Let him decide."

She nodded, thinking it through. "I'll think on it. We have many years during which to discuss this. It will be a long while before he's adult enough to even consider..." Her head came up, eyes bright. "Oh, but we must visit him! To have family again. Real family, from my own Gypsy clan."

"Your sister is the elder woman as well as the *Shuvani* now, my love. She won't likely let you near him."

Sarafina's eyes turned dark, her face deadly. "Nor will she stop me."

He nodded. "Remember the things I've told you. And remember that I love you, Sarafina. In all my centuries of life, I have never loved another the way I have loved you." He held up his free hand. "No, don't reply in kind, my love. I know it has never been the same for you. It doesn't matter. You've been kind to me, been my companion, my friend and my lover. I'm only sorry that I have to repay you so cruelly."

And with that he yanked his hand from hers, and, with his other, he shoved her. Sarafina stumbled down the stairs, falling the last few steps. She scrambled to her feet at the bottom, hiking her skirts in her fists and racing upward even as the trapdoor slammed down. "Bartrone!" she cried. She pushed against the door, but he had apparently blocked it from the other side. "Bartrone, don't do something foolish! Please!"

"Goodbye, my love," he called.

She heard his footsteps retreating back up the stairs. "No," she shouted. "No! I won't let you do this!" Turning, she ran back down the spiral staircase, seeing as clearly as a cat in the darkness. She was moving with such speed that the walls around her blurred. The sensation, to Will, who felt as if he were being propelled along in her wake, was dizzying.

Then she was at another door, jerking it open.

Sunlight streamed in on her, burning her as if she were on fire. Will *felt* it. Her arms flying up to shield her face, she staggered backward into the shadows. And then she lowered her arms slowly, breathing hard. There were burns on her skin. Will heard her thoughts. She would be all right. The burns would heal with the day-sleep, as all wounds to her kind would do. As Bartrone's would, if she could only get to him in time.

Then she looked up, through the open doorway, that threshold of yellow light, and she saw him. He stood on a small, grassy hillock in the distance, his back toward her, arms wide-open to the rising sun. As that glowing golden sphere rose higher, his form became only a dark silhouette. And then...a flaming one.

A cry burst from Sarafina—the keening wail of one in unbearable pain. She fell to her knees, watching in anguish as her companion seemed to dance in the flames, turning this way and that as his flesh was devoured. He never made a sound. He burned alive and never made a sound.

Then his form was no more, and the flames grew lower, nearer the ground. They flickered there only a moment, then died altogether, leaving only a scorched patch of earth where he had been.

Sarafina curled onto the cold floor, sobbing.

The door was still open, the sun rising ever higher in the sky. Its rays crept across the floor, closer and closer to where she lay.

"Sarafina," Will said. "Sarafina, you have to get up. Now, dammit, or you'll burn as he did!"

"Leave me alone, spirit," she whispered, the words coming very slowly, broken by sobs. "Allow me my grief, for I've lost my only companion."

"No. You haven't. I'm here. I'm with you."

She shook her head where it lay against her folded

arms on the floor. "You lie. I've not heard your voice nor felt your presence for fifty years. I don't even know...I don't even know what you are."

"For me, it's only been two months, Sarafina. And I'm not a spirit, I'm a man. I live in another time, a far distant time in the future. In a place called New York. I don't know how or why I find you this way, no more than I can understand why I love you so desperately. But I do. I do, Sarafina."

Sniffling, she lifted her head. "Everyone who has ever claimed to love me has betrayed me. They win my heart, my trust, my love, and then they take theirs away and leave me alone." She closed her eyes.

"I won't. I swear it."

Shaking her head, she lowered it again, weeping. "Oh, Bartrone, why? Why did you leave me all alone?"

"You're not alone."

"You do not count, spirit. Who knows when I will hear from you again? A day for you could be a century for me!"

Will racked his brain to think of something he could say that would give her something to cling to. Anything. And then he hit on it. "There's the child," he said quickly. "The one Bartrone told you about. Dante. Surely you can't give up without at least seeing him?"

She was silent for a moment, except for the sniffling. Then, finally, she struggled to her feet, pressing her palms to the walls to help her stand. Will wished with everything in him that he could help her, put his arms around her and hold her, carry her away from that dangerous sunlight.

She went to the door and closed it, secured the bolt from the inside, then slowly made her way into the depths of the underground lair. "Spirit? Are you still there?"

"I'm here."

"Stay with me until I sleep. And…try to come to me again—sooner, this time? Can you do that?"

"I don't know if I can. But I swear I'll try."

She nodded, then stopped beside a huge hardwood box. It wasn't a coffin. It was twice as wide, nearly twice as deep. She opened the lid, and he saw that the thing was lined with white satin sheets and pillows. And he knew with a stab of pain that Bartrone used to lie there beside her.

She lay down, lowered the lid and closed her eyes. She whispered Bartrone's name as she fell into a deathlike sleep.

Will let himself slip into sleep, too.

7

Sarafina had her driver drop her at one of her favorite places, a little bar on the lower east side. It wasn't quite lowbrow enough to be called seedy, but it was hardly uppercrust. She spent hours in this place, or places like it, when she was in the city. And she was in the city often.

Stupid, perhaps. It wasn't as if that imaginary lover had been real. It wasn't as if his words, about being an ordinary man, living in New York in the early years of the twenty-first century, were anything more than a dream created by her broken psyche as a trick to give her reason to go on.

He wasn't real. He hadn't come to her in a hundred years. He wouldn't appear now.

She spent hours in the bar that night, sitting in a dark, secluded booth, watching people, in between writing in her journal. She was trying to remember the exact details, to get them down on paper in a way that was true to what she had been feeling at the time.

What she had been feeling at the time was rage. Oh, not at first, not right away. There had been confusion, and there had been fear that night of her rebirth into a strange, new life. But when she returned to the camp, when she faced her sister, pretending to weep for her in Andre's arms, claiming to the tribe that the vampire had come to claim her sister at last, she had known only rage.

She had summoned every ounce of *Shuvani* magic in her blood, and she'd screamed her curse from the darkness for all those warmed by the firelight to hear. Andre would not live out the decade. But Katerina would—she would live long enough to see one of her own offspring, or theirs, become what Sarafina was. That was her curse.

And it had come to pass just that way.

At length Sarafina leaned back in the padded seat, setting her pen down and closing the velvet cover of the book. The journals she had chosen were not antique, nor leather bound, like her precious Dante's had been. They were new. She had made a quest out of finding just the right ones to fill with her memories, the tales of many lifetimes, and she had settled on these. The covers were coated in purple velvet. The pages were heavy, cream-colored velum, and each volume had a violet satin ribbon with a silver cradle moon dangling from the end, to keep one's place.

She liked to do her remembering in places like this one, though she hadn't analyzed her motives too closely and had no desire to do so. She found the smoke-filled bar comforting. She liked the smell and taste of tobacco, and sometimes indulged in it herself, not being likely to die of lung cancer anytime soon. She enjoyed the taste of vodka, as well, the burn of it on her tongue, and though her system could not digest the alcohol, she would often order a shot, just to swirl it around in her mouth for a while. She liked the din here. So many people lingering about, interested only in themselves and what they could get from each other. And the music, with the bass so loud it reverberated in her chest and behind her eyes with every pulse.

She liked this bar. No one knew what she was here. No one cared. And if they interrupted her work by hitting on her, it took only a look to send them scurrying away.

Something had happened to her, she supposed. Seeing Dante's story brought to life on the screen, seeing the way his life had become truly immortal, had made her long to share her own. But of course she had no one with whom to share it. Nor did she want anyone. Writing it down was an acceptable substitute. Though even if some future writer found her journals and shared them with the world, that wouldn't make Sarafina truly immortal. None of them were truly immortal, not really.

Some went mad and had to be destroyed. Others went mad and destroyed themselves. Like her dear Bartrone. So strong, so wise, so ancient. Even he had succumbed to the inevitability of death in the end. Others—far too many others—were killed by the vampire hunters. Stiles and his thugs had built up an impressive organization over the past several years.

Dante's journals had become fodder for films, and

though it had nearly been disastrous for him, Sarafina had begun keeping her own journals almost immediately after he turned his back on her, the woman who had borne him into darkness. He'd chosen his kitten-weak fledgling over her.

Her journals, Sarafina vowed, would be well guarded. She wouldn't leave them to molder in some dusty attic, and she wouldn't trust their well-being to anyone else. They represented her thoughts, her life, her history.

Someday, she would leave this body. And when she did, her stories would remain. Perhaps, if she were very lucky, she would find someone worthy of taking charge of the tales. Or she would bury them somewhere to be found in a few generations.

Closing the journal, she knew she was finished for tonight. Time to find an amusing diversion. She was hungry.

Tucking the journal into her shoulder bag, Sarafina slid from the booth and got to her feet. She came here often enough that she knew all the regulars. And she knew it would spoil her fun were she to hunt here. Should someone come up missing, the others would notice, questions would be asked.

She wore silk, burgundy silk pants with legs that draped as elegantly as any skirt. The blouse matched, and it was tiny, with spaghetti-thin straps. She wore diamonds at her throat and wrists. The coat was Arctic wolf—it had been a pet.

She took it from the back of her chair and slid her

arms into it, and then she walked slowly through the crowded bar, feeling the eyes on her, the appreciation, the interest. She ignored it.

Outside, rain had speckled the sidewalks and glittered from the cars. It still fell, a light, fine mist. She walked a block, then two, then three, enjoying the kiss of the rain on her face. She felt the night's dampness and chill, felt it more intensely than any mortal would, but she didn't shiver or feel in any way uncomfortable with it.

She kept walking. It wasn't a great neighborhood to begin with, and it got steadily worse in this direction. Garbage, rats, crumbling bricks, broken fire escapes and streetlights that didn't function were the scenery here.

It was one of her favorite places to prey, when she was in the mood to prey. She didn't have to. She had a pair of perfectly willing slaves at her house, who would feed her any time she commanded it. But sometimes you just needed a fresh kill.

The streets were dead tonight, she thought. Where was her next meal hiding?

"Hey, baby, that's some coat you got on."

She stopped in her tracks, smiling, turning to face the young tough who had come up behind her. "There you are," she said, looking up at him, since he was a good deal taller than she.

"Here I am," he said, grinning. He had a knife in his hand. "I'll take the coat. And that sparkly necklace, too."

"You think so?" she asked. She shot her hand forward far too fast for him to observe and gripped his wrist—hard. A bone cracked, and she eased off just a little as the blade clattered to the broken sidewalk.

"What? Jesus, what the hell...?"

"*Shhhhh.*" She put a finger to her lips, still holding his wrist. "I'd like you on your knees. I think that would please me very much." She squeezed, and he fell to his knees.

Then she stood, looking down at him. He had skin like bronze, deep brown eyes with thick, pretty lashes. A scar crossed the bridge of his nose, and a ring pierced his eyebrow. He had full, thick lips. He was young, strong.

"What are you doing, lady? Come on, I'm sorry, okay? I was only joking around, you know? Come on, let go of my wrist, man. You're killing me."

"Oh, I don't know, maybe not. God, you're going to be good," she whispered. She put her free hand on one side of his head, tipped it sideways, then bent low and put her mouth to his neck.

He shivered, tipped his head farther. She tasted his skin, felt the blood rushing just beneath the surface. Her stomach clenched in anticipation as she bit down.

He yelped, and then he relaxed. She released his wrist, knowing he wouldn't fight her now. No. He loved this. She drank, and he was as good as she had known he would be. Sweet and young and just bad enough to give the blood a luscious kick.

She drank while he melted against her, and when

she finally stood up, he fell over sideways and lay there on the concrete, his eyes open, staring at her. He was too weak to move.

"You've been a very good boy," she told him. "Now Fina's gonna give you a little reward, hmm?" She drew a tiny blade from her pocket, slit her forefinger just a little and watched the blood well up in the cut, warm and red. Then she reached down and slid the finger between his lips.

When the blood touched his tongue, his entire body jolted in reaction to its power. He blinked, shocked, and began sucking, as hungry for the force as she had been. But she withdrew the finger before he'd taken more than a few eager sips. "Ah ah ah, that's all for now. More later, though, hmm?"

He was quivering, craving her already. It was so easy with some. Others took longer. But eventually she could reduce any of them to mindless drones, living only to please her, utterly addicted to the few precious drops she gave them when she felt like it. Enough to keep them alive, relatively healthy and utterly addicted.

"Can you get up?" she asked him.

He struggled to his feet, even as the limo pulled to a stop at the roadside. Edward got out, came around the car and opened the rear door for her.

Sarafina rewarded him with a kiss that let him taste the blood on her lips.

"Are we to keep this one, my lady?" he asked.

She glanced at her new acquisition as he stood

swaying, weak. He was drooling. How utterly unbecoming. She sighed in stark disappointment. "No, Edward, I suppose not. He's not even a slight challenge, and I think I'd tire of him far too quickly."

"To the hospital then?"

"Why? Do you think I took too much?" Again she looked at the man. He was supporting himself by leaning on the car door. His skin was very white, and his eyelids tinted blue. "Oh, my. Yes, the hospital, I suppose." She rolled her eyes, gripped the young man by the front of his shirt and pushed him into the back seat. Then she got in beside him. "You're not to steal or use weapons against the innocent. Not ever again. Do you understand?"

He smiled at her, his lips wet. "Anything you say."

"No drugs, either. I've allowed you to live, and I won't have you wasting that gift. You're to get a job, support yourself through legal means, make something of your life."

"Yes, yes..." He reached weakly for her hand.

She pulled it free and turned her attention to the sidewalks they were driving past. Searching every face, a habit she couldn't seem to break. Her spirit lover had told her once that he was just a man. Had he died, then, as men were prone to do? Or had he simply abandoned her, the way everyone else she'd ever loved had done?

She sighed softly. It didn't matter. No one would abandon her again, because she wouldn't let them.

Her only companions were her servants—and she owned them, body and soul. They were incapable of leaving her. The very thought of it would be more than they could bear.

It was better that way, she thought as she silently scanned the faces they passed. At least she knew she could trust them. It was the only way she could imagine ever trusting anyone.

"Mom, come on, will you talk to him?" The eighteen-year-old pleaded with her mother but didn't expect it to help her case.

Angelica lowered her eyes and shook her head slowly. "I'm sorry, hon. Your father is right. It's far too dangerous."

"I'm *eighteen!*"

"If you want to see New York, you can see it with us," Jameson insisted. "And if you'd rather not be chaperoned by your parents, then I have no doubt Rhiannon or Tamara would be more than happy to—"

Amber Lily closed her eyes, clenched her hands into fists at her sides and stomped one foot. A vase flew from its stand, straight across the room, smashing into the wall on the opposite side.

"That will be enough of that, young lady," her mother said.

"Young lady," Amber repeated. "God, Mom, do you realize that you don't look a day older than I do?"

"Neither does your aunt Rhiannon, but she's several *centuries* older than you. And what does that have to do with it, anyway?"

Amber rolled her eyes. "Everything! I'm an adult. I can do what I want, and I will—with or without your permission!"

Her parents sent startled glances to each other, and Amber fully suspected they were exchanging more than a look. It frustrated her to no end that she couldn't hear their thoughts unless they wanted her to. Who the hell had parents like this? Why couldn't she just be a normal teenager, with a nice, normal, middle-class family in the 'burbs?

"Look, I've lived my entire life under your overprotective, smothering rules. I'm an adult now, and I've made up my mind. High school is over, college starts in the fall. I'm going to have some fun this summer. Alicia and I are going to New York City for two weeks. We're going to stay in a nice hotel, and we're going to see a show and we're going to shop and tour, and do things that normal teenagers would do. For once in my life, I just want to be normal."

Tears gathered in her eyes with the last sentence, but she turned away, so her parents wouldn't see them. Better they keep on thinking she was angry and spoiled than to know the truth.

Too late. "Amber," her mother whispered, coming closer. Then she hugged Amber close, stroking her hair. "Oh, baby, I'm sorry. I know it hasn't been easy on you."

"It's not that...."

"Of course it is. You're the daughter of two vampires. You're the only one of your kind, as far as anyone seems to know. And we don't even know the full extent of your—your—"

"Mutations," Amber filled in. "Let's face it, Mom, I'm a freak. I can hear people's thoughts, if they don't know enough to guard them. I can move things with my mind. I'm ten times stronger than a normal person. And God only knows what other latent freakishness is lurking, just waiting to make itself known. I'm not human, but I'm not a vampire, either. Unlike you, I age, but I don't know if that means I'm mortal. No one does."

"You're different, Amber. You're special. And those things you call mutations are gifts."

"Gifts? Mom, in all my life I've only had one true friend. Alicia. And she's had to live just as sheltered an existence as I have, because of her mother's loyalty to us. It's not fair to her, either."

Angelica glanced toward Jameson. "It's true. Susan's been with us ever since you girls were infants. Moving when we moved, never revealing our secrets. We couldn't have raised you without her help, Amber."

"Have you ever heard me complain?" a woman's voice asked.

They looked toward the door, where Susan Jennings had just walked in. Unlike Jameson or Angelica, Susan *had* aged with the years. She had laugh lines around her eyes, and a broadness to her hips that Amber found comforting. She was the sort of mother all the other students her age had at home.

"Amber," Susan went on, "your parents pay me an extremely generous wage to help care for you. They provide Alicia and me with a home and an income, and they're even going to put her through college." She glanced at Jameson, her eyes beaming. "But even if none of that were true, they'd still have my loyalty. And maybe it's time you knew why."

"Maybe it's time you knew a lot of things," Jameson said softly. "Sit down, Amber."

"Dad, do we have to do all this? It's a simple request. It doesn't require a family meeting."

"Sit. Down."

Sighing, Amber sat. She took the very center of the velvet-covered fainting couch, and her mother sat on one curving arm beside her. Susan took a rocker to the left, and Amber's father paced.

Jameson finally came to a stop, turned and looked his daughter in the eye. "When you were born, you were taken from us."

Amber blinked, glancing from him to her mother, and back again. "Taken?"

"By the Division of Paranormal Investigations. You've heard us speak of the DPI, haven't you?"

She nodded slowly as a cold little lead ball formed in her stomach. "They were some sort of shady government agency that harassed vampires."

"They did a little more than harass us. They hunted

us. Captured us. Kept us locked in cells and used us as guinea pigs in their endless experiments to learn more about our kind and how to annihilate us."

"Jamey, you're frightening her," Angelica said.

Amber put her hand over her mother's. "No. I want to hear this."

"But I don't think—"

Jamey interrupted his wife's objections. "Your mother was kept in one of those cells throughout her entire pregnancy, and that is where you were born."

Amber pressed her fingers to her lips unconsciously.

"The DPI couldn't resist the chance to get their filthy hands on the only child ever known to have been born to a vampire. You were to be their prize lab rat, Amber. And by the time I learned all that and went to get you out, they had already taken you away and left your mother sealed in a concrete box to die."

Amber's heart lurched, and her stomach clenched tight as she turned, wide-eyed, to her mother. "They did that to you?"

She lowered her gaze from her daughter's. "You shouldn't be telling her this, Jameson."

Amber sniffed, searching her mother's face. "You're still kind of claustrophobic. Is that why?"

"Yes," she admitted after a slight hesitation, finally meeting Amber's eyes and holding them.

"But Dad got you out. Right? And somehow you found me."

"He got me out. And we went looking for you."

"Your mother could sense you," Jameson said. "The bond between the two of you has been stunning, even from the very start."

Angelica nodded softly. "It still is. I always know when you're near, or when you're in trouble. Unless you're asleep, and only very deeply asleep at that."

"So you came after me."

"And it was lucky for me they did," Susan said, taking up the tale now, as she rocked. "Because on the way, they came upon the scene of a car accident. My car had overturned and caught fire. I'd been thrown clear, but my baby was still inside."

"Alicia?" Amber asked, her eyes widening even farther.

"Yes. Your father went to the car, even though it was blazing, and somehow he got her out. He was burned pretty badly in the process, and knowing what I know now, it makes it even more amazing that he did what he did. But he did it all the same."

Amber lowered her head, shaking it slowly. She knew, as Susan did, that a vampire's flesh was one of the most flammable substances imaginable. He could easily have been destroyed.

"Later, I had the opportunity to care for you, to keep you hidden and safe, until your parents came for you. And we've all been together ever since," she said, smiling toward Angelica and Jameson.

"I...I didn't know. I didn't know any of this." Looking up at her father, Amber smiled. "You're incredible, Dad. And you, too, Mom. To have survived so much and come through it so well. But—'' She broke off, bit her lower lip.

"But?" Jameson asked.

"But I still don't see what this has to do with my trip to New York."

Jameson closed his eyes, while Angelica rolled hers. Susan only shook her head.

"Well, come on. I mean, the DPI's long gone. I may not have heard the rest, but everyone knows the story of the day the vampires stormed DPI headquarters and burned it to the ground. It's legend. So you tell me how the threat of an agency that no longer exists has any bearing whatsoever on my having two weeks in New York."

"Baby, just because the DPI is gone, that doesn't mean there are no threats out there," Angelica said softly.

"Mom, there would be threats out there no matter what I was. Normal teenagers have to live with those same threats every day, but they don't become housebound because of it. And I'm not like them. I mean, I'm way stronger than any normal girl. It's not like I'd be mugged or something." She sighed. "Come on, you guys, it's just two weeks."

Again her parents exchanged a glance. Aloud, her father said, "One week."

Amber tried not to grin from ear to ear. "Really?"

"Jamey, I don't know—" Angelica began.

"There are conditions," Jameson went on. "We book the hotel, and we have a full itinerary. You phone us every single night. In fact, you'll be carrying a cell phone with you at all times, turned on, so that we can call you. There will be no bars, no nightclubs, no drinking.''

"Of course not,'' Amber agreed, nodding hard.

He held up a hand. "I'm not finished yet. This is only going to happen if this plan meets with Susan's approval. Alicia's going along, after all.''

Susan frowned. "I suppose, if you think it's safe…''

"Oh, it will be,'' Amber said quickly. "We'll be so good you wouldn't believe it, and so *totally* safe. We'll call constantly. I swear. Oh, God, I gotta go tell Alicia!''

Amber ran from the room. Alicia had preferred hiding out in her bedroom while Amber had this particular discussion with her parents. She was nowhere near as assertive as Amber was. In fact, Alicia was shy and timid. She hated confrontation of any kind.

Oh, but they were going to New York City. Two eighteen-year-olds on the loose in the Big Apple. Without a single parent supervising them. What a *blast* this was going to be!

Angelica glared at him, springing to her feet the moment Amber left the room, and Jamey knew he was in trouble, but he held up his hands. "I know, I know, but I have a plan. I wouldn't have given in if I didn't.''

She crossed her arms over her chest. "This had better be good, vampire. *Very* good."

"It is. I think." He went to the magazine rack in the corner, hunkered down to begin flipping through issues. "All we need to do is set someone up to watch her from a distance."

"Amber would know if there were another vampire around," Angelica reminded him.

"That's why we can't get a vampire for the job. Listen, I know this man, this really talented mortal, who happens to be living in New York City right now."

"So?"

"So we simply employ him as her bodyguard. We pay him enough to watch over her 24/7, and he contacts us the instant anything seems the least bit off-kilter."

"*Hmmph.*" Angel tossed her hair. "Just who is this man who impressed you so much that you'd trust him with our daughter's life?"

"Ah, here he is now." Jameson pulled out the magazine and showed it to her. It was an issue of *TIME,* and the cover held the granite hard face of a man, with an American flag waving as a backdrop. The headline read: They Couldn't Make Him Talk. And in smaller letters, "The amazing story of Colonel Willem Stone, captured, tortured, unbroken, he escaped his captors and lived to tell the tale."

"What makes you think this man will agree to take on the job?" Angelica asked.

"He helped me out of a tight spot once before," Jameson said. "When we were visiting Eric and Tam in Virginia, and I, uh, went to Bethesda for some takeout. He was there. He knew what I was in a glance, and he covered for me when I was nearly caught."

She frowned. "And what did he expect in return?"

Jamey shrugged. "He said he had some questions. I promised I'd touch base with him at a later date to answer them. But, uh, well, I never did. Now, though..."

"Now you need his help again. So you'll tell him what he wants to know."

"As long as it's nothing with the potential to be used against us, yes. He's a good man, Angelica. You need only a glance at him to know that."

"I suppose...Rhiannon's place is nearby. I'll make sure Amber has a key, and the address. Will Roland and Rhiannon be back from their trip by then?"

Jameson shrugged.

"Do you think this...Stone will agree to do this for us?"

"He will," Jameson promised. "I really think he will."

8

"I won't," Will told the pale, familiar man who sat across from him at the small, round dining table in his rather spartan apartment. Jameson Bryant was Will's first guest, so this was the first time he'd even attempted to see his place through someone else's eyes. It wasn't a bad apartment. Hell, it was a nice apartment. It just didn't look very lived-in.

Will had pretty much settled in over the past two months, though he didn't think it would ever feel like home to him. He wasn't exactly sure what "home" was supposed to feel like, though, so he couldn't be sure.

"You won't?" Jameson Bryant repeated.

"Look, I'm a retired soldier, not a baby-sitter. And besides..." He let his voice trail off, looking at the man again.

"Besides," Jameson said, "you're still not convinced I am what I say I am."

"I'm not even convinced you're sitting here having this conversation with me."

"You've spoken to me before. Covered for me that night at the hospital."

Will averted his eyes. "I was under the influence of some heavy-duty pain meds at the time."

"So you think you hallucinated our entire encounter? If that's the case, Willem, then how do you explain my being here now?"

Will forced himself to face the man—or whatever he was. He had piercing eyes that seemed to bore right into his skull. Into his mind. "It wouldn't be the first time my mind had...played tricks on me."

Bryant continued staring at him, probing with his eyes.

"So are you trying to hypnotize me, or just burn me to cinders with that glare?"

The other man blinked and looked away. "Actually, I was trying to read your thoughts. But you're adept at blocking them. I seem to recall noticing that about you at our last encounter."

Will shrugged. "It's not deliberate."

"That makes it even more interesting. Tell me about these other times your mind has...played tricks."

"No. It's none of your business."

Bryant nodded. "Fair enough. Tell me how you knew I was a vampire that night when we met."

"I didn't know any such thing. I don't know it now."

The man blew air through clenched teeth. Then he seemed to pause, to think, and then he spoke again. "You asked about a woman that night. Sarafina. Who was she to you?"

"Just another figment of my imagination."

"No. No, she's not. I knew it might take some work, Willem, to convince you to help me. Especially since I failed to keep my side of the bargain last time. So I took the liberty of checking into the name—discreetly, of course. She's a vampire, as am I. And she's right here, in New York."

A shudder worked through Will's body. He tried hard to keep it hidden. But his mind raced back to the day he had arrived in New York. The woman he'd seen just outside the airport—getting into the limo and speeding away. He'd caught only a glimpse—her hair, the shape of her cheekbones. The way she moved. It had been more than the way she looked that had hit him that day. He'd felt her, sensed her, felt her tugging at him the way magnetic north tugs at a compass needle. He'd convinced himself it hadn't been—couldn't have been—Sarafina. My God, what if it had?

"Willem?" the vampire prompted.

Will cleared his throat, focused on the here and now. "That's impossible," he said. "She's not real."

"She's as real as I am."

Will started to argue that *he* wasn't real, either, then stopped himself. The man was sitting here at his table at two in the morning, solid flesh and bone. He wasn't like other men. Most people might not notice it in passing, but Will was trained to notice things, especially abnormal things. The man's eyes took on a slight glow when he became angry or agitated. His skin was pale, but not in the same way an unhealthy, anemic human being's would be. It was pearly. Almost lustrous.

"From what I've been able to learn about Sarafina, she comes from Gypsy stock. A small band that roamed Italy. She was transformed by a vampire who went by the name of Bartrone, sometime close to two centuries ago, and..." He stopped speaking, smiled slowly, and Will saw the tips of his incisors, slightly longer than the other teeth, and sharp. "You knew these things about her?"

"I...imagined them. But they aren't real."

Bryant started to get up, but before Will saw him straighten all the way, he was standing right beside him, clutching his upper arm. He drew Will to his feet bodily, without seeming to exert much effort at all. Will felt a single jerk on his arm, and the floor beneath him was gone. When he felt it beneath his feet again, they were standing in the apartment's bathroom, in front of the oval mirror mounted to the wall.

"How the hell...?"

"I told you, I'm a vampire. I'm far stronger, and light-years faster, than a mortal. Now look, and see the truth." He nodded toward the mirror.

Will looked. There was only his own reflection looking back at him. And even as he watched, his comb rose from the counter beside the basin, floated this way and that way all on its own. Will shot his gaze to the vampire—for that was surely what he was—and saw him holding the comb, moving it back and forth in front of the mirror. He looked at the glass again, and again saw only the floating comb.

"All right." Will had to look away from the mirror. It was too disorienting to keep watching that damned floating comb trick. "All right. You are what you say you are."

"At last."

"But I still don't know why you want me for this job. It ought to be pretty clear to you that I'm not up to it. Hell, with all your superpowers, why don't you just do it yourself?"

Sighing, the vampire walked slowly out of the room. Will followed, limping badly without his cane to help him. He sank into his chair, and the vampire took his own. "I can't do it myself. Amber would know if I were there, just as she would know if I assigned another vampire to watch over her. I don't want to break her trust in me forever, but I am not incorrect in feeling she will be at risk without protection. So it has to be a mortal."

"I suppose that makes sense. But there must be a hundred men more qualified. Men who do this sort of thing for a living."

"That's true. But we do not go around announcing our existence to mortals if it can be helped. You already know we exist. You knew it that night in the hospital."

"There must be others who know about you."

Jameson Bryant lifted his brows. "Oh, there are. That's part of the problem. They're mostly dedicated to hunting us down like animals. Slaughtering us, if possible.''

Will brought his head up slowly.

''And besides those things, Willem Stone, I trust you.''

''You barely know me.''

''I know what you did for me that night in the hospital. And I know the kind of man you are. I'm very good at sensing these things—just as you are.''

Will lowered his head, thinking it over. He didn't have a job right now. He had all the time in the world.

''I'll pay you whatever you want,'' the vampire said.

''I have more money now than I'll ever want or need.''

''Then what? What can I do to convince you to do this for me?''

Swallowing hard, Will met and held the creature's eyes. ''Show me Sarafina.''

They walked along the rain-damp sidewalk, past concrete and brick facades, and windows protected by bars, past well-cleaned stoops, the pattern broken only by the occasional alley, until the vampire stopped in front of a red metal door. Cars hissed past, their lights waxing and waning in time. Horns blew now and then. Not with the constant, unending taxicab language of midtown Manhattan. In midtown the horns spoke in loud voices, arguing and cussing each other out in a code only they and their drivers could understand. The yellow cabs spoke to one another with a little more civility in the Village.

"This is where she is?" Will asked. He was impatient, his good leg tired of bearing most of his weight, while his injured one ached mildly as his meds wore off.

"I don't do this thing lightly, Stone," Bryant told him. "Revealing the identity of another vampire to a mortal is—well, it's not done."

"Because of those who hunt you," Will said, nodding in full agreement with the wisdom of it. "But you know I'm not one of those."

"I know you're not one of those. And I know you're no threat to this woman."

He should have been insulted. "Because of my injury," he said, again filling in the blanks on his own.

"No. Because of her power."

Will dragged his gaze from the red door and the sign above it that read The Red Lion, with its stylized scarlet lion silhouettes on either side of the words, and focused on Bryant. He didn't show any sign that he was joking.

"I knew you'd ask about her in exchange for your help before I ever showed up at your door tonight, my friend. As I told you, I did some digging before I arrived. What I've learned about Sarafina—it's less than pleasant."

Will lifted his brows. "Then she's not the right woman. The Sarafina I knew—or imagined—was young and trusting. Too trusting, I'm afraid."

"How much different are you today from the child you were at, say, eight years old?"

Will knew what he was getting at and didn't bother answering. The answer was obvious. He was a completely different person now.

"She's lived five times as long as you have, Willem."

He nodded once. "So what are you telling me? That she's not a *tame, friendly* vampire like you?"

"Are you patronizing me now?"

He looked away. "I'm sorry. You didn't deserve that."

"No, I didn't." He drew a deep breath, sighed. "From what I understand, Sarafina is...dangerous. Most of us today live on animal blood, or what we can steal from blood banks. Some drink from living beings, but only in small amounts, leaving them unharmed."

"They don't remember and run screaming to the tabloids the next day?" Will asked.

"They remember what we let them remember."

Will digested that without asking any of the questions that were swirling in his mind, though Bryant paused to give him time to ask them. He didn't care about their methods. He wanted to know about Sarafina.

"Sarafina is different. Rumor has it she...well... her victims sometimes disappear."

He blinked. This couldn't be the same gentle woman he'd encountered in his mind. Then again, he had seen what she'd been through. Had losing Bartrone twisted her mind?

"She is not overly fond of humans, I think," Bryant said.

"Then why would we find her here, at a bar full of them?"

The vampire shook his head slowly. "I don't know. But I was told she comes here often, sits at a booth in the back and writes in a book of some kind. She never hunts here, so it's the safest place for you to approach her."

"Why does she never...hunt here?"

"It would stir up too many questions, attract the vampire hunters in droves, and that would mean she would no longer be able to come here every night. It would ruin it for her. The place without a single sign of a vampire is the place where you'll find them in droves, Willem. A place where there has been a kill, or a blood bank break-in, or any other sign of our presence, is the last place you will find us."

Again Will nodded. "You'd make good soldiers."

"In a way, that's exactly what we are." Jameson paused for just a moment, then reached for the door. "Are you ready?"

He nodded. Inside, he was preparing himself for disappointment. This woman was not going to be his Gypsy enchantress. She wasn't. There was no way that the Sarafina of his dreams could have become a killer.

"I'm not going in with you. She'll sense the pres-

ence of another vampire immediately and might per-
ceive you as more of a threat. She tends to shun the
company of others like her, or so I'm told.''

"So she's not overly fond of humans *or* vampires,'' Will said, thinking aloud. "Maybe she just
likes being alone.''

He looked through the door Bryant held open. People milled around carrying drinks, while others sat at
small square tables on impossibly high stools. Still
others lined the bar. The place was smoke-filled, the
music a little too loud for his taste. A little too hip-
hop for his taste, as well. He preferred classic rock,
probably a sign of his age.

"I'll meet you tomorrow night at your apartment
to finalize our bargain, Willem,'' Jameson Bryant
said.

"All right.'' The vampire didn't seem to harbor
any doubt whatsoever that this was going to be the
woman Will sought.

"Be careful.''

Will nodded, barely hearing him as he stepped into
the bar. The door closed behind him. He limped to
the first vacant stool he spotted, sat down to rest his
leg and ordered a shot of Black Velvet.

Sarafina sat in the back, at her usual place, her pen
moving slowly and deliberately over the parchment-
like pages of the large, velvet-covered book. She was
writing about Dante now. About his betrayal and their
resulting estrangement. He had been her only surviv-

ing family member, her grandnephew. But they'd been more than that to each other. She'd become his mother when she'd found him near death on the ground and fed him from her veins, making him immortal, as she was. She'd become his sister when he had grown in power and wisdom until he was nearly her equal. And then he'd become her betrayer when he'd chosen his precious lover over her.

Dante and Morgan lived in bliss like a pair of happily wed mortals in Maine. Dante had been neutered, she wrote. His fangs filed off, his claws clipped. He no longer lived the life of a lone predator. The life of a vampire.

She did. She relished it. And she always would.

An odd chill brushed over the nape of her neck, and Sarafina's pen stilled. She lifted her head slowly, *feeling* the room around her. There was someone there. Someone familiar.

Turning, she searched the bar, her gaze guided by instinct. There was a whisper tickling her mind, one she couldn't quite hear, but the sensation was so like one from long ago. It had been a century since she'd felt this particular presence. But the last time, he had told her his name. Willem. And that he lived in New York. And while she hated to acknowledge it, that was part of the reason she had come here after her break with Dante. She'd vowed never again to become dependent upon another living being for her happiness. They only let her down; it never failed. But perhaps her friend from the spirit realm would contact her here. And, she had to admit, she would welcome that. It had been so long....

"Sarafina?"

The voice came from behind her. It was the voice of her familiar spirit. It was a voice she would never mistake. And yet it came not in a mental whisper but as an actual sound. How could that be?

She turned her head slowly, not getting up.

A man stood there. A mortal man. She'd seen her spirit once, in her crystal. This man looked harder. Less mystical, more physical.

He extended a hand in greeting. "My name is Willem Stone. Do you remember me?"

She glanced down at the hand he offered. "You're just a man." He couldn't be the one. He couldn't be. He only sounded the same—and looked similar, too. But her spirit could not be flesh. She didn't trust people on this plane the way she'd trusted him. He couldn't be the one. Please, God, she thought, don't let him be the one. Not an ordinary man.

He withdrew his hand slowly, nodding once. "Yeah. Do you mind if I talk to you? Just for a few minutes?"

Blinking slowly, she let her gaze explore him. He was, perhaps, not so ordinary. His build, his physique, spoke of power. He must be strong, for a mortal. He used a cane to help him walk, which she supposed was a flaw, but a recent one, she sensed. He was in pain. She knew that immediately. He kept it pushed to one side of his awareness, as if he were the one in control of it, rather than the other way around. He wore suede hiking shoes, khaki trousers that fit loose in the crotch, making her wonder what they hid. His sweater was a pullover in olive drab, with leather patches sewn onto the shoulders and elbows, and a patch on the front that bore foreign letters.

Perhaps he was not so ordinary at all.

"Sit with me...for a moment."

Nodding, he came around the table, limping, and slid into the booth opposite her. There was a candle burning inside an amber glass jar in the table's center. Its light played on his face, which was not handsome, but hard. Sharp lines at the jaw and nose. An iron brow. Arctic-blue eyes in stark contrast to the dark, closely cut hair and deeply tanned skin.

"What did you want to speak to me about?" she asked, leaning back in her seat, enjoying her exploration of him. Enjoying even more that it didn't seem to bother him or unsettle him in the least.

"Excuse me? I'm sorry to interrupt," a waitress said, standing beside the table.

Sarafina lifted her brows, sending daggers with her eyes, but the twit was too focused on the man to notice.

"Are you Colonel Stone?" she asked. "'Cause I saved the issue of *TIME* that had you on the cover, and I'd just love to get your autograph to go with it. I think you're just—"

He held up a hand, which stopped the woman's mindless chatter, thank the stars. His eyes met Sarafina's, then shifted to the little redhead. "Sorry," he said. "I get this a lot, but I'm not him."

The girl frowned, as if confused. "Oh. I'm…sorry, then." She walked away, puzzling things over in her very tiny mind.

Sarafina looked at her mortal companion. "So it's *Colonel* Willem Stone."

"Retired."

"And you're some kind of…war hero?"

"I was captured and tortured and lived to tell the tale. To some that makes me a hero. Given the choice, I'd have foregone the pleasure."

She felt her lips pull at the corners. And she remembered a vision of her spirit lover—bound and being tortured by red-hot irons. It drove a deep chill up her spine, and she had to shake the image away. This wasn't him, though he used the same name and appeared in the same place her spirit had told her he would.

"I know you," he said. He dropped the words and just left them lying there.

She was unsure what he expected her to do with them. "I doubt that, Willem. No man truly knows me."

"I do. I know all about you. I know about the camp. I know about your sister, Katerina, and how she and Andre betrayed you. I know about Bartrone and the way he died. And I know what you are."

She sat very still, watching him, listening to him, a sense of unholy dread spreading in her chest. When he stopped speaking, she leaned across the table, curling her hand around his nape and drawing him closer to her to whisper against his ear. "And you think that I can allow you to live, now that you've confessed all you know about me?"

His own whisper, just as soft, and spoken so close that his lips moved against her ear with the words, startled her. "I'm not an easy man to kill, Sarafina. But if you want to try, I'd be more than happy to play."

The feel of those lips, that warm breath against her ear, set a fire in her loins. Images of the night her spirit had come to her in her dreams—made love to her in a way no man, mortal or vampire, had ever done—made her shiver with desire. She drew away sharply, flicking her eyes to his. "Perhaps we'll play first. And you can die later."

"However you want to do it."

She nodded slowly, reminding herself that he wasn't the one. It was safe to love a spirit. Not so a man. "How do you know all the things you know about me, Willem Stone?"

He held her gaze as a vampire might do, probing, trying to read her thoughts with his eyes. "My God, Sarafina, you have to remember. I was there. I was with you. I was the voice that spoke to you inside your mind. You called me your beloved spirit. I told you I was just a man."

She nodded slowly, searching her mind for an explanation besides that one. He was going to put out the one remaining sliver of light in her life—the hope that one day her spirit would return to her, love her again as he had so long ago.

"That's impossible," she whispered. "You weren't yet born when I was experiencing those things."

"I know it's impossible. I also know it happened. I used to doubt it, thinking maybe it was because of the torture or some kind of mental illness, but now that I've seen you…" He shook his head. "I know it was real, Sarafina. Do you?"

She studied his face. "The things you describe… happened. There *was* a voice that spoke to me at those times. He said the very things you claim to have said to me. I've never told these things to anyone, nor even written of them in my journals."

"Then there's no way I could know them—unless I was there."

She nodded slowly, realizing it was true, and trying to keep the fact that his words had shattered what remained of her heart hidden from him. He was real. Physical. Physical beings lied and betrayed and died, and left their beloved alone and in pain. She couldn't love her spirit lover if he were a physical being. She *wouldn't.*

She kept her eyes averted. "What do you want from me now?"

He seemed stunned, maybe a bit hurt. "I…I don't know. I guess I just wanted to see you. To convince myself I wasn't losing my mind."

"You needed your experiences validated." It was difficult to keep her voice from trembling with the pain. "That's done. What else?"

He blinked, perhaps taken aback at her directness. "I had to know that you were all right. When last I saw you, you were..."

The pain overwhelmed her restraint. "When last you *saw* me, you promised to try to come again as soon as you could. But I never heard from you again until now. It's been a hundred years, Willem."

"It was the night before last," he told her.

That brought her head up, her eyes to his. She held his gaze only a moment, then looked away from the power of it. "I'm fine."

He nodded. "I can see that." He drew a breath. "You've changed."

"People do. It's irrelevant. What else do you want from me, mortal?"

He took his time about answering, leaning back in his seat, studying her as freely and openly as she had studied him. Perhaps hiding some pain of his own behind those eyes. If he was, it didn't show. He had a good deal more self-control that she did.

"I want to know how it happened. I want to understand how I was able to tap into your memories and your past the way I did."

She smiled just a little at that.

"What? That's amusing somehow?"

"It's only typical. You mortals and your curious minds, wanting answers, always answers. Over the centuries, one learns that things simply are. There's no rhyme or reason. Young ones of my kind, fledglings, go through an inevitable period of demanding to know why. Why do we exist? What is our purpose? It usually takes at least a mortal lifetime of living as an immortal before they stop questioning and simply accept.''

He tilted his head to one side. ''You don't believe there's a purpose to it all? A grand design?''

''That you and I were soul mates, connecting through time and destined to meet at last in this time and place?''

''Yeah, something like that.''

She rolled her eyes and fought to keep a sob from ripping free of her chest and giving her away. ''It's rubbish.''

''All right. Maybe it's rubbish.''

''Then we've nothing left to talk about. And your time is up.''

He reached across the table, clasped her hands in his. ''I want to know you, Sarafina. I want to know what's happened to you since Bartrone's death.''

She studied his hands on hers and felt flushed with warmth, and a longing almost too intense to ignore. He had some foolish romantic attachment to her, just as she had to him. But his was all based on the woman she had once been. She wasn't that woman anymore. And yet she wanted him. God, how she wanted him. And that was dangerous. It gave him the power to hurt her, to destroy her, perhaps. She'd long ago determined it was best to associate only with those she disliked, or those who left her utterly unmoved and uninterested. Or the slaves, for whom she really did come to feel affection—safe in the knowledge they would never betray her.

Willem Stone was none of those things, and because of that, he was dangerous. And she had a feeling he wouldn't stop coming to her, especially not if he had felt as strongly for her as she had for him. She'd had a century to get used to being without him. He'd had—what had he told her? Two days?

Maybe she should just show him that she wasn't the innocent girl he thought he had loved once. "Would you like to know what I want from you, Willem Stone?"

"I really would," he told her.

She gripped the front of his shirt and drew him across the table toward her. She knew he was a strong man. She wanted him to resist, so she could demonstrate that she was far stronger, but he didn't oblige. "I want to ride you until you're too exhausted to stand anymore. And then I want to sink my teeth into your throat and drain you dry. I want to pleasure myself with your body and gorge myself with your blood. And that's *all* I want."

"You really think so?"

"I know so."

He slid his hand around her neck, tangled his fist in her hair and pulled her head forward, mashing her mouth to his. She didn't fight him. She let him kiss her, let him drive his tongue into her and taste her. Let him feel the razor edges of her incisors.

Then he broke the kiss. "I think you want more, and I think you're fighting it, but I'm damned if I know why."

"You delude yourself. And risk your life by doing it."

"You wanted me to come back to you when I was nothing more than a spirit, a voice in your head. You didn't want my blood or my body then, because for all you knew, I didn't have either one. You wanted *me*. You loved *me*, Sarafina. I know you did."

"I wanted company. A stray cat would've done just as well. But I've cured myself of that flaw, Willem Stone. I no longer need companionship. In fact, I revile it."

He released her, and she released him. They sat back in their seats, staring at each other. "Then I guess I should leave," he said.

"While you still can," she advised.

He smiled slowly at her, got to his feet, reached for the cane beside the chair and walked out of the place without once looking back. Sarafina swallowed hard. God, she'd missed him so. She wanted him. Exactly the way she had told him she did, with one exception. She didn't want to kill him. He fascinated her, in spite of herself. She wanted his voice, his friendship, his comforting presence in her dark times, the way she'd had it once.

But those were desires she would not satisfy. He

was a mortal. Not even one of The Chosen, just an ordinary mortal. She would not allow herself to become even passingly fond of a creature who would inevitably leave her alone. She knew that pain too well and had no desire to experience it again.

No. Not ever. And especially not with him.

Sarafina closed her eyes, turned her face toward the rear wall, and, for the first time in a very long time, she wept. Tears rolled down her cheeks against her will.

She still felt him with her. She didn't know where he was, but she knew he was aware of her crying. And she knew he was bleeding inside.

9

Will returned to the apartment. The vampire, Jameson Bryant, was there waiting.

"I thought you said tomorrow night," Will asked, unsurprised when he walked in to see the creature there at his table. He helped himself to a beer, then turned, holding the bottle up in question.

The vampire shook his head no. "I never drink... beer."

"So why are you still here?"

"I couldn't wait." Bryant said, then frowned. "You looked more dead than I am, earlier tonight. Now there's color in your cheeks. If you were one of us, I would say you'd just fed."

"That's disgusting." Will took a long pull of his beer, then sat down.

"I used to agree." Bryant shrugged. "You spoke with Sarafina?"

"Yeah." He sighed. "Yeah."

"And?"

Will met the man's eyes slowly. "You kept your end of the bargain. I'll keep mine."

"I already surmised as much. But what happened between you and the vampiress?"

Will looked him dead in the eye, making every effort to let the vampire read his thoughts this time, if such a thing were possible. He let his expression tell the vampire that he was treading on sacred ground, and then he changed the subject. "Tell me about your daughter."

Bryant smiled slowly, and Will knew he'd received the message loud and clear. "She's eighteen," he said. "And she's not a vampire."

Will was surprised by that statement. "How is that possible?"

"It's a long story, and one I'll tell you some day. I was mortal when she was conceived. My wife was not. Amber Lily is the only child of her kind, and those who hunt us would give anything to get their hands on her."

He nodded slowly. "So she's...normal?"

Bryant shook his head left, then right. "Not exactly. She isn't a vampire. She ages normally, so far. She can go out in the sunlight. She doesn't need to drink blood. She can eat normal food, though she seems to require excessive amounts of protein—which is an extreme challenge now that she's declared herself a vegetarian."

Will laughed out loud. He clamped his jaw to stop it at an impatient look from Bryant, but then the vampire grinned, as well. "It *is* rather ironic, isn't it?"

"Slightly," Will said.

"Amber has the same antigen in her blood that all vampires had as humans—the Belladonna Antigen.

Though from the tests we've run so far, it appears to be mutated in her.''

"What does this...antigen do? In those who have it, I mean?'' Will asked. He was deeply interested in this now.

"Only humans who have the antigen can become vampires. If we attempted to change anyone else, they would simply die. It's very rare, and mortals who have it rarely live past the age of thirty.'' His voice quieted when he said that last sentence.

Will thought of Sarafina, those first few times he'd seen her. How easily she had tired, and how she worried that she was becoming ill. It made sense to him now. Then he reminded himself that this man was speaking about his own child and jerked himself back to the present.

"You say the antigen is mutated in your daughter. So that may not be the case, right? And even if it were, couldn't you just make her a vampire like you and she'd be okay?''

"We have no way of knowing whether the antigen will cause Amber Lily to die young or not. Just as we have no way of knowing whether she would survive the transformation. As I said, she's one-of-a-kind.''

Will saw the ache in the other man's eyes. It was the same ache he would expect to see in the eyes of any man who was forced to consider the mortality of his own child. "I'm sorry.''

Jameson cleared his throat, busied himself removing a billfold from his pocket and opening it to a photograph of a teenage girl. He held it out to Will.

Will took it, looked, then looked again. "She's... stunning."

"The photo doesn't do her justice. We thought her hair was going to be raven, like her mother's. But it's not. It's this rich, dark auburn—like fire when the light hits it at a certain angle. She has eyes of such a deep shade of blue that they appear ebony most of the time." Bryant took the folder back. "She's stronger than ordinary girls. Faster. She's good at reading thoughts that are not guarded. And she seems to have some telekinetic ability, though it's far from under control at this point."

"Telekinetic...you mean she can move things?"

"Mmm," Bryant replied with a nod.

"Anything else?"

"Yes. She's stubborn as a mule. She's spoiled rather rotten. She's a hopeless romantic, and she is far too adventurous for her own good. Like us, she has a condition similar to hemophilia, though milder. If cut, she bleeds excessively, though eventually clotting takes place. Unlike us, she doesn't heal while she sleeps—but she does heal far more quickly than an ordinary mortal would. Other than that, I'm not sure what her vulnerabilities are. I hope to God I never have to find out. She's never been ill. She's never broken a bone. But then again, we've spent every moment protecting her. Watching over her."

"No wonder she's so eager to get out of the nest."

Jameson shot Will a look that should have incinerated him. He tried a smile in return. "Sorry. I was kidding."

"Too accurately, I'm afraid." He got to his feet. "She's booked at the Marriott Marquis on Saturday. Here's the flight information." He slid a scrap of paper across the table. "Her best friend Alicia will be with her. She's a petite blonde. They'll be traveling as sisters under the name Howe. All right?"

"Got it."

Bryant reached into his jacket again, this time pulling out a thick stack of bills, wrapped in a paper seal. "One hundred thousand dollars," he said, slapping the money onto the table. "I know you said you didn't need it, but I can hardly expect you to work for free, now can I? My daughter's life is worth a thousand times this, and more. There will be another payment of the same size sent to you when she returns safely home."

Will glanced at the money. "And she's in town for…?"

"One week."

"One week." Will pursed his lips, reached out and took the cash. "Two hundred grand for a week babysitting Super Girl. Hell, I'm robbing you, Bryant."

"You may well demand more by the time we finish. I wouldn't quibble if you did."

Will yawned, doubting he would have any trouble with the child.

"The most important thing is that she not know

I've hired you. She must think she's on her own, otherwise this trip will be wasted and she'll be looking for some other way to try her wings."

Will crooked a brow. "You *are* talking metaphorically, right? I mean, she doesn't actually *have* wings."

The vampire sent him a look, but he only shrugged. Shit, if there could be vampires and teenagers with superpowers, why couldn't there be wings?

"I'm trusting you with my daughter's life, Willem. Don't let me down."

"Don't worry," Will told him. "This is the easiest assignment I've ever had."

Amber and Alicia were on their feet, screeching at the tops of their lungs along with several thousand other teens while a shirtless young man whined and cussed about his terrible childhood with the help of massive speakers. His three companions hopped up and down, abusing their guitars and drums.

Will was exhausted. He'd barely been able to keep up with the two girls, and it was only their first day in town. He didn't know what he'd expected. Some whispy, ethereal, mystical creature or something, he supposed. Instead the vampire's daughter was far more frightening than that. She was a typical teenage girl.

The two girls had laughed and talked and danced their way through the airport, barely paying attention to anything around them. But *drawing* plenty of attention. They hadn't checked baggage. Their luggage consisted of a pair of backpacks stuffed to bursting, slung over their shoulders. They'd hopped a taxi to the hotel, spent approximately five minutes in their suite—yes, suite; Daddy vamp had deep pockets—and then they'd taken off again.

Apparently Amber had scored the concert tickets well in advance of her trip. It was a sold-out show, so the only way Will managed to get in was to slip into the security area and lift a T-shirt and ID tag. The face on the tag didn't resemble his, but that hardly mattered in the dark auditorium.

The bashing and banging and shouting on the stage—he refused to think of it as music—was deafening. It jarred his teeth *and* his foot. It had gone on for nearly two hours now, almost making him homesick for his former torturers, who'd inflicted far less pain.

The girls were having a ball, though. On their feet, arms over their heads, hair flying back and forth as they growled out the lyrics along with the singer, cuss words included.

Finally the band stopped playing, flipped off the crowd and headed off the stage. This only resulted in the loudest screeching, squealing round of applause yet. Then Amber was tugging Alicia out into the aisle.

He managed to hear her say, "Nah, Men in Chains *never* do encores. They're probably in their bus by now."

Sighing, he headed out after them, equally glad to

beat the crowd, most of whom were shouting for an encore, not being as in-the-know about such things as Amber Lily Bryant. Thank God. He would have lost them in the crowd for sure.

He was more likely to be questioned now, limping along with his cane, than he would have been inside, where he'd been mostly standing still, so he ducked behind a pillar and peeled off the yellow security shirt and name tag. He'd worn his own black T-shirt underneath. He dropped the stolen items into a garbage can and kept going, never losing sight of the two girls.

He was fortunate, he supposed, that they were such a striking pair. Alicia was platinum blond, and Amber's auburn hair was so dark it was more like black hair with maroon highlights. Tough to lose sight of those two heads weaving through the thickening crowd toward the exits.

They got outside. He did, too, trying to keep a safe distance. Amber was sharp. Twice she'd paused to glance behind her—almost as if she sensed someone's interest. She hadn't pegged him yet. She would if he wasn't very careful.

"So what now?" Alicia asked. "Back to the hotel to crash?"

"Are you kidding? We only have one week, girl. Let's go to a club and dance till they close it."

Will moaned inwardly. Obviously he was going to have to resort to alternative means with these two. A week of this would kill him.

* * *

Frank Stiles eyed the men who had been tracking Jameson and Angelica Bryant and their freak offspring for the past several years. Every time they traced the couple to one area, the monsters would pack up and leave without a trace. This time, though, he had them.

"They put two teenage girls on a flight to New York under the name of Howe. We had operatives waiting. They trailed them to the Marriott Marquis."

"And one of them is the girl we want."

"Yes, but we aren't sure which one."

"And why not?" Stiles asked, his good eye raking the men. "It shouldn't be that difficult to ascertain, if you've been watching them."

"Sir, there's very little difference. They both go out in daylight, they both have been observed eating regular food, and so far neither of them has shown any signs of being anything other than a, well, a typical teenage girl."

Stiles ran one hand over his face, a subconscious gesture. His palm moved from the smooth skin of the right side to the puckered, scarred flesh of the left, reminding him that vampires were nothing more than animals—rabid ones in need of putting down. His research was getting close to adding another weapon to the arsenal to be used against them. The most powerful weapon yet.

"She's not a typical teenage girl, gentlemen. She's the bitch pup of a pair of killer dogs. She may look human, but she's not. Keep it in mind. If you don't have the stomach for what needs to be done, then we have ways of dealing with that.''

The men exchanged glances. They were not stupid. Stiles didn't recruit stupid men. They knew no one left his group alive. He wasn't about to risk having former operatives running around telling tales.

''We'll take them both,'' Stiles said, when he sensed his message had been delivered. ''And then I'll find a way to determine which is the human traitor and which is the mutant half-breed.''

Willem was exhausted by the time the girls called it a night, which was far closer to his wake-up time than his usual bedtime. Still, Will knew he couldn't rest. Not yet. While the girls lay safely locked in their suite, sound asleep by all appearances, he had to move and move quickly. He had not expected them to be this much of a challenge.

By noon, he had booked himself a suite near theirs and made a fast trip to a ''hard to find'' weapons and equipment merchant by the name of Mike Mulcahey, who'd been a fellow Special Forces soldier years ago. He was one of the good guys. Not exactly legal, but he only dealt with relatively legit private operatives— nothing shady or un-American. He prided himself on his patriotism, in fact.

Will picked several cleverly designed surveillance devices that would make his job one hell of a lot easier. Mike talked him into taking a few other items from his ''clearance'' rack. Hell, Will didn't know what the hell he would ever need plastic explosive and timing devices for, but Mike needed them gone for some reason, so Will figured the least he could do was help an old buddy out. He put that carefully bundled package in his trunk, underneath the spare tire. It was illegal as hell. But he took the bag of surveillance equipment into the front seat with him.

He was just heading back into his newly acquired suite with his sackful of goodies when the two adventurers emerged from their room next door, smiling and talking. He glanced sideways at them while pretending to search for his key, taking mental notes. They were dressed similarly, in tight-fitting, low-rise jeans, and blouses that showed off their tiny waists. Amber's jeans were slightly darker blue, her top a robin's-egg-colored tank top with the words 'Boys Lie' on the front. Alicia's top was a pale lilac skintight T-shirt that made him wonder if it were designed to be that small, or if she'd bought it in a child's size. He hadn't paid much attention to what young girls were wearing since he'd been their age. The shirt had a kitten on the front, and her belly button had a silver ring poked through it. Amber didn't have a ring in her belly. He wondered briefly if that was a style choice, or one based on her tendency to bleed a lot, which made him look up to her earlobes. No holes in them, either.

"So breakfast in the hotel and then shopping on Fifth Avenue," Amber said.

"Then the MTV studio to see if we can spot any stars, and then..." Alicia frowned. "Then what, Amber?"

Amber shrugged. "We'll play it by ear. Definitely clubbing tonight."

"Definitely."

The two headed down the hall toward the elevators, but Amber stopped walking, just stopped. Then she turned slowly and looked directly at him.

Will made sure his full attention appeared to be focused on unlocking his door. But he felt those eyes on him like a physical touch. Had she caught a glimpse of him last night? Was the girl on to him already? Damn, she was good.

He slipped inside but didn't close the door all the way, so he could listen.

"What's wrong, Amber?"

There was a pause. Then a sigh. "Nothing. Except that I'm starting to get as paranoid as my parents."

"No way. No one is as paranoid as your parents—except maybe my mom. Come to think of it, we'd better call my mother over breakfast or she'll send out the National Guard."

"Worse yet, Aunt Rhiannon once the sun goes down. She's closer. If she's home."

"God help us if she is!" They both laughed; then he heard the bell of the elevator ping, the doors closed, and their voices faded.

Perfect. He would have time to work while the girls

had their breakfast, and hopefully he would still be able to catch them before they left the hotel.

He used the magnetic key card his pal Mike had provided to open the girls' suite. It was easy enough that it made him nervous—because it would be just as easy for anyone else. He didn't think Jameson Bryant was the paranoid type, contrary to his daughter's opinion. He came off as intelligent and genuinely concerned for his child's safety. Will had to assume the man had reason to be.

Will was quick, and he was thorough. Within ten minutes he'd planted a listening device in the girls' suite, so he would be able to hear if they got into trouble, and he'd lined the door with a sensor wire so thin it was almost invisible. The magnetic strip on the door frame was no more noticeable than a strip of transparent tape would have been.

He closed the door and took the indicator—a box with an on-off switch and two lights—from his bag of tricks. When he flipped the switch on, the green light lit up. Will opened the door. The green light went out, and the red light came on as a soft "chirp" emanated from the box.

Perfect. He would know any time their hotel door was opened.

He dropped the box back into his bag and left the girls' room, returning to his own. It only took a few more minutes to complete the work there. He left the indicator box on his bedside stand, set up the receiver and headphones for the listening devices right beside it, and he was done.

Checking his watch, congratulating himself on his time, he took the two remaining items from the bag—two calculator-size tracking devices and an ordinary-looking ballpoint pen. He tucked the "pen" and one of the trackers into his pockets, putting the other one into a drawer for safekeeping. Always have backup—especially when it came to electronics—that was part of his training. Finally he headed down to the hotel dining room.

He didn't have time to eat. The girls were already signing their check, heading for the nearest exit. God help him. He managed to grab a Danish from the continental breakfast buffet. No time for coffee. They were going to kill him before the week was out. He hadn't even slept.

He gave them a few paces, then went through the revolving doors behind them.

Sarafina rose at sundown, and her devoted servants were awaiting her. Misty had been an addict of a different kind before Fina had found her. She'd been about to sell her infant daughter to a dealer in exchange for a bit of the crystal-like substance she called "rock."

The dealer's mind was easily pierced, easily read, and his intentions toward the girl child had been so ugly that Sarafina had only taken the briefest glimpse before retreating in revulsion.

When she had finished her work that night, the dealer had been lying dead in an alley. She hadn't had the stomach to drain him, so she'd broken his neck instead.

She'd fed, instead, from the mother, who hadn't had any of her drugs in several days, so the blood was fairly uncontaminated, though weak and lacking in body. When Misty had hovered on the brink of death, Sarafina had given the woman a few precious drops of her own blood. Not enough to transform her. One couldn't transform an ordinary mortal, anyway. But one could addict them and thereby enslave them. Especially one with the will of a gnat.

She had tossed the limp, barely conscious woman into the back of her limo that night, gotten into the back with the infant and told Edward to proceed.

The baby didn't cry. Nor did it laugh. It had very little expression whatsoever. It was filthy, emaciated and bruised. She would be surprised if the child survived at all.

Sarafina was far from soft. But children were, unfortunately, a weakness of hers. She'd never borne one of her own. It was her one regret. Had she had a child, born of her own flesh, surely it would be the one being in the universe she could trust not to turn on her. To walk away.

Then again, there was no guarantee of that, was there?

She had Edward drive the limo up to the main entrance of the closest hospital. There she spotted a group of people in green scrubs, standing outdoors having a cigarette break. She lowered her window. "You there. Come quickly!"

They looked up, frowning, but they came closer to the car. When they were close enough, she thrust the baby out the open window, into the arms of one of them. She had only a glimpse of the man's wide, stunned eyes before Edward hit the gas and the limo sped away.

And now she had Misty. No longer a crack whore but an efficient and utterly devoted drone who would give her life for her mistress and a few precious drops of her new drug of choice.

Misty came the moment Sarafina opened her eyes, sensing her mistress's wakening. She stood now beside the bed, holding a robe of black satin. "Did you rest well, my lady?"

"Quite well, thank you." Sarafina slid her arms into the whisper-soft sleeves and pulled the robe around her.

"There's a bath freshly run and waiting."

"Very good."

Misty pushed back her sleeve, thrust her arm forward, wrist turned up.

Sarafina glanced at it, at the many tiny wounds dotting the skin. Then she shook her head only once. "I'm not hungry this morning, Misty. I have a lot on my mind." She turned and headed into the bathroom. "Bring the emerald silk. And choose my jewelry. I'm feeling...big and bangly tonight."

Misty nodded and scurried away toward the dressing room with the walk-in closet. Sarafina went to the bathroom, shed the robe and stepped into the sunken tub, descending into the hot water and letting it ease some of the tension from her body.

She had to find another place. The bar she had come to love so much was no longer an option. She didn't really know why she had developed this habit of going out at night to sit in crowded places. She didn't like associating with people, especially mortals. But she enjoyed observing them as they associated with each other. She enjoyed the noise and constant interaction around her while she sat alone, penning her thoughts and memories into a journal, wondering why she bothered.

Still, she'd become fond of the bar in the Village. It was a shame that man had found her there.

That man.

Sarafina closed her eyes and called his image to mind. He was so achingly familiar to her. From the moment he'd approached her, she had known him. He was that voice she'd heard in her mind any number of times throughout her mortal life. The day of her cousin's death, the day she'd learned of her lover's betrayal. The day she'd been transformed into one of the mighty ones. She had believed him to be a familiar ghost or a spirit guide, or perhaps a guardian angel of some kind.

Any of those things would have been preferable to

what he claimed—and she had to believe—he was. An ordinary mortal.

God, he didn't even possess the Belladonna Antigen! He was not one of The Chosen. There was no earthly reason why she should feel this...this powerful bond with him. No reason why he should have been able to journey, somehow, through time and across continents, to be with her during the most pivotal moments of her life.

But it was even more impossible to believe that he was making it up, lying to her. No. She had told no one of the strong, gentle, loving voice in her head. No one. She hadn't even written of it in her journals. And yet he knew, he knew details, and he gave the same name.

And he was in New York, where he had told her he would be, during the time he had told her he would be there. But more than any of that, she knew he was the same—she knew. She felt him. Sensed him.

Loved him.

No! Not that. Never that.

Her spirit lover had abandoned her. And while she had vowed never to care about anyone again so much that she would miss them in their absence, she had come to New York all the same. Perhaps just to find out for sure if her spirit lover had ever been real.

Now that she knew, she wished she didn't. She would rather have gone on believing him a god or a ghost than to know him for an ordinary man. A mortal, at that.

No. She mustn't return to the bar. He knew where to find her, and she did not want to see him again.

It was a lie. She *did* want to see him again. She was longing to see him again. But she couldn't. It was a matter of self-preservation.

When she emerged from the tub, Sarafina found her clothes waiting on her bed and Misty hovering nearby, a hairbrush in her hand.

Sarafina took it from her. "I'll brush my own hair tonight, love. Go and tell Edward to get the car ready. We're going exploring tonight."

"Right away, my lady."

10

"So far, we're totally striking out," Alicia said.

She wasn't whining. Not yet, anyway. Amber knew it wouldn't be long, though, before Alicia insisted they go back to the hotel and call it a night. The list she'd found on the Net of the best clubs in the city was apparently outdated. She glanced down at the printout in her hand, and then out the window at what looked like an office building, and not a nice one, either.

The cabdriver, a dark-skinned man with brown eyes and lashes to die for, glanced back at the girls. "This the place?" he asked.

"I don't think so," Alicia said.

"Let's go look. Maybe the club's in the basement or something."

Amber reached for the door.

"Your friend is right," the driver said. He had the sexiest accent, Amber thought. She wondered how old he was. He didn't *look* a day over twenty. "This place…no good for you."

Amber sighed, glancing up and down the street. She could have argued with him but decided against it. Instead she just handed the man some cash and opened her door.

"Amber!"

"I just want to check."

The driver sighed, shaking his head. "I wait here."

"Fine."

"I'm waiting with him," Alicia pointed out unnecessarily.

Amber thought that was a good idea. God forbid something should scurry in the shadows and give her timid sisterlike friend heart failure. She walked along the sidewalk, located a stairway that led downward and saw a door at the bottom. Beyond the door there was light. She supposed there could be a club down there. The address was right.

She had taken two steps down before three young toughs stepped out of the stairwell at the bottom, looking up at her.

"Mmm, mmm, mmm," one said, looking her up and down, stepping up the stairs toward her. "You come here lookin' for me?"

She tilted her head to one side. "In your dreams, maybe. I'm looking for a club called The Iron Mill. You know it?"

The young men exchanged glances. She heard them clearly, their minds a clutter of thoughts, all along the same lines. The club had closed several years ago.

"Sure, honey. You found it. It's right through these doors. Come on, I'll walk you down there."

She smiled slowly. "Nice try." Shaking her head, she turned to go back up the stairs. The three shot up the stairs, two flanking her. The leader, the guy she'd been talking with, came up right behind her, slid his arms around her waist, one hand cupping her crotch, another, one of her breasts, and jerked her back against him.

"Don't be walking away from me, bitch. That's rude. I just wanna get to know you."

Amber's heart was in her throat, but she kept her voice level. "Yeah? Okay, then, if you insist."

"That's better," he said, nuzzling her neck as he spoke the words.

"Not for you, it isn't." She slid her hand up to cup his head, then bent low and jerked him hard, driving her elbow behind her into his ribs for good measure.

He flipped over the top of her, landing on his back on the sidewalk. The two on either side of her grabbed her arms. So she used her feet, kicking the one on the left first, catching him in the groin and sending him stumbling right back down those stairs. A spinning back-kick upside the head floored the one on the right. The one on the ground in front of her started to get up, so she pressed her foot to his throat. "Don't even move."

He nodded as much as he could, sucking air through his pinched windpipe.

She took the foot off and stepped over him, toward the waiting cab.

And there was Alicia, halfway between the cab and

the stairway, a broken bottle in her hand. Shy, timid, easily frightened Alicia, white as a sheet, with eyes so round Amber thought she could have fallen into them. She'd been about to jump into the fray.

Amber smiled. "You're the best, you know that?"

"Are you okay?" Alicia asked. Her voice was shaking.

"Sure I am." She took the bottle, tossed it toward the nearby Dumpster, where Alicia had, no doubt, found it in the first place, then looked past her.

The cabdriver was still inside, tucking something shiny and metallic back underneath his seat. The cutie had a gun, and while he hadn't leaped to her defense, Amber thought he wouldn't have let her get killed, either. She was listening to his thoughts when she sensed someone watching them.

She turned, looking back down the street.

There was a tall man getting into a dark-colored car. He was familiar, but she wasn't certain why.

"Who is that?" Alicia asked.

"I don't know. He seems...I'm sure I've seen him before."

Alicia frowned. "Do you think he was rushing over here to help?"

"That was my first impression."

"Mine, too," Alicia said. "Hmm, people always say New Yorkers never do stuff like that. You know, get involved. Try to help someone out."

"Maybe people are wrong."

"Maybe."

The guy in the black car drove on by them. His windows were tinted, so she still couldn't see his face.

Alicia opened the cab door and got in. She picked up the printout, which had fallen to the floor, and handed it over the back seat to the driver as Amber got in. "We want to go to a decent dance club in a nice area. Can you recommend one?"

"You haven't had enough excitement for one night, even now, eh?" He gave a nod. "Lock your doors." Then he perused the list, muttering, "Closed, out of business, full of hookers, drug den, closed—ah, this one. This one is good."

Amber locked her door and watched the three guys helping each other to their feet and limping away, their backs to the cab.

Alicia took the list from the driver. "Star-Crossed?"

"That's the one. They have loud music, many kids, much dancing. And it's uptown. Safe for you. I take you there now?"

Amber took the list from Alicia, found the club near the bottom. "Sure, why not?"

Will parked around the next corner, in a spot where he would see the taxi when it left. It was a one-way street, so it would have to pass by him. He left the car running, put it in Park, and then sat there mentally replaying what he had just witnessed.

The girl fought like a commando.

He closed his eyes, gave his head a shake. He'd

pulled over, seen her get out of the taxi, and thought she didn't have the common sense of a ten-year-old to be poking around the way she was, in the places she was. Then the young thugs were on her, and Will was out of the car, heading over there as fast as his limp would allow, fully intending to break some heads. He was afraid for the girl, angry at the punks. But part of his mind was thinking about how angry her father would be if he let anything happen to her. That wasn't any part of his reason for keeping her safe—he had more honor than that. His mission was reason enough. Always had been. But for the first time it occurred to him that he had got himself into a rather dicey situation here. Should he fail, he doubted Amber's vampire relatives would rest until they made him pay.

Until that moment, he hadn't considered that, mostly because failure was beyond the scope of his imagination. He'd never yet failed in a mission. Then again, this was the first job he'd undertaken since the injury. He wasn't the same man he'd been before.

He'd been halfway to the girl when she'd sprung into action. Within a heartbeat, all three of her assailants were on the ground, and she was standing on the throat of one of them.

Now that he had a minute to process it, he reviewed what he had seen. The flips, the elbow, the kicks. Her form, ease, confidence. She'd obviously had some martial arts training. Lots of it, maybe. Her father had said she was stronger than ordinary girls. So maybe her poking around in dangerous parts of the city wasn't as much stupidity as it was confidence that she could handle anything that might come up.

That kind of confidence, Will knew, could get a person killed.

The cab drove by, and Will put the car into gear and followed. This girl was going to be even more trouble than he'd feared.

"Okay, okay. Once again, I'm forced to admit you were right," Alicia said as she and Amber wound their way through the club. "This place is great! And to think it was only a couple of blocks from our hotel the whole time."

Amber's senses were on full alert. She felt... something. Something besides the powerful bass beat echoing in her chest. The band was loud. Not great, not bad. Definitely loud. The people lining the dance floor seemed to like them well enough. And there were plenty, so many bodies gyrating in the place that you couldn't walk through without brushing up against strangers. The red and green strobe lights gave an otherworldly effect to the place. But Amber didn't think it was the lighting or the loud music or the bodies of strangers giving her the odd sensation in her belly.

"Let's dance!" Alicia said, for once losing her shyness. She tugged on Amber's hand, until they created a spot for themselves amid the crowd, and they began to dance.

Amber told herself to relax. Her parents had gotten to her, in spite of her certainty that they were nuts. Oh, she loved them. She loved them with everything in her. But she had to show them that she was grown up now, strong and sure of herself, and perfectly capable of surviving a week without them hovering over her. Maybe once she proved to them that the world would not come to a bloody, brutal end the moment she spent a night on her own, they would ease off a little bit. She knew they loved her, but they were smothering her.

So why was she undermining herself now by getting all nervous and jerky? Probably the fact that, for the first time in her life, she was without her mom and dad's protective wings wrapped around her was making her feel vulnerable. Heck, she should have expected it.

Like the guy in the room next to theirs in the hotel. He seemed like a perfectly okay guy. Just because she couldn't read him very well, that didn't mean he was up to no good. Some people were naturally guarded. Most didn't even know it. And just because the guy in the car earlier had looked similar to him, didn't mean it was the same guy. It was dark outside, and he wasn't near a streetlight. She could see in the dark better than a mortal, but nowhere near as well as a vamp.

And whatever she was sensing here, now, was different. It wasn't him. It wasn't a threat, exactly, it was...

She stopped dancing, her eyes scanning the crowded room.

Alicia stopped, too, searching Amber's face. "What's wrong?"

"There's a vampire here."

"Shit." Alicia looked around the room, too. "What are you getting, Amber?"

"Old. Powerful. Female, I think."

"Jesus, Amber, we should get out of here."

Amber glanced at Alicia, saw the fear in her eyes. "I really don't think we have to worry."

"Yes, we do. Look, Amber, you may be half-vamp, but I'm not. We both know they aren't all like the ones we know. Some are rogues. Some are... killers. How many times has your dad told us never to go anywhere near a strange vampire?"

Sighing, Amber nodded, once again scanning the room and seeing no vampire. She must be staying out of sight. "Fine. We'll go back to the hotel and call it a night, okay?"

Alicia sighed her relief, and the two turned to make their way to the exit—only to bump into the broad, solid chest of a tall, dark man, who walked with the help of a cane.

Amber looked up, into his face, and she knew suddenly. He was the same man who was in the suite next to theirs. He was the same man she'd glimpsed at the concert last night, and the same man who'd been on the street when those thugs had attacked her.

He was following them.

She held Alicia's hand, squeezed it and glanced at her, a single message in her eyes. *My parents were right.*

Sarafina was unsure this new place she had found was going to work any better than the three she'd already dismissed. The lights flashed too much, and the music was a bit too loud. Ah, but it was full of life. Full of youth. That part of it was perfect. Perhaps she could work on the minds of the management, convince them to make a few changes and—

Her thoughts came to an abrupt halt as she sensed someone near. Her head came up, eyes scanning the crowd, particularly those nearest the door.

Two girls. One of whom was not quite mortal.

Sarafina squinted, focusing her senses on the child. But the signals were confused and messy. The girl smelled human, but not precisely. She emanated vibrations like a vampire, but not exactly. She bore the antigen—or something very much like it.

What was she?

A moment later, the man came in behind the two. The owner of the voice in her head. Willem Stone.

How the hell had he found her here?

Sarafina gathered her things, ready to find a rear exit and slip away. But she realized that he wasn't looking for her. No, his attention was riveted on the girls who'd entered just before him. And in a moment he bumped into them as they tried to leave, making every effort to make the collision appear accidental.

What was he up to?

I know you're here, vampire. I need your help!

The words rang clearly in Sarafina's mind, the message sent by one accustomed to communicating mentally. She knew, instinctively, it came from the girl with the hair that looked as if it had been rinsed in blood to achieve its deep burgundy highlights.

Smiling slowly, Sarafina relaxed in her seat. Well, now, this night might prove amusing after all. *Why should I help you, little girl?*

She watched the child's face as she opened her mind to receive her answer—assuming, of course, the child was talented enough to have received her reply.

This man is following me. I think he might be DPI.

Sarafina frowned. How would this child know about the DPI? True, the organization itself was no more. But there were survivors, rogue agents who sought to carry on its work. She knew that only too well. But Willem? Never.

What would they want with you?

She felt the girl struggle with her decision, wondering how much to tell, how much to trust this stranger. Sarafina still didn't know what to make of the creature, what she was. She probed and sought, but the child had guards around her thoughts. And then, quite suddenly, the blocks fell away. As if the girl had let her guard down deliberately to allow Sarafina to read her.

Fina caught her breath. My God, this child was the one she'd come to believe was only a legend. Half vampire, half human. A result of the DPI's experiments long ago, and the only one of her kind in existence.

Go outside, child. If he follows you, I'll follow him. And I promise you'll have no more need to worry about his intentions.

She felt the girl's confirmation, saw her grab her mortal friend's hand and the two went out the door.

Sarafina watched Willem, her heart wrenching painfully. Could he be working with the vampire hunters? If so, did that mean he had been working with them all along? He didn't follow the girls. Instead he limped to the bar, ordered a drink and waited for it to arrive. Sarafina relaxed. God, but she did not want to believe this man could be evil or mean to do harm to her kind. More than that, she didn't want to believe everything he had been to her had been a lie—some kind of mental trick implanted in her mind by those bastards.

Will received the drink, tipped it to his lips and swallowed it whole. Then he got to his feet and went out the door.

Sarafina's disappointment weighed heavy on her heart. But she knew what had to be done.

She crossed the room easily and exited the bar behind him.

Will followed the two girls from a distance. He wasn't overly worried about losing them at this point. He'd dropped the pen into Amber's little handbag when he'd bumped into them so he could track them now if he needed to. Still, he preferred to keep them in sight. If they got too far ahead, something might happen faster than Will could catch up to prevent it.

A fact that ticked him off, because for just a second, back in that club, he'd been sure he was going to turn around and see Sarafina. He hadn't seen her. Hadn't heard her voice, exactly. It was more like a feeling. He sensed her. And now he wondered if it had been wishful thinking on his part, or if, had he searched that club, he would have found her sitting in a corner somewhere, writing in that velvet-covered book of hers.

It didn't matter. He didn't have time to find out, not now. The girls were in sight, just a few yards ahead of him, walking rapidly toward the hotel, visible now two blocks ahead and across the street.

Amber glanced back over her shoulder, but very quickly. Almost as if she knew he was following and didn't want him to know she knew it.

What the hell was up with that?

A touch, featherlight, whispered across his nape, and a voice said, "What's your hurry, Willem?"

He jumped, because for the life of him he hadn't heard her approach. And he was too well trained not to. But then he reminded himself what Sarafina was and decided all his training was probably worthless. God, it was good to hear that voice. It sent warm, fluid pleasure seeping into his limbs.

He stopped walking, turned but only halfway,

keeping the girls in his line of vision. "I *thought* I felt you in that club."

Her brows rose, and she smiled. "Did you?" she asked. "Then why did you leave?"

His gaze shifted in the direction of the girls, who were a block ahead now. "I assumed you didn't want me bothering you," he told her. "I went back to that other bar...several times. But you never showed. My guess was you just didn't want me to find you."

"You've found me now."

"Unfortunately now is...not a real good time." The girls were crossing the street. Soon they would be safely inside the hotel, inside their room. And he would be inside his. Alone.

"I've been thinking about you," she told him, stepping a little closer, sliding a hand up his chest. "I wanted to see you again."

He couldn't take her to his room, he told himself. She would see the damn equipment, or hear it, or—

Oh, God, look at those eyes, he thought, when his got trapped in them. Dark and so full of need. Hunger. He couldn't look away. And then he didn't want to. He dropped his cane to the sidewalk, slid his arms around her waist and pulled her against him. And then he kissed her. And it was as if a dam broke. He hadn't been with a woman since before his capture. He'd doubted himself, felt less than a man because of the injuries. But when her mouth parted and her body pressed against his, he forgot all his doubts.

By the time he could stop himself from feeding at

her mouth and lift his head for a breath, his heart was hammering, and he was so hard it was painful. But he couldn't—dammit, not tonight. The girls...

"My knees are shaking," she whispered. "Just hold me. Hold me, Willem."

He pulled her close, and she nestled her head on his shoulder, in the crook of his neck. He threaded his fingers in her hair and massaged her there. "I can't do this tonight, Sarafina. God, you don't know how bad I want to, but, I—"

"Shhhhhh." She pressed a finger to his lips. "Don't worry. Let Sarafina take care of everything." When she spoke, her moist lips moved against the skin of his neck, and it made him so hot he thought he was going to go into meltdown.

And then he felt her teeth. There was no warning. She just opened her mouth and bit down, hard, stabbing deep into his throat. He jerked and tried to pull away, and he was strong, despite his leg, but she held on. Biting down harder, and sucking, and the pain jolted through him, and then it sizzled and changed into pleasure. Her mouth. Her tongue. Her teeth embedded deep in his flesh. God, it was good. She was drinking him, and he was loving it, whispering to her to take him, take all of him, to drink her fill.

And then he was fading, falling. He didn't feel the sidewalk when he landed. He didn't feel any pain, or heat or cold, or much of anything at all except this haze of pleasure.

A car pulled up beside the curb. A man got out,

and dragged him into the back seat. Sarafina got in beside him, and the other man climbed behind the wheel, and then the car was moving.

Sarafina stroked his face, his hair. "I couldn't drain you. No, not you—even though..." She sighed, started over. "I need to know everything you've been up to, Willem. And you'll tell me, won't you, precious?" She drew her hand to her lips, pierced her palm with an incisor, and then pressed it flat against his mouth.

Blood, her blood, welled and touched his lips, his tongue. A jolt of heat and an orgasmic shudder ripped through his entire body, and he grabbed for that hand, held it to him, lapped at the tiny amount of fluid, shivering in pleasure with every taste.

Then she drew her hand away. "Yes," she whispered. "You'll tell me all about it. This connection between us. How you found me. And why you were following those two girls. Won't you, my precious one?"

He thought, at that moment, he would probably do anything she wanted. And he wondered why she had twin rivers of tears flowing down her cheeks. Then he closed his eyes and knew nothing for a while.

11

"Ohmygodohmygodohmygod, did you see that?"

Amber tried to tug Alicia away from the tall windows in the hotel lobby, but the second she let go, Alicia was back again, peering across the street. Amber grabbed her again, jerked her away and held on this time.

"I think she killed him. My God, I think she killed him," Alicia said. There were tears standing in her eyes.

Amber's throat went dry. She moved nearer the window, peered outside. "No, she didn't kill him. She took him with her. If she'd killed him, she'd have just left him there, right?"

"I don't know."

"She would. She would have just left him." She didn't really believe it herself. She'd never seen a vampire kill someone before. It shook her. "Sarafina," she said softly.

"What?"

"The woman's name was Sarafina. She never said, but I picked it up clearly. We should probably remember it. She might be...trouble."

"She saved us," Alicia said. "But, Amber, why

would she take him alive? What could she want with him?''

"I don't know." Amber tried to shrug off the heavy sense of guilt that was weighing on her. "I don't care. Why should I? He was following us, Alicia. He couldn't possibly have been up to anything good."

"How can you be so sure?"

Amber pursed her lips. "Fine, you want to be sure, we'll make sure." Again she took Alicia's hand, tugging her firmly toward the elevators. "Come on."

Alicia came. She kept craning her neck to look back, but the limo was long gone, Amber knew. She wouldn't see a thing. They took the elevator up to their floor, got out and went not to their own room, but to the one next door. Amber didn't even hesitate, just twisted the knob and pushed with her shoulder until the lock gave.

"Jesus, you're going to get us thrown out," Alicia whispered.

Amber dragged her inside, closing the door behind them. Then she let go and began going through the man's things. There wasn't much. A handful of clothes in the dresser. A little calculator. Some shaving stuff and a hairbrush. Some pills in a brown plastic prescription bottle.

She noticed the two boxes on the bedside stand—one of which had headphones attached. "See?" she asked, pointing.

Alicia looked at it, shook her head.

"It's some kind of spy crap. He probably has our room bugged." Amber yanked up the headphones and snapped them over her ears, then turned on a switch.

Then she froze as a tinny male voice came through the device.

"So where the hell are the girls? Shouldn't they have been up here by now?"

"Amber, I don't know—" Alicia began, but Amber held up a hand to silence her. Alicia's eyes widened, and she came closer. "What? What is it?" she whispered.

Amber held one of the earpieces away from her head, and Alicia leaned in and listened.

"The boss said he saw them come through the lobby. They'll be here any second. Will you just be patient?"

"I'm gettin' sick and tired of waiting."

"What the hell is our option? Go back to headquarters without them?"

"I was thinking more of popping 'em in the head on sight, tossin' their carcasses into the trunk and taking 'em somewhere to wait and see which one wakes up."

"Shit, we don't know for sure that either one of them would."

"Not even the half-breed?"

"No way to tell. That's why Stiles wants her. We let her get past us again, he'll have our heads."

"You're not shitting. I was with Stiles the first time

he got his hands on the 'breed. I was a rookie. It was only a couple of weeks old.''

"Yeah? What did it look like then? I mean, you know, was it...gross?''

Amber and Alicia locked eyes.

"Nah. Looked like a regular baby. You'd never know it wasn't human.''

"Half-human, I thought.''

"Not the way Stiles sees it.''

Amber tugged the earphones off her head, set them quietly on the bedside stand. "That guy Sarafina took—he must be one of them,'' she said to Alicia.

"We have to get out of here, Amber.''

Amber set her jaw. "Do you know what those assholes did to my mother?'' she whispered. Some of the things on the man's bedside stand started vibrating, and the pictures on the walls shook slightly. "I'm gonna kill 'em, Leesh. I'm gonna kill those two, and then I'm gonna go find the other one and finish him off, if that vampiress hasn't already done it.''

Alicia grabbed her arm and said just one word. But she said it with so much fear in her voice that it got Amber's attention, made her stop up the rage that was building inside her.

"Please?''

Amber paused, closed her eyes, got herself under control. The room stopped shaking.

"Amber, they're not talking about just you. They're talking about both of us. And I can't fight them, you know that. If they get the best of you, I'm history. Please, don't do this. Let's just get out of here and find somewhere safe to hide out and call your parents to come and get us. Okay? Please?''

Amber closed her eyes, lowered her head. For the first time in her life, she felt capable of murder. She remembered the things her father had told her—how she'd been born in captivity, how those men had left her mother locked in a concrete box to die once they had the baby they wanted.

"Oh, they were so tough then, weren't they?" she muttered. "Let them come and get me if they think they can. I'm not a helpless little baby anymore, Leesh.''

"I know. I know you're not.''

"Stiles. That was the name one of them used. Remember it. I'm gonna get them. I swear to God—''

"But not tonight. Not now. Please, Amber, can we just get the hell out of here?''

Amber looked at her friend. She was crying, twin streams streaking her cheeks. "Okay. Okay, come on. Let's go.''

She took her hand, pulled her toward the door.

"They have someone watching outside. Someone who told them when we came in.''

Amber bit her lip. "Yeah. Tell you what, we'll find a back way out of here, okay?''

"Okay.''

As they went, Amber pulled out her cell phone. Then she shoved it back into her backpack. The men had been in her hotel room; they'd bugged it. They might easily have bugged her phone, as well. She would have to find a neutral one from which to call home. She walked as quickly, as quietly, as she could, keeping her mind open, hoping she would pick up on any danger signs before it was too late.

Silently the two crept past their own hotel room door, where men waited in ambush, past the elevator, to the stair door. Once through it, they ran.

Sarafina had Willem Stone taken to the finest room in her house. Then she sat beside him and waited for him to wake.

She should have simply killed him. She knew that, but, God help her, she couldn't bring herself to do it. She had very little contact with her own kind, especially since her beloved Dante had abandoned her. But even *she* knew of the legend of Amber Lily Bryant. And she, more than most perhaps, knew that the DPI hadn't been completely destroyed all those years ago, when the vampires had revolted and burned its headquarters to the ground.

Stiles had survived. He'd been steadily building his network of vampire hunters ever since. It had been more than a decade, thirteen years, perhaps—a mere blip in the life of a vampire as old as she—since he and his skeleton crew of thugs had tried to murder Dante. She'd gotten the best of them then, and they'd been hunting her ever since.

And now they were onto Amber Lily, the only child of her kind.

Sarafina was not soft. But she wasn't about to allow Stiles or his thugs to get their hands on the girl. And yet, somehow, some idiotic fool deep inside her had trouble believing that Willem, who lay swathed in satin bedding, was working for them. With them.

He might be, though. It would explain so much. They had obviously devised some method for getting inside her head. They had tricked her into coming to New York by planting those conversations, that feeling of closeness to Willem, in her mind, knowing she would come here hoping to find him. She had likely been the main target all along. That Amber Lily and her pale, trembling mortal friend had shown up here must have been an added bonus. And no doubt they hoped to capture both their trophies in one fell swoop.

She smiled slowly, watching him as he stirred awake. "You don't have a clue who you're dealing with, mortal. You stand no chance against me."

He opened his eyes, blinked at her.

And she weakened again. God, when he looked at her...

She should have killed him. But she couldn't. Instead she had made him her devoted, mindless servant. When he woke now, his only desire would be to please her. She hated that she had been forced to do it to him. But it was too late to take it back now. He'd had enough of her blood that he stood no chance.

And it was a better alternative than death.

He parted his lips to speak her name in a voice coarse and weak. "Sarafina...?"

"Yes, my pet?" She leaned closer, studying him, waiting for his plea. He would beg to serve her any time now.

"What...what the hell did you do to me?"

She narrowed her eyes on him. "I drank from you," she told him softly, trailing her fingernails over his cheek. "And then I gave you the honor of tasting my power. And you loved it. Now you crave only more."

He pressed one hand to his forehead, closed his eyes tight. "I'm so goddamn weak."

"That will pass. Though not entirely. Not until I'm certain of your loyalty, at least."

He lowered his hand slowly, and looked at the room around him, then at her. "Shit. I have to go." He sat up in the bed.

Sarafina frowned, placing a hand on his chest, pushing him back down onto the pillows. "You'll go only when I say so. And I haven't finished with you yet."

"Well you'd better *get* finished, Fina, because I've got a job to do." He moved her hand off him, not gently. Not with the loving, devoted touch of a drone, but with a hint of anger and impatience. Then he sat up again, swinging his legs to the floor.

"Yes, you must be in a great hurry," she said, getting to her feet. She stood in front of him as he lowered his head to his hands, as if getting upright too quickly had left him dizzy. "You wouldn't want those two girls to get away from you, now would you?"

His head came up slowly. "I...don't know what you're talking about."

"You know exactly what I'm talking about, Willem Stone. The girls, the ones you've been following. I know what you're up to. You cannot hope to outwit me, Willem, nor to outfight me. So I suggest you relax back on the bed so that I'm not forced to kill you and be done with it."

He surged to his feet. "Listen, Sarafina, I don't know what the hell you think this is, but—"

She hit him—just once—with the back of her fist, and his head snapped back and his body left the floor. He landed hard, faceup on the bed.

"Misty! Edward! To me!"

The door was flung open almost immediately, and her two faithful servants appeared at her side, flanking her, their eyes flashing protectively.

"Bind him. Quickly."

They sprang into action at her command, falling on Will, gripping his arms. He shook them off, sending them tumbling to the floor in either direction. Then he sprinted unevenly for the door.

Sarafina got to it first, moving in a blur of speed, locking it tight, then standing in front of it.

Will grabbed her shoulders and tried to move her aside. "Jesus, Fina, what the hell are you *doing?* Have you lost your freaking mind?"

"You will *not* defy me!" She hit him again, with her full force this time. His body flew across the room, slamming into the wall, cracking the wood. Then he slumped to the floor, unconscious.

She glanced at her two servants, who were getting to their feet. "Go. Bring chains. I want him restrained before he comes around again."

They scurried away to obey, and Sarafina went to stand over the powerful mortal. "You're named aptly," she said. "Will of Stone. It will hurt me to do it, but I have no choice now that I know the truth—that it's all been a lie. I will break you."

His eyes opened, mere slits in his face, shooting fire. His lips moved to form the single word. No sound emerged, but she heard it all the same.

"Never."

Amber held Alicia's hand as they ran down the endless flights of stairs. Forty-six of them. And then still more. She didn't dare emerge anywhere near the lobby, where there might still be someone watching. So they kept going, down another flight, to the underground garage.

There they stopped. Alicia leaned back against the block wall, panting. She was hot and breathless from the long race down the stairs. Amber could have kicked herself for forgetting. She wasn't even winded. She let Alicia rest for a moment, while she peered through the square of glass in the door. The garage was dimly lit, lined with shiny cars. She didn't see anyone walking around. Closing her eyes, she opened her senses, tried to *feel* anyone out there, waiting for them. But she got nothing.

"Okay?" Alicia asked.

"I think so. You ready?"

She nodded, and the two opened the door and moved quickly across the open space into the darkest shadows in sight.

The ramp angled upward, to the street. The exit was a pale gray square right now, but it would be lighter soon. "The sooner the better," she muttered.

Alicia nodded, and they ran for it.

The garage entrance was around the corner from the hotel's lobby entrance, and that was good. Holding hands, they ran down the sidewalk. The streets were nearly deserted this early in the morning. Even traffic was light. Amber didn't figure that was to their benefit. They would have been much harder to spot in a crowd.

They hurried, and only after they'd put seven blocks between themselves and the hotel did Alicia turn to her and say, "Amber, where the hell are we going?"

"As far from that hotel as we can get."

"What about Aunt Rhiannon's place in the city?"

"If we go to her, she'll call my dad."

"Amber, we have no choice. This is serious. We have to get out of here."

Amber knew her friend was right. Damn, how she was going to hate to have to admit to her father that he had been right. And who knew when he would ever let her leave home without an armed guard again, after this fiasco? She would never live it down.

But she supposed staying alive and eluding capture was more important than her own pride or independence. It just killed her to think she was about to hand the keys to her cell back over to her parents, though.

"Aunt Rhi's place is on Long Island. Um, shit, I can't think. Wait, yes, yes, it's in my address book. Now if we can just find a cab."

"What about this?" Alicia pointed at a set of stairs descending into the earth and a sign that said Subway.

"I don't even know what train to take."

"Let's just take the first one that stops. Then we'll be far enough from here to be safe, and we can ask someone. Or find a map. Or catch a taxi from there. Come on, Amber, there are no cabs in sight, and I'll feel better down there, off the street."

"Okay, okay, let's go."

They found a machine to buy subway tokens, and then they got on the first train that stopped. They took it to the end of its run, got off, and emerged from the underground into brilliant morning sunshine.

Somehow things didn't look anywhere near as frightening as they had before. Amber sighed in relief. She flagged down a taxi, rather proud of herself for having caught on to the method for doing so as quickly as she had, and then they got in.

"We need to go to this address on Long Island."

She showed him her now-open address book. "Can you take us?"

The cabby looked over his shoulder, eyebrows raised. "You're in Brooklyn."

"So?"

"So that's quite a haul. Can you afford it?"

"I think so. You take plastic?"

"Cash. And a tip is always nice."

Sarcastic little bastard, she thought. "How much you think it will be?"

"Thirty-five, give or take a few bucks."

She dug into her minibackpack, thumbed through the wallet. "I have enough."

"Then we're outta here." He put the car into gear.

Amber leaned back in her seat. "I don't even know for sure if Rhiannon and Roland will be there." She looked out at the sky. "Even if they are, they won't be up."

"Then how are we going to get in?"

She pulled a yellow envelope out of her bag, opened it. "Remember mom's emergency kit? I laughed at her for insisting I bring it. Aunt Rhi's address, a key to her place, a can of mace—"

"There a stun gun in there?"

The cabby glanced at them in the mirror. "That stuff's illegal around here."

"So arrest me," Amber said, continuing to paw through the contents of the envelope. There were extra cash, credit cards and passports bearing their faces, with false names. "Good grief, you'd think we were on the run from the Feds or something."

"Too bad she didn't put an extra cell phone in there."

"There will be a phone at Rhiannon's place," Amber promised. But she was already wishing she could come up with some better plan than using it to call her father.

12

———————

William had a craving. A vague need gnawing at his gut so powerfully that it woke him from a sound sleep more surely than the pain in his bad foot.

He opened his eyes slowly, let his vision focus. He was not in his bed—his bed didn't have red satin sheets. He was not even in his own apartment, but in a large, lush bedroom with cream-colored walls and dark rich woodwork. He closed his eyes, trying to get his bearings, trying to think beyond the unidentifiable hunger inside him. Sarafina. Yes, he remembered. She was…a vampire. Unbelievable, but true. And he loved her, and she…she had bitten him. *Drunk from him…*

He lifted a hand to touch the wounds on his neck, as if to prove to himself that they were really there, that all this wasn't just part of some slow-growing insanity. But his hand stopped short of his neck, and there was a metallic clanking sound when he tugged.

He looked up sharply. A shiny steel bracelet encircled his wrist. A chain ran from it, through a ring attached to the post of the bed's headboard, and its twin held his other hand to the opposite post. From those rings, he couldn't see where the chains led. They disappeared behind or underneath the bed.

He studied his wrists for just a moment, a vague sense of disbelief slowly giving way to other feelings. He would have laughed at the absurdity of it if he hadn't been so angry.

The bedroom door opened slowly, and he lifted his head, watching, ready to rip into her with his words, even while he felt an odd stirring of anticipation in his gut and arousal in his loins.

He wanted her. He wanted her as much as he ever had—maybe more.

But it wasn't Sarafina who entered the room. It was a gaunt, pale-skinned woman who might be thirty but looked fifty. She carried a tray of food in her hands and closed the door behind her with one foot.

"Where is she?" he asked.

The woman's head turned sharply, her eyes wide with something like surprise, or maybe fear. They were blue, her eyes, and ringed in dark circles. Her blond hair was knotted in a neat bun, and she wore a kaftan in such bright colors that it only emphasized her own washed-out hues.

"The Mistress is asleep. She won't rise again until sundown."

"Then I guess it's up to you to take these cuffs off me. Immediately."

She brought the tray closer, studying him as she did. "I can't do that. But I did bring you food. The

Mistress left strict instructions as to your care. You're to have anything you ask for—aside, of course, from your freedom.''

She set the food on a stand beside the bed, where nothing else rested, other than a vase full of red roses, their stems lined in thorns.

Will studied the woman. Her blank expression, the slightly dead tone of her voice. Was she drugged?

"And how am I supposed to eat, chained up like this? Or use the bathroom, for that matter?"

"I can let out the chains." She got to her hands and knees, fiddling with something underneath the bed. There was a humming, motorlike sound, and the chains holding his wrists to the bed went slack.

He pulled at them, and they gave. Stupid move on her part, he thought, as he sat up in the bed, his hands in front of him now.

She set the tray on his lap. "The chains are very long," she told him. "You can move around the room freely. The bathroom is through that door." She pointed. "You can even shower, if you like. The Mistress has left you fresh clothing and toiletries in her favorite scents."

"Oh, she has. That's...thoughtful of her, isn't it?"

She smiled, a wan, weak-looking smile. "She is always thoughtful. And kind and generous. I love her." Her eyes flicked over Will's face, and her smile died. "You will, too, in time."

Something twisted in his chest, but he ignored it.

"Now that's interesting. Why would I love someone who would lock me up and try to keep me here against my will? Hmm? Why do you?"

She blinked as if confused.

"Do you think she loves you, too? Is that it?"

"Of course she does."

He nodded, setting the tray aside, flipping back his covers, surprised to find himself stark naked underneath them. What the hell, he was anything but shy. He got to his feet. "If she loves you, then why did she tell you it was all right to loosen the chains when she knew perfectly well that, once you did, I could kill you with my bare hands?"

The woman didn't back away or seem afraid in the least. She only stood there, facing him. "She knows I would die for her. Gladly. But if you kill me, I promise you, she will be very angry when she wakes."

He was surprised by her reaction. Her lack of fear. He'd expected her to run for the door, and he'd been prepared to lunge and grab her before she could get away. His foot was throbbing. He ignored the pain. He stepped closer, sliding his hands to either side of the woman's pale neck. "I won't kill you. Not if you do as I say. Get the key and unlock these cuffs."

She stared into his eyes. "I don't have the key." She said it in a calm monotone.

"Who does?"

"The Mistress."

He set his jaw, tried to school himself to patience. "Then you can get it from her while she sleeps."

"No. I cannot."

"I could break your neck with my bare hands, lady. You're going to get that key."

"No. Break my neck, if you will. It makes no difference to me. I can't disobey the Mistress."

He narrowed his eyes on her, searching her face. "Why? What the hell power does she have over you?"

"I don't know what you mean. I love the Mistress. Serving her is my life. It will be yours, too. You'll see."

She turned away, walked to the door and left the room. He heard the locks turn from the outside.

Fury raged to the surface. Will spun around, grabbing the vase of thorny roses and hurling it across the room. It hit the wall, smashed to bits, water, roses and glass exploding everywhere, littering the floor.

"Damn you, Sarafina!" he shouted. "What kind of sick game are you playing?" But he knew she couldn't hear. He jerked at his chains, promised to throttle the beautiful Gypsy the first chance he got, swore and raged and threw things, including the food. Hell, he wasn't going to eat anything she had sent to him. It was probably laced with whatever drug she'd been feeding her zombielike servant to keep her in line.

An hour later he sat in the center of the bed, the

room in shambles around him. He'd spent enough of his fury to leave him rational again. Calmer now, he got to his feet and examined the chains that held him. The only thing he found under the bed was a hook and a place where the chains met in the center and ran through the floor. The hook could be set through the links, to keep his chains at any length desired. At present the hook wasn't through them at all. There was a motorized winch somewhere on the floor below. How she'd turned it on from here, he didn't know. She might have had some kind of remote control he guessed. Or there was someone on the other side.

The chains were fixed fast, the passage through the floor secure. He couldn't break it open, couldn't pull more chain through. And he couldn't get the manacles off his wrists.

He focused next on exploring the limits of his reach. He couldn't reach the windows, couldn't reach the door. The bathroom door was nearer, just past the head of the bed, and he could get into it. It was a small room with a seat, a basin and an upright shower stall.

He explored the room fully, looking for flaws, for mistakes on which he could capitalize to make his escape. He looked for anything that could be used as a weapon, or even a tool to use to free himself.

Nothing. There was nothing. He was trapped like a rat in a cage.

But he'd been held captive before, by men who were experts at it. He hadn't escaped them only to let a mentally ill women who'd managed to enchant his soul get the best of him. He would escape.

He just hoped the two girls he was supposed to be protecting would still be alive by the time he did.

13

Sarafina rose at dusk and went to the room situated just below her captive's. In it were the controls. A hydraulic winch that could reel in the chains, a video monitor so she could keep an eye on him. There was a hidden button beneath the bed, as well, that could retract or extend the chains.

It wasn't as if she hadn't had captives before. She'd been prepared to have troublesome servants. But this was the first time she had ever had to use the safety features she had devised in case she ever got her hands on Stiles and his fellow DPI renegades.

Always before, her chosen servants were hers to command after the first taste of her blood. Addicted to her, craving her, loving her—not because of any real feeling, but because her life force lived within them.

But Will was different. She'd known it from the beginning. But she had never believed him to be an evil-doer, undeserving of life—at least, not until the girl, Amber, had told her the truth about him.

He had deceived her. Played a game with her mind. Endeared himself to her by getting inside her heart and soul before ever approaching her. Worse yet, he'd made her love him. But he'd only been using her all along, working for those animals who wanted to see every vampire destroyed.

She should have killed him outright. But she couldn't. Something about him just wouldn't let her. Perhaps he'd used his skills at mind manipulation to make her feel this odd softness toward him, even now that she knew the truth. That must be it. He was playing with her mind. She hated the weakness inside her that allowed it.

He was wandering now, naked, around the room. Still looking for some means of escape. She watched him for a time, enjoying the ripple of muscle in his thighs, even though he limped when he walked. His flanks, too, were toned and firm. Hard. He was a beautiful man despite the many scars that marked him, a strong man. His chest and belly were powerfully made. And his shoulders...

Tearing her eyes away from the monitor, she hit the button on the winch. It growled to life and began to turn at a steady pace. Glancing back at the monitor, she saw Willem stumble, tug against the chains as they pulled him toward the bed. They grew shorter, pulling him nearer, and he soon realized fighting them would be useless. He hit the bed facedown but rolled onto his back to prevent his shoulders from being torn from their sockets as the chains drew his arms to the bedposts. And then he lay there, fury coloring his face, his eyes blazing.

He wanted to kill her, she knew it.

Sighing, she left the control room, locking its door behind her.

Misty and Edward stood in the hallway, submissive and silent, awaiting her command.

"How has our guest been today?" She asked the question of Misty, who alone had been commanded to see to Willem's needs. Somehow, Sarafina sensed he would be less inclined to kill a woman. Edward might not have fared so well.

"Angry, my lady. And he refused to eat. He made a terrible mess of the room, but I've cleaned it all."

She nodded. "Come with me, then."

They followed, and she walked up the stairs to Willem's room. Unlocking the door, she stepped inside.

He lay there, naked and still, hating her with his eyes.

"Hello, Willem. I'm sorry about the chains. We'll be able to dispense with them very soon, I promise you."

"Oh good," he said. "Because I'm going to murder you the moment you do."

Even then, as angry as he was with her, the words didn't sound sincere. She wondered for a moment if he were as incapable of harming her as she was of harming him. And if he was—was it real, or was it the effect of her blood on his mind? "No, you won't," she told him. "We both know you won't."

She walked to the bedside, feeling his eyes on her. But she spoke not to him, but to her pets. "You've been a very good girl today, Misty. I will reward you now."

"If it pleases you," Misty whispered, but her eyes looked hungry and wet, and she licked her lips in anticipation.

Sarafina drew a pin from the skintight black sheath she wore and pricked her own forefinger, just a little. Blood welled, and she offered it to Misty, who took the finger into her mouth and drew on it. Fina let her have only a few drops, but she kept her eyes on Willem the entire time, and she knew he felt the hunger, the craving. She could see it. He couldn't take his eyes off Misty's mouth, where she suckled the finger. And she thought his breathing quickened just a little.

She took her finger from Misty and offered it to Edward. He, too, suckled the finger. Willem's tongue darted out to moisten his lips—involuntarily, she was sure. Sarafina let her gaze slide down Willem's naked body, and she saw his member growing hard with arousal.

She tugged the finger away.

Misty fell down to her knees, kissing Sarafina's feet. "Thank you, Mistress. How I love you."

Edward only bowed, taking Misty's hand, drawing her upright and leading her from the room.

Sarafina let them go, watched the door close behind them; then she sat down on the edge of Willem's bed. She took a small bandage from her pocket and stuck it over the tip of her finger. The wound would seep blood all night unless she stopped it.

"So it's the blood, is it?" he asked.

She only looked down at him, brows raised.

"I thought you had them drugged. Brainwashed, maybe. But it's not a drug, and it's no mind-control technique. It's the blood that addicts them. More than addicts them—it makes them mindless drones, with no will of their own. My God, I thought I knew you."

"Don't pretend you're not dying to taste me yourself, Willem. I can see you are."

"You're using these people like animals."

"They are animals," she snapped. "Misty was a crack whore who'd neglected and abused her own baby girl until she was barely alive when I found her. She was going to sell what was left of the child for more drugs."

He went silent for a moment. Then, softly, he asked, "And Edward?"

"Edward beat his wife—the last time so badly she nearly didn't survive it. She wanted to leave him, but she knew he would kill her if she tried." She shrugged. "I needed a new driver, so..."

"What happened to the old one?"

She lowered her head. "He was a pedophile. I thought I was doing him a favor by keeping him as a servant rather than killing him outright—but even as soulless and evil as you no doubt believe I am, I couldn't bear the sight of him. I told him to walk out into traffic one night, and he did."

He nodded slowly, studying her, his face different now. As if she had revealed something about herself that made him want to know more. "So you only make slaves of people you believe deserve it. Maybe you *do* still have some twisted sort of morality left in you."

She shrugged. "I make slaves—or meals—of whomever I choose. I'm a vampire. They're mortals. It's the natural cycle. Morality, or lack thereof, has no more to do with it than it does when a lion devours a gazelle on the Serengeti."

"Bullshit. The lion preys on the weak and the feeble. You prey on criminals. That's a moral judgment, Sarafina, though a perverted one."

"I find it far more entertaining this way. There's a poetic form of justice to it all."

"But you make yourself their judge and jury."

"And executioner, at times. I'm above them. Like a goddess among the mortals, so I do as I please. Is there some point to this discussion?"

She met his eyes. They probed hers. Her insides warmed and clenched. How did he make her feel this way with no more than a look?

"I was just wondering what crime I had committed, Sarafina. What makes me deserve this?"

She jerked her eyes away. "Are you going to tell me you've done nothing to merit imprisonment?"

"Nothing you'd consider worthy of it, no. Most people think I'm some kind of hero."

"I am not most people, Willem. And you were following two teenage girls when I took you."

He looked up at her quickly, obviously startled by her statement. "I didn't realize you knew them."

"I don't. But even I will protect one of my own kind—at least in a situation like this one."

"The problem is, you have no clue what the situation is."

"Don't I?"

He drew a deep breath, pinned her eyes with his. "I was hired to protect them, Sarafina."

She lifted her brows. "By whom?"

"By a vampire, just like you. The dark girl's father."

She lowered her head, sighing. "A vampire hired a mortal to protect his child? Really, Willem, I'm sure you can do better."

"Sarafina, I am telling you the truth. Look at me. Jesus, you *know* me. We have this connection—or had."

His eyes held hers, probed them. She forced her gaze away, got to her feet, and put some distance between them. She couldn't listen to his lies. There was something in her that wanted to believe them, and she knew too well where that would lead.

"You'd like me to believe that, wouldn't you? You'd like me to think that what I felt for you was real, that this bond we have is anything more than just some mind trick you've mastered. Then you could really do your worst, couldn't you? Lure me, convince me, win my trust, then use it to destroy those girls, or, worse yet, to destroy me. Better men than you have tried, Willem Stone.''

She paced the floor. He remained silent, just watching her, studying her, looking for some weakness, she knew.

''Unfortunately for you, I've lived a long enough time to know that anyone who claims to love you has a knife hidden somewhere, just waiting to plunge it into your back. I trusted you—foolishly—because I thought you were some kind of spirit. My guardian angel.'' She closed her eyes to stop their burning, tipped her head back, smiled bitterly at her own idiocy. ''You'd think I would have known better.''

''Just because I'm a man and not a spirit, doesn't mean I'm a liar, Fina. It was real, what we had. It was *real*.''

She had to turn her back on him to blink away the tears without him seeing them. ''Where did you learn it, this game you played with me? This mental trick? Was it something you picked up from your captors in the desert lands?''

''No.''

''Where then?''

''It's not a trick, Sarafina. I don't know why we connected the way we did. But you...you were where I went when the torture got to be more than I could bear. You were my haven.''

''Stop.'' She whispered the word.

''All I had to do was wait until the pain got bad enough, close my eyes and search for you. And I'd find you there. I'd stare into your eyes, and the next thing I knew, I was with you. Inside you, somehow, but outside you, too. I could see and feel everything you did. I could hear your thoughts. But I could see you, too.''

''Lies. All lies.''

''When they released me, I couldn't find you again, the way I did before. I tried, I tried everything. I only managed that once, when I became so goddamn desperate to see you again that I was close to losing my mind with it. I lay on my bed, and I slammed my cane into my mangled foot with all my might and…it worked. The pain was enough. I found you again.''

''Stop!''

He went silent, but only for a heartbeat. ''It's true. I only wanted to find that innocent, beautiful Gypsy girl I'd fallen in love with—to find out what had become of her.''

She swallowed the lump in her throat. Her heart ached.

''You were the only thing that kept me alive and sane those months I was held and tortured. Tell me that girl still lives in you somewhere. Tell me she hasn't turned into a monster without a soul or a conscience.''

She whirled on him. ''If you think those men in the desert caves tortured you, Willem Stone, you had better think again.'' She gripped his shoulders, lifting his upper body from the pillows. ''What I do will make the pain they inflicted pale by comparison!''

Then she bent and sank her teeth into his neck. She tasted him, and she lost herself inside his mind.

Willem tugged at the chains that held him, but he wasn't sure whether he wanted to push her away or pull her closer. God, the feel of her mouth on his neck, the gentle suction. He found himself arching his neck toward her. Let her drink him, let her drain him, he didn't care, if she would only just get closer.

As if reading his thoughts, she slid her body over his, lying on top of him. Inexplicably she released his throat, her lips sliding over his jaw, to his mouth, and he kissed her then. He let his mouth and his tongue do what his hands couldn't. He made love to her mouth with his, and he felt her entire body trembling in reaction. He tasted her tears, and he knew her threats were all just an act, a defense mechanism borne of past pain and betrayal.

Her legs straddled his, and one of her hands reached behind her to bunch her black skirts up around her hips. He couldn't see her, but he could feel her flesh, bare against his. When she lowered herself over him, he moaned and arched his hips. It was heaven and hell all mingled and confused in his mind. He craved her, he wanted her, and, in that moment, he loved her as much as he ever had.

She lifted and lowered herself rapidly, her body slamming down over his so powerfully it hurt, and yet the pleasure was so intense it didn't matter. It all blurred together, the pain and ecstasy, melding into one blinding sensation too potent to identify.

The orgasm rocked him to the core. And as the waves subsided, he realized her forefinger was in his mouth and he was sucking at it like a nicotine addict sucking on a cigarette.

He turned his head away, letting her finger go. And only when she moved her hand away did he dare to look up at her face. She wasn't looking at him but straight ahead, or maybe within herself. She looked...off. Upset. As if someone had just hit her upside the head with a two-by-four and she was still seeing stars. He hoped that was how she felt. It was how *he* felt, and he would have hated like hell to be there alone.

"Sarafina," he whispered. "I felt everything you felt, just now." He arched against her, still inside her, causing delicious friction that made her close her eyes and shiver with pleasure. "God, I still do," he said.

"Quiet."

"But, Fina..."

She pressed her forefinger to his lips to silence him. A scarlet drop beaded there, and he couldn't stop himself from licking it away.

"Sleep, Willem. Sleep and let the elixir of my blood do its work. Once it has..." A single tear rolled freely down her cheek. "Once it has, you won't lie to me anymore."

He was tired, some heavy weight settling over him, even as she slid hers off him and got to her feet on

the floor. "It won't work, Sarafina. Not on me. I'll
never become like your drones are. Mindless, obeying
without question. It's gonna be different with me,
Sarafina."

"Silence." She smoothed her dress down over her
hips, leaned over him to press her mouth to his again.

When she lifted it away, he said, "It's already different with me. You're drowning in me as much as I
am in you, aren't you?"

"Sleep," she commanded, straightening, turning
toward the door.

But before she did, Will saw more tears welling in
her eyes. They flowed like rivers over her flawless,
pale skin. A sob was torn from her chest as she fled
from him.

Rhiannon liked the modern conveniences, though
Roland detested them. She liked flying by jet, when
she could get a red-eye flight that posed no danger of
exposure to the sun. She liked fast cars, though Roland's dislike of motor vehicles bordered on the pho-
bic. She liked clothes and furs and jewels, and she
liked music and art and travel.

Roland had very few likes and only a handful of
passions. She was, of course, one of those. His dear
Jameson was another; like a son to him, though
Rhiannon herself had been of the opinion the young
one could use a good thrashing more than once since
she'd known him. And this was one of those times.

"I'm so sorry that Amber Lily isn't here to see

you," Jameson said as he hugged Roland, slapping his back in manly fashion.

"No matter. We didn't exactly warn you we'd be stopping by. We're just back from a cruise to Hawaii. Driving cross-country by night in one my beloved's cursed autos, naturally, and we couldn't pass by without stopping to say hello."

Rhiannon listened to Roland fill Jameson in on the details of their cruise, her eyes locked with the meek and mild Angelica's the entire time. She waited for Roland to pause in his conversation before saying, "What do you mean, Amber Lily isn't here?"

Angelica sighed, looking away. "I was against it, Rhiannon."

"I have to say, this is a *nice* place you've found," Roland said, as always, trying to play the peacemaker.

"It's a gloomy, isolated, ancient mansion on the foggy, rainy shore of Lake Michigan," Rhiannon said. "Of course *you* think it's nice. Now, if you don't mind, can we find out where my precious niece is?"

Roland sent her an adoring, indulgent smile, nodded once, and Rhiannon turned to Jameson, crossing her arms over her chest and waiting.

"She and Alicia are celebrating their high school graduation with a week in New York."

She blinked slowly. Her hands curled into fists so that her nails pierced her hands. "By themselves?"

"Rhiannon, I'm her father. I know her. And trust me when I tell you that if I hadn't let her go, she would have run off on her own."

"And you couldn't at least wait for a time when we were in residence so I could keep an eye on her?"

"Rhiannon, Jameson and Angelica surely know what's best for their own daughter," Roland said softly. Though she knew he had doubts.

"Angelica has already stated she was against the idea," Rhiannon said. "Obviously she hasn't yet learned to stand her ground."

"Or maybe it's just that I trust my husband's judgment," Angelica snapped, then she turned on her heel and left the room.

"What judgment?" Rhiannon shot after her.

Jameson stepped in front of Rhiannon before she could go after his wife. "Easy, princess," he said to Rhiannon. "I'm not as stupid as you seem to think. I was practically raised by vampires, after all. Give me some credit for picking up a little caution along the way. Amber and Alicia are perfectly safe. I have someone keeping an eye on them."

Rhiannon lifted her brows. "Who?"

Angelica reentered the room, a magazine in her hand. She thrust it at Rhiannon. "Him. That's who."

Rhiannon glanced down at the cover of *TIME.* The rugged face of a man, superimposed over a rippling American flag, stared back at her. She looked at it, then looked up again. "A *mortal?* You've put my niece's safety in the hands of an ordinary mortal? Has the constant rain in this godforsaken place mildewed your brain, Jameson?"

"Spoken like a true desert dweller. This man is no ordinary mortal. Read the article."

"As if there's time to read when our precious Amber Lily is on her own in the city. Stiles and his rogues have been hunting for her forever."

"They have no way of knowing what she looks like. Besides, she checks in every night by phone."

"And has she checked in yet tonight?"

Jameson glanced at Angelica, who glanced at the clock.

"Call her," Rhiannon said.

When the cell phone in her purse bleated, Amber Lily almost jumped out of her skin.

She and Alicia had spent the entire day safely ensconced in Aunt Rhiannon's posh Long Island home. The place had everything. A hot tub and a sauna, a home theater with a huge screen and surround sound, state-of-the-art DVD player, stereo and computer systems, high-speed Internet, and an endless supply of movies and music.

They'd been trying on some of Rhiannon's trademark gowns, all of them skintight and floor-length, with daring low necklines and high leg slits, when suddenly the cell phone wept pitifully.

Both girls went dead still and silent, their eyes meeting.

It rang again, and Amber hurried to where she'd left her bag slung on a chair, rummaged inside, pulled out the phone. As it rang for a third time, she looked at the digital panel. "It's coming from home."

Alicia sighed in relief. "Your mom, checking on us. We haven't called in yet tonight."

It rang a fourth time.

"It's not like we didn't try," Amber said. "It's not our fault my parents are dead to the world during the day, or that your mom was out somewhere. And this isn't exactly the kind of news I could leave on the machine."

"Aren't you going to answer it?" Alicia asked.

"No. We already decided they might have bugged the cell phone, or maybe they have some other way of tracing it. We'll just call them back from Aunt Rhiannon's line."

"Good thinking."

As the phone rang again, Amber pushed the power button to turn it off. Then she dropped it back in her pack. The two girls walked to the living room, moving carefully on pairs of Rhiannon's stiletto heels, and sat down. Amber picked up Rhi's telephone and dialed her own number.

Her mom picked up on the first ring, sounding anxious. "Amber?"

"Yeah, it's me, Mom. Sorry I didn't answer before. The, uh, the reception's kind of funny here. Comes and goes, you know?"

Alicia frowned at her. Amber covered the mouthpiece and whispered, "There's no point in us scaring her to death, is there?"

Shaking her head, Alicia sighed and sat back in her chair.

"I'm just glad to hear your voice and to know you're okay. And I—" There were muted voices, then, "Oh, for God's sake, all right! Amber, um, your aunt Rhiannon is here, and she really wants to talk to you."

Amber shot a look at Alicia. "Aunt Rhiannon is there?" She covered the mouthpiece with one hand and whispered to Alicia, "New plan. Aunt Rhi is there."

"Yeah, just a minute, let me put her on before she has a coronary."

Amber scrambled to her feet, studying the telephone on the end table, and finally finding the speakerphone button and pushing it.

"Amber? Where are you, child, are you all right?"

Amber licked her lips. "I'm fine. For now. Listen, don't say anything to scare Mom, okay?"

There was a pause. She could picture Rhiannon's face so clearly, could imagine her looking worried, then covering the expression easily. She was so smart. God, of every woman she had ever known, vampire or mortal, she admired her aunt Rhiannon above them all. She might not have to confess to her father after all.

"Of course, love. Please, tell me all about the adventures you've been having."

"We really are fine." Amber was so glad to be able to tell someone what was happening, besides her parents, who would overreact. They *always* overreacted. "But our hotel room was broken into. And we think it was bugged."

"Oh, I agree, the Metropolitan Museum is spectacular. And what did you do next?"

"We thought we were being followed. But then I ran into this vampire—I know I'm not supposed to interact with those I don't know, but she was all right, Aunt Rhi. In fact, she reminded me a little bit of you."

Rhiannon sniffed. "Her name?"

"Sarafina."

"I have heard of that actress. She's a recluse. A loner. Some say she has a dangerous temper."

"Maybe so, but she got rid of the guy who was following us. We didn't want to go back to the hotel, so we came to your place. That's where we are now."

"Ah, a lovely choice. And you're comfortable there?"

"Comfortable and safe. No one knows where to find us."

"Well, that's good to hear. I think you should continue with that plan."

"You mean...stay right where we are?"

"Exactly, child. Roland and I will be on the first flight, and we'll be sure to see you the instant we arrive back in New York."

"Thanks, Aunt Rhi. I promise, we won't leave this house until you get here."

"I'll hold you to that."

Rhiannon handed the telephone to Angelica, so she could speak to her daughter. She drew the necklaces from her silk handbag. Each was made of pink-toned pearls, alternating with tiny shells, on long strands. She'd picked one out for her darling Amber Lily, and then decided to purchase one for Alicia, too. She was a dear thing, for a mortal.

Turning, she wondered whether to betray her beloved Amber's trust, or head home and deal with this on her own. She eyed Jameson and Angelica, as they held their heads close together near the phone to speak to their daughter, smiling and fully reassured by whatever she told them. God, Amber Lily knew her mother very, very well. Jameson was as tough as any vampire ten times his age. But Angel was fragile. Like Rhiannon, she'd been a captive, a lab rat for the DPI once, long ago. Unlike Rhiannon, she'd emerged from the experience damaged and broken, with wounds that would never heal.

No, Amber Lily was right to want to protect her mother from the truth. Perhaps Rhiannon should simply rush home, pack Amber Lily and Alicia up and personally escort them back here to their dreary lakeshore mansion.

And then she would deal with whoever had frightened her niece.

Rhiannon was certain it was the right thing to do. Angel need never suffer the horrible fear for her daughter that she had suffered once before. The tender vampiress could not survive going through that kind of torment again.

14

———————

"**I** can't believe you didn't tell your mom what was going on." Alicia used her most annoying tone, but only after Amber had finished speaking to her mother and hung up the phone. "And you didn't even ask if I wanted to talk to mine!"

Amber did feel a little guilty about that. "She wasn't there. Mom and Dad gave her a spa weekend to enjoy while we were gone. That's why she didn't answer the phone earlier today."

"Maybe there's a number where we can reach her. How do you know, when you didn't even ask?"

"Look, Alicia, if you talk to her you'll spill the whole thing. You know you will. And then the whole bunch of them will come charging to the rescue like the vampire cavalry, with your mom and mine both scared out of their wits for no good reason."

"No good reason? Hello? We're in trouble here, Amber. Or haven't you noticed that?" Alicia paced the living room, pushing a hand through her platinum curls.

Amber stayed where she was, sitting comfortably in a leather chair that hugged her in luxury. "We're not in trouble. We're perfectly safe here. Rhiannon and Roland are on their way, and they'll see us safely home.''

"Right. And have you noticed what time it is?''

Amber frowned, glancing first toward the windows, which were still dark. But then again, they were lined in tightly drawn miniblinds and black velvet drapes. So she looked at the antique grandfather clock—which must have been Roland's contribution to the decor. It was almost midnight. She'd been putting off her call home, fully expecting Roland and Rhiannon to arrive at any time, unaware they were so far away. She should have called home far sooner.

"There's no way Roland and Rhiannon will get here before sunrise. So we're on our own for another entire day.''

Amber sighed. "Alicia, don't worry. We're safe. No one knows where we are—except for Rhiannon, and she's certainly not telling. We'll just hang here for the day.''

Alicia sighed, pacing to the sofa and dropping herself onto it. "I still think we should have told your parents the truth. Just in case.''

"In case of what? Real danger?''

Meeting her eyes, Alicia nodded.

"Don't you get it, Alicia? If there's real danger here, that's even more reason to keep your mom and my mom safe at home, as far from this mess as they can get.'' She licked her lips, hugging a pillow to her waist. "I don't want anything to happen to my mother, Alicia. She's been through enough because of me.''

Alicia sighed, but at least she didn't argue. They both knew she didn't want anything to happen to her mother, either. Amber got up and went to sit beside her on the sofa. She slid an arm around her friend, pulled Alicia's head down onto her shoulder. ''Before another night passes, we'll both be safe at home in our own beds. I promise, Alicia. Come on, let's get some sleep. We both need it.''

''All right.''

The two got up, still arm in arm, and walked into the bedroom. Amber had checked the locks a dozen times, but she found herself glancing at them again as they passed by the entry door.

They hung Rhiannon's dresses in the enormous walk-in closet, put her shoes back into their spots on the wall-size shoe rack, put on T-shirts for sleeping and curled up in the king-size bed.

They were sound asleep when, hours later, something smashed through the front door.

Why? Sarafina asked herself the same question over and over after leaving her captive alone in his room. Why had she let herself be washed away by the tide of passion he set loose in her? When she left the room, she had been trembling, weeping, her lips tender and tingling from the delicious assault of his. How long had it been since she had allowed a man to kiss her?

She'd kissed Dante. But never in passion. No, it had been a century. It had been Bartrone. And even with him, it had only been a companionable sort of love. Not the explosive fury she felt with Willem.

But she'd done more than kiss Willem. She'd impaled herself on him. She had reached climax, and it had been shattering. When she'd climbed off him, she honestly hadn't been certain her legs would support her. My God, she knew better. Passion, in her kind, mingled with the bloodlust, each magnifying the other. She could have killed him.

She could have killed him.

And now, as she lay in the safe haven of her crypt-like bedroom, deep beneath the house, reviewing the events of this night as she waited for the day-sleep to claim her, there were still tears dampening her face.

Tears! How many times had she wept since he'd come charging into her life? Too many. God, she'd vowed long ago never to allow another living being to have this kind of effect on her. And yet she had. Dammit to hell, she had.

She'd made a dire mistake in bringing him here. He held a power over her, one she did not understand. One she feared.

She closed her eyes, vowing that, come sundown, she would have to set him free. He wasn't like the other slaves. He wasn't like any man she had ever known. Willem Stone could not be broken. Will of Stone, she thought, as her eyelids grew heavy and the lethargy stole over her body. She would locate the girl and her mortal friend first. She would take whatever steps were necessary to ensure their safety, even if it meant returning them to their home personally. And then she would have to turn him loose.

Because the only alternative was to kill him. And she knew she was incapable of doing that. No matter what kind of evil he had done, or planned to do, she couldn't kill him. She couldn't.

Will knew exactly what he had to do.

After Sarafina left him, his chains were once again loosened. Misty appeared, bringing him a fresh change of clothes that were not his own and a morning meal. He greeted the timid woman with a weak smile, taking the clothes, thanking her for the food. He dressed right there in front of her, and then he sat down and obediently ate the meal.

There was no reason not to. The food wasn't drugged, as he had at first suspected. It was Sarafina's blood that drugged her prisoners, and he'd had enough of it to understand that now. He craved her. It was like a hole in his gut that only she could fill.

But he would never let her own his soul the way she owned Misty's and Edward's. He could not be broken.

Not ever.

The breakfast consisted of sausage so perfectly seasoned it must have been imported, an omelet oozing with cheese and mushrooms and ham, thinly sliced fried potatoes, seasoned with bits of onion and green pepper, freshly ground, freshly brewed coffee, and a pastry so delicate it nearly floated from the tray. It was delicious, all of it, and his stomach was beyond empty. He relished the food, wondering if the other meals had been this good and regretting that he'd refused them.

Only the best for Sarafina's pets, he thought as he ate.

Misty lingered. He was certain she must be under orders from "the Mistress" to watch him and report back. So he ate with enthusiasm, keeping that dumbass blank expression on his face, except to smile wanly every now and then, and compliment her on the food.

When he finished, she picked up the tray, no longer wary of getting too close to him. "It's good to see you feeling better, Willem. I told you everything would be all right. Our lady loves us. And you most of all, I think."

"What makes you think that?"

She shrugged. "She was weeping when she went to her rest. I've never seen the Mistress weep before. At first I thought you'd harmed her in some way, but when I asked, she nearly took my head off. Said if Edward or I harmed a hair on your body we'd spend the rest of our lives regretting it."

He took all that in, knowing it was insane of him to believe that Sarafina was still harboring some trace of the girl she had been. The one he had fallen in love with, even when he was just a voice in her mind.

He closed his eyes, remembering everything that had happened between them the night before. She'd fed from him as if he were prey and she was a hunter. She'd mounted him and worked him as if he were little more than a sex toy she'd purchased to pleasure herself.

But when she'd kissed him...all that had changed.

Her pace had slowed, her movements becoming languid and almost...tender. Definitely needy. He could feel everything she felt, and he thought maybe she could feel what he was experiencing, too. The way she took him deeper when he needed to go deeper. The way she moved still faster when he neared release. The way she took him to the hilt at the moment when he exploded inside her. And she did, too. He felt her shuddering climax as powerfully as he had felt his own. And she had still been kissing him.

Loving him.

He'd felt it.

Or was that just the power of her blood working its dark magic inside him?

He had never had sex that intense. Never.

And in spite of everything, he wanted her again.

Misty left him alone, returning later with a selection of books. Edward showed up a short while after that with a portable television set.

They were buying it.

But would she?

The day passed at a snail's pace. He plugged the

television set into the wall, managed to maneuver the rabbit ears until he got a viewable picture, and passed the time answering game show questions and critiquing the acting skills of soap stars. When that grew too monotonous, he dug through the books.

And finally night fell and he sensed her coming. He didn't hear her, which was odd. He didn't have a clock to go by, but he knew she was coming to him. He felt it.

Jesus, maybe her blood really *was* having some effect on his anatomy.

His chains didn't suddenly begin winding up, dragging him to the bed to be held there by a short leash. Apparently her drones had informed her of the change in his attitude. Not that she had much reason to be afraid of him anyway. The woman was as strong as he was—stronger, though he hated to admit that. And even if she hadn't been—hell, he couldn't have hurt her if he'd tried. And that wasn't the blood. That was a preexisting condition.

His door was unlocked and opened. She stood there wearing a red satin robe. She hadn't even dressed yet. He almost smiled, thinking maybe she wanted a repeat of last night. But then he forced his face to be expressionless and simply stared at her, pretending to adore her as mindlessly as her whipped puppies did.

"My beautiful lady," he said, his voice soft. "I've been so alone without you."

She blinked in surprise, and he thought he saw a hint of suspicion in the bend of her brows. She was beautiful. God, he'd never seen a woman as beautiful. But she was not convinced.

He fell to his knees, bending low to press his lips to her feet. Soft, pale skin, cool to the touch. She smelled clean, freshly bathed. For him? The thought made him hot. He slid his mouth around to her ankles, kissing a path up her calf to the hollow behind her knee.

"Enough, of that. Get to your feet, Willem. If you think I am so easily fooled, you should think again."

He got to his feet, keeping his head lowered. "I'm sorry. Please don't be angry with me."

She narrowed her eyes on him, studying his face. He thought she was trying to read his mind, but he remembered Jameson Bryant saying he couldn't make that particular trick work on Will. That he had his thoughts naturally blocked. He hoped that was the case with her, as well.

Her frown of frustration hinted that it might be.

"So you're my servant now. Is that what you'd have me believe?"

"Your devoted servant."

"And how do you feel about me?"

"I adore you, Sarafina. I love you with everything in me." His stomach knotted when he said it. He tried to ignore that.

She paced the floor, circling him, tapping one finger against her chin in thought. "How shall I put you to the test?" She stopped behind him, and he could feel her eyes boring into his back. He waited, knowing he had to make this convincing. Obey her without question, though it would grate on him to do so.

"Your mistress is hungry, Willem."

Will closed his eyes. Jesus, not that. Not again. It made him lose his mind to wanting her, and it left him weak and barely able to function.

Still, he lifted his hands to the front of his shirt, ripped it open and turned to face her. "Then drink," he told her.

She came closer, watching his face closely, waiting, he knew, for him to flinch or shrink back or in any way indicate resistance. He gave her none. In fact, when she bent her head to his chest, he threaded his fingers into her hair and urged her forward. She touched his skin with her cool, damp lips, and he shivered. How he could be so turned on by a woman he had every reason to hate was beyond him. Her mouth opened wide on his chest, and he whispered, "Do it. Drink me, Sarafina."

Fangs pierced his skin just below the collarbone, cutting, but not too deeply. Then they withdrew, and she lapped the blood up with her tongue. His entire body shuddered with awareness and need.

"Now your turn." She stepped away from him, just a little. His jaw was set as he fought the sensations this woman could bring to life in him. He tried not to shake visibly and battled the urge to just fling her down on the bed and take her, force her to drop the dominatrix act and admit that she was as wild for him as he was for her. That she loved him.

Sarafina drew a tiny blade across her palm, leaving a trail of scarlet beads in its wake. She offered it to him, but when he reached for her hand, his stomach knotting with hunger, she drew it away. "Not until I say. This is a test of your obedience, after all." She studied him, watching for the slightest hint of temper. "On your knees."

He didn't hesitate. He dropped to his knees. The awkward landing hurt his bad foot, and he winced, then saw her notice it. She offered her palm again, and he took it in both of his chained hands, drew it to his mouth. Told himself to pretend not to be revolted and realized he didn't need to pretend. He licked the blood, kissed the palm repeatedly, and licked some more.

Her breathing quickened. Good. She *should* be affected. Hell, every taste was sending shock waves jolting through his entire body.

He wanted to devour her, but he was still in control. He recalled what Jameson Bryant had told him about the way a vampire would bleed to death from a minor wound. So he drew his head away, removed his shirt and tore a strip from it with his teeth. Then he took her hand again, gently wrapping it, tying a knot, sealing it with a kiss. "You should be more careful, Sarafina. You cut too deeply."

Trembling, her hand moved through his hair. "And you would care if I were to die before sunrise?"

Slowly he rose to his feet, slid his arm around her waste. "I would die, too, if you did."

She didn't pull away, only stared into his eyes as he lowered his mouth to hers and kissed her. He kissed her deeply, tenderly. He didn't ravage or demand, the way every cell in his body wanted to do. He kissed her like a devoted slave, asking, pleasing, utterly selfless. And when he finally lifted his head away, he stared intently into her black eyes and whispered, "I love you."

Sarafina jerked out of his arms, spinning around to put her back to him. "You must never say that!"

Why?

He moved closer, slid his hands over her shoulders. "I've made you angry. I'm sorry. If it distresses you to hear those words, I'll never say them again."

"See to it you don't."

He lowered his head to kiss her neck. "Let me please you. I can balm your soul like nothing else can. If you would allow it...?"

She said nothing. Instead she stood as she was, moving only her arms to slide the robe from her shoulders. It pooled at her feet. She wore nothing else.

Will traced the curve of her spine with his fingers and then with his lips. Oh, yes. She thought she was in complete control, didn't she? That she'd made him a mindless drone like those other two zombies she had sleepwalking around this mausoleum? But she was wrong. He dropped to his knees. She liked him on his knees, didn't she? He kissed her buttocks, which was no doubt exactly what she had in mind, though perhaps not so literally. Then he gripped her hips, and he turned her around.

Her fingers tangled in his hair as he spread her open with his thumbs and fed from her in a far different way. Her head fell backward, and her hands clutched his head as he made her entire body shiver and quake. He kept feeding as he pushed her backward, until her legs hit the bed and she tumbled down onto it, her legs still over the side. He pushed them wider and burrowed deeper, kept pushing her, eating her, wishing he could go on until there was nothing left. Everything left his mind except for her, her taste, her scent, the sounds she was making as he pushed her beyond endurance. And then she screamed his name, mashing his face into her so deeply he could barely breathe, nor did he care, as he obediently lapped her juices. Then, just as suddenly, she shoved him away with so much force he skidded across the floor until he ran out of chain.

She sprang from the bed and followed, looking hungry, predatory. "Get those pants off," she whispered.

And he did, quickly, had them off before she reached him. It was a good thing, because she mounted him immediately. As she moved, her breasts bounced in front of his face, so he caught one in his mouth and suckled her. She liked his mouth, he could tell, so he kept using it, until she was crying out again, spasming around him, and he was pouring into her.

She fell forward, her teeth sinking into his throat. She drank, and she drank some more.

God, how far was she going to go?

He was getting dizzy. Weakening. Jesus, would she do him in this time? His hands moved to her chest as if to push her away, but he stopped himself. That would blow his cover. He had to play this thing through to the end, carry the bluff to the very edge.

"Take it all, Sarafina. I'll gladly die in your arms tonight."

It worked. The sucking at his neck stopped, and Sarafina jerked her head upright. He stared up at her, saw the sudden hint of panic widening her dark eyes. She pressed a hand to the wounds in his throat, cursing under her breath.

He let his head slump to the side, let his eyes close to mere slits. He could have forced them open wider, but they wanted to close anyway, and it couldn't hurt the situation.

"Willem," she whispered. "God, what have I done?"

She climbed off him, quickly fetching her robe and pulling it on. Tying the sash and giving it a brutal tug, she went to the door and jerked it open. "Edward, Misty!"

The two came quickly. Will heard their footsteps—though they seemed more distant than they should.

"What's happened to him, my lady?" Misty asked.

"That's none of your business," Sarafina snapped. Then, in a softer tone, "I never meant...just get him into the bed. And remove the chains. Here. Here is the key.'' She started out of the room, then turned. ''Watch over him tonight. He'll need fluids. If he dies, there will be hell to pay.''

''Yes, ma'am,'' Edward said. ''Don't you worry, we'll see to it.''

The door closed.

Will felt his lips pull into an almost smile. Great. The bluff had worked. He felt Edward's grip on his shoulders, felt himself hauled upward, and then the bed was underneath his back. Covers were tugged over him, and Misty, he thought, because of the softness of her hands, dabbed something soft and moist against the wounds in his neck.

''He's awfully pale,'' she whispered.

''He must have displeased the Mistress,'' Edward replied. ''No doubt he deserved it.''

''If he displeased her, she wouldn't want his chains removed.'' Even as she said it, he heard the rattle of a key, a tugging at his wrist. The manacle slipped away. While she moved to the other side of the bed to free his other hand, Will began to plan his escape. This was going to be easy. Escaping from that nest of vipers in that desert cave made this little challenge look like child's play. Sarafina wasn't half as good as she thought she was. And he was going to beat her at her own game.

Just as soon as he woke up.

15

It had been impossible to make arrangements to transport a coffin by air on such short notice. A standard ticket was impossible. No flight leaving would arrive in New York before dawn. It would have been even more impossible to leave in haste without alarming Jameson and Angelica, who would likely have baked themselves in the sun in an effort to reach their daughter if they knew the truth. Which was why she had a plan.

Rhiannon booked four tickets on a flight leaving Michigan an hour after sunset and doubted even the day-sleep would relieve the worry in her mind.

But, as always, the sleep came and took her, with or without her will; it never seemed to matter. It seemed only moments before she felt life returning to her body, stirring her cells, activating her heart.

She rose in the guest room of Jameson's home. Angelica had never been able to bear sleeping in a coffin or in any other enclosed space. Not since what those DPI animals had done to her. There were no such places in this house. Just locked, secure bedrooms without windows, invisible from outside, with doorways that doubled as bookcases or solid walls.

Jameson had been clever, and he'd had help from the vampire Eric Marquand, no doubt. Eric was Roland's best friend and as close to Jameson as Roland was. He was also something of a scientist among the undead.

Rhiannon was already showered and dressed by the time Roland rose. He looked at her, a crook in his brow. "Are you going to tell me what's going on, or are you still determined to keep me in the dark, so to speak?"

"That's a very bad pun, love. And you're terrible at guarding your thoughts from Jameson."

"So there's something you don't want him to know?"

"If there's anything he needs to know, he'll know it soon enough." She had made a decision, one she thought for the best. She would both get Jameson and Angelica to their daughter's side *and* prevent Angelica from unnecessary worry. If she could pull it off.

There was a tap at the door, just before it opened and Angelica stood there, dressed in ordinary jeans and a sweater. "We should go out tonight, the four of us. See a film or something."

"So long as it's in New York," Rhiannon said. She smiled brightly. "I've booked all four of us on a flight that leaves in just under two hours. You're coming for a visit."

Angelica lifted her brows. Appearing behind her, Jameson said, "Look, we promised Amber we wouldn't come spying on her. I think it's important we keep that promise.''

"Pish,'' Rhiannon said with a wave of her hand. "You're not spying on her, you're visiting me. Amber Lily knows me well enough to know I don't take no for an answer.'' She drew her brows together, deepened her voice. "She, at least, knows better than to try *giving* me no for an answer.''

"But it's such short notice,'' Angelica insisted.

"Just a minute here,'' Jamey said. "Something's going on.''

Rhiannon turned away from him.

He lunged forward, gripped her upper arm and turned her around to face him. "You tell me what the hell this is about, Rhiannon.''

She glanced down at his hand on her arm. "You're dancing on the edge of oblivion.''

"Rhiannon, just tell him,'' Roland said.

She shot him a glare, then met Jamey's eyes and held them. "Who am I?''

"Do we really have time for this?''

"Who am I?'' she repeated.

He sighed, rolling his eyes. "You've had many names. First you were Rianikki, firstborn daughter of Pharoah, princess of the Nile, yada, yada, yada.''

"That's right. I'm a vampiress, more than two thousand years old, Jameson Bryant. I am not a frivolous woman who makes requests without a reason.''

"*Requests?* You're not the kind of woman who makes *requests* at all. You just deliver commands.''

"And I *expect* them to be obeyed." She glanced past him at Angelica. "Gather your things. We leave for the airport in twenty minutes."

Angelica stared back at her. "It's Amber, isn't it? Something's happened."

"Amber will be waiting for us at my house when we arrive." Rhiannon went to her. "I swear to you, as far as I know Amber is perfectly fine. Now go, get ready, so you can see for yourself."

Angelica rushed away. Jamey turned to Roland. "What's going on?"

"I don't know, Jamey. She has told me no more than she's told you."

He faced Rhiannon again. "Is she in trouble?"

She glanced toward the doorway, but Angelica was gone. "She might be," she said, keeping her voice to a whisper. "She was fine when I spoke to her. Safe. There's no cause to plummet your wife into the hell-fires of worry until we know for sure, and we can't know until we get there."

"All right. But if you're keeping anything from me—"

"Must you challenge me at every turn, Jameson? I'm more tired of it than you can imagine, and if you weren't my precious Amber Lily's father, I'd have ripped out your heart long ago."

"Sure you would, princess. You keep telling yourself that."

She bared her teeth at him, and he left the room.

Roland turned to her. "You've reason for concern."

She nodded. "Enough so that we'll go directly to the house when we return. Pandora will have to wait a few more hours for us to retrieve her from the sitter's."

Jameson and Angelica got their act together, fortunately for them. They were all on the plane in time for takeoff. They never used their own names when traveling and all had plenty of fake identification. A vampire couldn't survive long in the modern world without it.

Angelica was pale on the flight, and totally focused. Rhiannon guessed she was trying desperately to pick up some sense of her daughter's well-being. She'd always had a powerful bond with the child, but it weakened over great distances. Perhaps as they drew closer to New York she would sense that Amber was all right and recover a bit. Because, despite Rhiannon's efforts to spare the woman pain, Angelica was already nearly sick with worry.

As the plane's wheels touched down on the runway at LaGuardia, Angelica suddenly pressed her hands to her chest and began gasping for air. She couldn't speak for the rapid breathing. A flight attendant rushed to her side.

"What is it? Is it asthma?"

"A panic attack," Jameson lied quickly. "She's afraid of flying. It's all right, Angel. It's okay, we're on the ground. We're here."

The attendant ran away and returned with the news that they were taxiing directly to the gate, and that Angelica could get off the plane at once.

It didn't help. Jameson held her, soothed her and whispered, "What is it? What's wrong?"

"They've taken her, Jamey. They've taken our baby," she rasped.

Amber Lily had sensed something an instant before she heard the sound—sensed something so strongly that she'd instinctively rolled off the far side of the bed, pulling Alicia with her. They hit the floor at the moment they heard the crash, the splintering of wood and the heavy, hurried footfalls.

And then three men surged into the bedroom, stopping just inside the doorway, scanning the room. Amber crouched as low as she could beside the bed and silently lifted the bedspread, hoping they could crawl underneath.

There was room! She nudged Alicia, nodded at the space. Swallowing hard, nearly frozen with fear, Alicia forced herself to move, flattening her body to the carpeted floor, sliding, inching, bit by bit, underneath the bed.

The men were coming farther into the room, weapons—odd-looking handguns that didn't really look like handguns—pointing the way. One yanked open the door of the closet, then cautiously ventured inside.

Another explored the adjoining bathroom.

It was the man who remained in the doorway, still

as stone, nothing moving but his eyes, who frightened her. Amber could see him from her position. Half his face was mottled and pink, like a glob of unshaped Silly Putty. He wore a bad hairpiece. His mouth was normal on one side, pulled out of shape at the other. And he stood there as if he were listening, or maybe smelling the air.

"I know you're here, Amber Lily. There's no point in hiding. We found a sweet little note from your mamma, tucked into a jeans pocket in your hotel room. It had this address on it."

He was looking toward the bed. Alicia's hand came groping out from underneath, finding Amber's and tugging. But Amber was afraid to move, afraid he would see. She cursed herself for forgetting about her mom's note. How could she be so careless?

"Closet's clear," said the man who'd been searching it.

"Bathroom's clear." The other one came out, stood there.

"And the rest of the house?" He said it loudly, tipping his head, so she could see the left eye. It was a pale blue in color, filmy, milky, and the skin around it drooped like icing down the side of a cake frosted when it was still warm. His ear was a series of lumps on the side of his head.

From somewhere in the living room, a man's voice called, "Clear, sir!"

"Well, that only leaves the bed," he said in a sing-song tone, as if he were reciting a nursery rhyme to a baby. "Are you hiding under the bed, Amber Lily?"

Alicia sucked in a breath, probably startled that he had known Amber's name. Smiling, sort of, the scarred man moved closer to the bed. He was bending over, reaching for the bedspread to lift it up.

Amber got to her feet on the far side of the bed. "I'm right here."

He lifted his brows. "Are you the half-breed vampire or her faithful companion?" he asked.

"I'm Amber Lily Bryant," she said. "The girl you're going to wish you had never heard of, before too long." Her voice was shaking, but maybe he wouldn't notice.

"You have your father's fight in you, don't you, girl?"

"Most people think it's my aunt's."

"Your aunt?" He smirked. "Oh yes, Aunt Rhiannon. She was mentioned in the note. We've been after her for years."

Amber pursed her lips, refusing to say more.

"I'm Frank Stiles," he told her. "You may call me 'sir.'" He glanced toward the man on his right. "Best continue the search. We can't be sure she's the right one. Her friend would likely lie to protect her."

The man nodded, started for the bed, the one place they had yet to search. As he reached for the covers, Amber shot her gaze to the vase on the bedside stand, then jerked her eyes toward the man. The vase shot from the stand, hit him in the forearm and shattered to bits.

"The next one will take off your head," she stated.

The man moved toward her, but the scarred one held up a hand. He dug a microrecorder from his pocket, depressed a button with his thumb. "Extremely well-developed telekinesis," he said. "Nicely controlled."

Amber was shaking down deep. She hoped it didn't show that she was so afraid she could hardly stand up. And she hoped to God she could get these men out of here before they discovered Alicia hiding under the bed.

"Where is your friend, the girl who was with you earlier?" Stiles asked.

"There's no one else here. I sent my friend home as soon as we realized we were in trouble."

"And where is home?"

She met his eyes, shook her head left, then right.

"Why didn't you go with her?" he asked.

She shrugged.

He smiled as if he knew. "Ahh, it was the daylight, wasn't it?"

"Boss, we've glimpsed her outside in full daylight."

"And you're never mistaken, are you?"

The man just looked at him blankly. Stiles returned his gaze to Amber. "It's daylight now, Amber Lily. We can always put it to the test."

The two men on either side of the room lunged

forward, gripping her upper arms. She thought she could have flung them off her pretty easily, but she didn't try. Let them get her out of here, away from Alicia, first. Then she would give them something to remember her by. But there was no way she was getting her friend hurt.

They moved her toward the window, maneuvered her to stand in front of it, and one of them jerked open the dark drapes.

Brilliant sunlight streamed through, hitting her squarely in the eyes, and damned if it didn't blind her. She jerked one arm free, raising it to shield her eyes even as she jerked her head away.

"Enough! Get her away from there!" Stiles shouted.

The men tugged her into the shadows. One of them reached back to close the drapes.

"I'd like her alive, in case I hadn't made that abundantly clear by now," Stiles said.

They muttered apologies and, regaining their hold on both her arms, marched her out of the bedroom, into the living room, where two other men and a woman stood like sentries. The two men at the windows, the woman at the door.

"Where are you taking me?"

Stiles smiled, his gaze meeting one of the other men's as he said, "Oh, it's an old place, in Byram, Connecticut. Been in the family for years." The two grinned wider, sharing an inside joke.

"Your family?" Amber asked.

"No. Yours." He laughed, but the sound turned into a cough that doubled him over for a moment. Then the six of them wrapped her in some sort of heavy, dark blanket and led her out of the house. The minute they set foot outside the door, the woman jabbed Amber's arm with something, and within another heartbeat, she was sinking to the floor. Whatever it was, it hit her like a train wreck.

When she woke, Amber was in a bedroom that could have been an ordinary bedroom in an ordinary, if very old, house. Except that the door had been removed and a barred iron one stood in its place. Similar bars lined both the tall windows, she noted, when she went to them to stare outside. The house stood above steep, rocky cliffs that dropped straight to the sea. Or maybe not—she could see a shore on the far side, even though the only light was from the brilliant nearly full moon shining down on the water. A lake, then? Where the hell was she? God, she must have been unconscious for hours.

There were men—soldiers—down below the bedroom window, standing among the brush on the ill-kept lawn. There was a tall wrought-iron fence with a leaf and vine pattern, and spikes at the top, that seemed to surround the place.

She remembered, then, the things her father had told her about these people—because they had to be the same people, didn't they? The DPI might have been destroyed in the vampire rebellion in the year of her birth, but some of its hunters had survived. *Still* survived. Her father had told her of capture, of torture. The cruel experiments they had performed on vampires. And how badly they had wanted her when she'd only been a baby, to use as their prize guinea pig.

And now they had her. God, what would they do to her?

Fear stabbed her in the chest in the form of a painful, wrenching sob. She closed her eyes, but the tears fell all the same. Brushing them away angrily, Amber wrenched the window open, wrapped her strong hands around the bars and shook them with all her strength.

They didn't budge. Not even a wiggle.

She tried the other window, with the same result. Crossing the room, she gripped the barred door and pulled. Again. And again. She pulled until the skin on the pads of her palm had rubbed away, with no resulting give in the bars.

Trapped. She was trapped here. A prisoner of the DPI. Just as her mother had been, when they'd buried her alive in a dark, concrete tomb and left her to die there.

Amber sank to the floor, hugging her knees to her chest and crying hard enough to shake her heart to pieces.

Sarafina fled the room, the house. She didn't take the car; she went on foot, out into the night, wearing only the red satin robe, barefoot. She was weeping as she ran. And running from something, though she had no idea what. Not from Willem. He couldn't hurt her. Not anymore.

For one instant it was almost as if she had been swept back in time, far, far back to the days of her youth. Her *true* youth. Certainly she looked as young now, but she felt every one of her years. Then she'd been new, young, fragile and innocent. And she'd raced through the night after Bartrone had changed her, made her feel everything a thousand times as intensely as before—made her hurt more, want more, hunger for more.

She had denied all the things he'd told her, and she'd raced back to her home. Her camp. Her family. Barefoot, dressed only in her nightdress, she had run in the darkness.

And there she had found them, all of them, her kin, gathered around a small child, a boy, who lay very pale and still.

"I've tried to cover for my sister as long as I can," Katerina said softly. "But I cannot do it any longer. She is in league with the demon. I saw her myself, saw her murder this innocent child, just as she murdered Belinda before him, and so many others."

A gasp went up from the family. Katerina looked across the fire, meeting Andre's eyes. "It's true," he said. "I've seen it myself. Katerina and I hoped we could save her from the evil, but it has her in its grip now. It has her. I loved her, but she is no more."

"She must be cast out," Katerina said. "God, how

it breaks my heart to say it of my own sister!'' Covering her face with her hands, she wept loudly. Andre, too, lowered his head and dabbed at his eyes.

The others all nodded in solemn agreement.

"Sad as it is, it must be done," Gervaise agreed. "Go, gather her things, all her belongings. Bring them to the fire. We must burn them, just as we would had she died. For she is dead to us now. It is the only way."

Nodding, they all moved away. All except for Katerina, because Sarafina's betrothed took her by the wrist when all eyes were turned away and tugged her into the cover of the trees. And there he stared intensely into her eyes. "You've hidden away anything of value?"

"Of course. Sarafina had pouches of gold and silver, from her readings. And there's her crystal, and her jewelry. I have them all hidden safely. Don't worry."

He smiled at her, wrapping his arms around her slender waist and pulling her close to him. "And what about her?"

"Dead by now. I left her for the demon to feed upon."

"Then we can be together," he muttered. "At last." He pulled her close, kissing her passionately. "Your sister no longer stands in the way of our happiness."

Sarafina's heart broke when she saw what they had done to her. Her own sister and her own beloved.

They had plotted against her, demonized her, tried to murder her, and then turned the entire clan against her. And the child. Had they sacrificed an innocent child in order to make her appear guilty?

She looked at the dead boy and knew by some instinctive sense that he had not died at the hand of any vampire.

She stepped out of the shadows, into the small clearing in the trees where they embraced. "Make no mistake, my loved ones. I will *always* stand in the way of your happiness."

Gasping, the two tugged apart, whirling to stare at her, shock in their eyes.

"You told me she was dead!" he hissed.

Some of the others heard Sarafina's cry and gathered around.

"Look at her!" Katerina cried. "Look at her eyes, how they glow. Her skin, how pale." She yanked a polished metal mirror from her pocket and held it up. "She casts no reflection!"

"Don't be a fool!" Sarafina shouted, and she yanked the mirror from her sister's hand and stared into it, disbelieving what she saw. Her tongue ran over her teeth, and she felt the incisors, longer and sharper than they had ever been.

Bartrone had been telling the truth!

"Go!" Katerina shouted. "Before we send our men to hunt you like the animal you are."

"Animal I may be, but *Shuvani* still!" Sarafina lifted her hands and made the sign of the oldest curse she knew. "You, my beloved Andre, will die young for your betrayal. Not another decade will you see. And I declare now that one of your offspring, or their offspring, or one of theirs, will share this curse I must bear, for I am your sister, Katerina, and my blood is your blood. What lives in me lives in you, and as I am, so will one of your descendants be. *Vampire!* And you will live to see it."

"No!" Katerina made the warding sign with her fingers, but it was too late, Sarafina knew. She had felt her curse wing forth with a power all its own, and she knew—*she knew*—it would come to pass.

Then she turned and ran into the forest, ran toward the demon who was the only being she could trust.

She had loved Andre, and she had believed him when he said he loved her, too.

She had loved Katerina, and she had believed her love, too, was real, deep down beneath the animosity and jealousy.

She came to love Bartrone, in time, and more than ever before, she had believed his declarations of love for her.

But Andre had blasphemed her love, and Katerina had betrayed her to death, and Bartrone had abandoned her to life alone, with no one.

Until Dante. With Dante, Sarafina had let herself love just once again. Until he, too, had betrayed her, chosen another over her.

And now, tonight, she ran until she finally sank weakly upon a boulder and lowered her head to cry.

It had been ages since a man had touched her as deeply as Willem Stone had done. Had pleasured her as intensely. Had kissed her as passionately. Had whispered words of love to her as sincerely...

God, he said he loved her.

But only because she had made of him a mindless drone, like Misty and Edward. Only because he craved the blood only she could give him. They said they loved her, too, and thought they meant it.

But *his* declarations had been different. More intense. More real. Or maybe it was only that some idiotic, weak-willed part of her wanted them to be.

It terrified her that her heart had responded so readily, so hungrily, to hearing those words. As if love were the drug to which she was addicted. Love, the thing she could not live without.

Even when it was only an illusion.

When she looked at Willem, she didn't see a man whose will had been broken and twisted until all that remained was the desire to please her. She saw the man he'd been before. It was *that* man, in her mind, who made love to her. That man who declared that he loved her, would die for her, and made her believe it was true.

But it wasn't. It couldn't be. Not ever.

And that was why she wept. And it was the desire for that from which she ran.

16

By the time the four of them reached Rhiannon's exclusive neighborhood, Angelica was barely able to stand on her own. Rhiannon knew better than to doubt the woman's sense that something was terribly wrong.

Before she had even exited the cab, Rhiannon saw the broken remains of her entry door, which looked as if it had been smashed in with a battering ram. As the taxi pulled away, Angelica saw it, too, and screamed. Jameson took his arms from around her for the first time since they had left the plane, and he ran into the house, shouting for Amber Lily. Without him to hold her upright, Angelica sank to the ground, weeping, shaking her head. "She's not here," she said. "She's not here."

Rhiannon shot Roland a look and a message. His eyes replied. He would see to her. And even as he bent to scoop Angelica up into his arms, Rhiannon raced into the house.

Her home.

They hadn't trashed it. But they'd been messy. Careless. Things were toppled, strewn about as if they'd been searching the place. She went into the bedroom, opening her senses, feeling for any hint of a presence. And she felt one. She met Jamey's eyes and knew he felt it, too.

She dropped to her knees and peered under the bed.

Alicia shrieked and folded her body more tightly around itself, hiding her face.

"Come out, child, it's all right. No one can hurt you now. Come."

Trembling, Alicia lowered her hands from her face, revealing only her eyes. "Aunt Rhiannon?" she asked.

"Yes, it's me. Roland is here, as well, as are Jameson and Angelica. You're safe now. And you have to come out."

Alicia closed her eyes against a flood of tears. "Angelica's here?"

"Child, I am growing weary of having a conversation while standing on my head. Contrary to pop fiction, I do not double as a bat. Come out from under that bed before I'm forced to pull you out by whatever appendage I can reach."

Alicia nodded in jerky motions and uncurled her body, rolling from her side onto her back. Then she slid out from under. The moment she did, Jameson gripped her hands and hauled her to her feet. "What happened? Where's Amber?" he demanded.

"I don't know. Some men came. She shoved me under the bed. They took her." Her chest heaved between words, breaking her sentences into barely intelligible barks. "Where's my mom?"

"She'll be here soon," Jameson said. "We phoned

her from home.'' Rhiannon sent him a sharp glance.
''I knew something was wrong here, Rhiannon, even
though you refused to tell me. I had to let Susan
know. She will meet us here.'' Then he returned his
attention to Alicia. ''Now tell me what happened to
Amber.''

Alicia's body bent, jerking with her sobs. ''Amber
only went with them to protect me. She could…have
fought. But they were searching. They'd have…found
me.''

''Where did they take her? Where, dammit?''
Jameson had the girl by the shoulders and was a
heartbeat away from shaking her.

Rhiannon grasped one of his shoulders and spun
him firmly away from her. ''This child is trauma-
tized.''

Roland came in, Angelica at his side, walking under her own power now. She went to Alicia, gathered
the girl into her arms, and held her close as they both
cried. ''It's not your fault, Alicia,'' she said softly.
''Don't think any of us blame you for this. They stole
her from me once, too. I know you'd have stopped it
if you could.''

''I should have tried,'' she whispered into Angelica's hair. ''I should have tried even if it killed me,
but God, I was so scared, I couldn't even move.''

Rhiannon often thought Alicia was far more like
Angelica than Amber was, but she would never say
it aloud. ''Come to the kitchen. I keep herbal teas for
the housekeeper. I believe there's a chamomile and

lavender blend that will help calm you, Alicia. And then you have to tell us everything, as calmly as you can.''

''But it's too late,'' she sobbed.

''Nonsense. It's 11:00 p.m. Which gives us plenty of time to hunt these suicidal thugs down and make them wish they'd never been born.''

She nodded. Rhiannon hurried to the kitchen, put water on to warm, quickly located the box of herbal teas and pulled out a chair. Angelica brought Alicia in slowly, the two of them shuffling along as if they'd been severely beaten. Rhiannon had to bite her lip to keep from snapping at them.

Angel helped Alicia into a chair, then took one herself.

''Time is of the essence,'' Roland said, very gently, and Rhiannon knew he'd felt her impatience. ''Please, tell us all that transpired.''

''Well...we kept seeing this man. Several times when we went out, he...seemed to be following us. And he took a hotel room right next to ours. I think he was DPI, or one of those rogue agents we've heard you talk about—the ones who survived. Then we met this vampire at a club and—''

''What *kind* of club?'' Jameson demanded.

Alicia looked up, guilt all over her face, as she searched for an answer.

''I hardly think that's of any importance at the moment,'' Rhiannon said.

He scowled at her, but nodded. "What about the man? What did he look like?"

She lowered her head. "He looked...hard. Strong. He was tall and had dark hair...and he walked with a cane."

Jameson closed his eyes as if in pain.

"What is it?"

"That was Willem Stone, the man I hired to watch over the girls."

Alicia clapped a hand to her mouth as fresh tears welled in her eyes. "Oh my God! I didn't know. We...we didn't know."

"We're aware of that," Rhiannon said. "Go on, child."

Alicia nodded. "I didn't think we should approach the vampiress, but Amber said she thought the woman was okay. So she told her about the man following us."

"And what did she do?"

Alicia sniffled. "I didn't think she would, at first, but as soon as she realized who Amber was, she agreed to help. She told us to just go back to our hotel, that she would take care of it. At least, that is what Amber told me. They didn't speak to each other out loud, you know?"

The teapot squealed. Rhiannon started to rise, but Roland placed a hand on her shoulder. "I'll get it." And to Alicia, "Go on."

"We—we left the club. And he followed us, just

as he'd been doing. But she followed *him*. Oh, God,
I didn't know he was only trying to protect us.''

"What did she do to him, Alicia?'' Jameson asked.
He stood beside her chair, his hands clenched into
fists.

"She...we saw her—she fed from him.''

"Killed him?'' Rhiannon asked.

"I don't know! Amber didn't think so. She—the
lady—she tossed him into a limousine and took him
away. We thought our problems were over, but then
we got back to the hotel. Amber wanted to search his
room, to try to find out what he was up to. So we
did, and we found these headphones, and when we
listened to them we could hear voices. Men's voices.
They were coming from our own room, next door.''
She sucked in a spasmodic gulp of air. "They were
waiting for us!''

Roland set the tea in front of her. Rhiannon thought
it fortunate he'd cooled it with tap water or she would
have burned her mouth, as quickly as she gulped from
the cup.

"We thought he must be working with them.'' Alicia's tears flowed like rivers.

"But you eluded them,'' Rhiannon prompted.

"We took the stairs and used the rear entrance.
And then we made our way here. We thought it was
safe here. But they found a note in Amber's jeans
pocket back at the hotel. The address was on it. They
smashed the door in, and they took Amber.''

"How long ago?'' Jameson asked.

"It was about midmorning. We'd been up late, and we were still sleeping, but it must have been…I don't know. Maybe 10:00 a.m.''

Angelica winced as she glanced at the kitchen clock.

"It doesn't mean anything," Roland told her. "You know as well as I that they'll want to keep Amber alive.''

"And you know as well as I what they want to keep her alive for!'' Angelica shot to her feet, gripping Jameson by the front of his shirt. "We have to find her.''

"We will.'' He covered her hands with his, lifted them to his lips, kissed her knuckles. "I swear to you, we will.

"Alicia, I want you to remember everything you heard from the moment those men came in until they left with Amber. Did they say anything—*anything*—about where they were taking her?''

"No. Nothing.'' She closed her eyes. Then popped them open again. "Wait. There was something… something about an ancestral home in…oh, God, help me remember.'' She squeezed her eyes closed very tightly, screwing up her face as if trying to force the memory out. "It was like an inside joke, the way they said it. Amber's ancestors, not their own, they said. And they laughed.''

Jameson frowned hard, staring from Rhiannon to Roland to Angelica.

"Connecticut!" Alicia burst out. "Brian or Byron or…"

"Byram," Jameson said.

"My God, Eric's old place," Roland said.

"Then you know? You know where they've taken her?"

Angelica searched Jameson's eyes, her own echoing Alicia's hopeful question. Jameson nodded. "Yes."

"We'll go at once," Rhiannon said, rising to her feet.

"There are one or two things to consider first," Roland said, taking her hand. "We'll need to get Alicia to safety. We'll have to arrange for shelter in Byram, in case we can't get Amber out before sunrise. And I should think we'll want to find the strange vampiress, learn what she's done with this Stone fellow."

Rhiannon thought she would rather enjoy dealing with the addle-minded vampiress who had attacked the girls' bodyguard, leaving them defenseless against the vampire hunters. Then she modified her thoughts. Amber Lily was anything but defenseless. "This vampiress, Alicia. Remind me, what was her name?"

Alicia lifted her head. "The one Amber told you about on the phone. Sarafina."

Rhiannon's eyes narrowed.

"You know her?" Angelica asked.

"I've heard of her. I make it my business to know what other immortals haunt the places where I live."

"She may not have killed him after all," Jameson

said. "I believe they have…a history. What else do you know about her, Rhiannon?" he asked.

"She's a hermit, keeps to herself in a palatial estate north of the city."

"We can't take time to search for her now. Not even for the sake of this Willem Stone," Angelica said. "God only knows what they might be doing to my baby. We have to go to her. *Now.*"

Rhiannon stared at Alicia. "Darling, are you certain they didn't know you were hiding in the room when they said what they did?"

Alicia nodded. "Amber told them I'd gone home. They wondered why she hadn't gone with me, but then they just assumed it was because of the daylight. She didn't correct them."

Rhiannon sent Roland a glance and a message. *It's too easy. Something's wrong.*

He heard her thoughts just as clearly as if she had spoken them aloud, and from the worried frown he returned, she thought he agreed. But she knew, as he did, that they had to go. They had no choice.

"For the love of God, what's happened?" a woman's voice asked from the next room.

Alicia surged to her feet. "Mom?"

Susan came hurrying into the kitchen. Alicia met her in the doorway, hurling herself into her mother's arms, weeping all over again. "I got your message at the spa, caught the first flight out. What on earth is going on?"

"We'll explain it all in the car. You...you do have a car here, don't you, Rhiannon?" Jameson asked.

"Several, in the garage in back." She left the room and returned with several sets of keys. She didn't speak again until they were in the garage. Rhiannon's private collection of cars could only be accessed by punching a combination into a keypad. Once inside, she went on. "I would suggest you two take the Ferrari," she said, tossing one set of keys to Susan. "It will outrun just about anything on the roads. Go to Eric and Tamara's place in Virginia. You remember how to find it?"

Susan nodded, turned and pressed the button on the keyring to unlock the small red Ferrari. Alicia hugged Angelica. "I'm so sorry. I'm so, so sorry."

"I know, darling. It's not your fault."

Alicia sniffled, then glanced at Rhiannon. "Get Amber back."

"Don't doubt it, Alicia. We will."

When Willem woke, he felt as if he'd been on a three-day drunk. His head alternated between swimming and throbbing, and when he got to his feet, he fell over. God, his balance was shot to hell, and his bad foot was screaming. He hadn't had pain meds since he'd been here.

He had been dressed, possibly bathed, as well, but he didn't want to think about that. He was barefoot, and he didn't see his shoes anywhere nearby, much less his cane. But he wasn't chained, and he knew beyond any doubt that if he didn't get the hell out of here—now—he might never. This might be his only chance. He wasn't sure how many more times he could play the lovesick zombie convincingly.

Bullshit. It was easy, pal. Maybe a little bit too easy.

He shook away the voice in his head, told himself it didn't mean a damn thing that he hadn't really had to do all that much acting. Hell, he was a red-blooded man—assuming he had enough left in his veins to qualify. She was a beautiful, desirable woman. Even if she was a vampire. He would have to be considerably deader than she was not to want her. He would have to be ten years in the grave. It didn't mean he was becoming addicted to her. This was normal physical attraction. Powerful, yes. Hell, he'd loved the woman—loved her before he'd ever met her. But not anymore, not after what she had tried to do to him.

Only, that was a lie, and he knew it. There was something powerful gnawing at his belly that he didn't want to examine too closely. Just let it gnaw. Maybe it would get its fill. And if it didn't, hell, then maybe it *was* the blood. The addiction thing. A weakened version of the spell she'd cast over her two lapdogs. It hadn't taken him over, as it had them. He wasn't sure why; maybe his will was too strong. But anything that felt like an emotional attachment to the woman must surely be because of it. She'd held him against his will, for God's sake, tried to make him her slave.

He lurched unsteadily to the door, tried the knob, found it unlocked. When he opened it and peered out, he saw no one. Just a long hallway, lined by an Oriental runner that was mostly red. The better to conceal the bloodstains of her victims, he told himself, even though he knew it wasn't true. She wasn't the villainess he wished he could believe she was. He followed the runner to the top of a staircase that widened at the bottom. Gripping the dark hardwood railing, he made his way down.

At the bottom he had to look up, because the room was like something out of *Lifestyles of the Ancient and Immortal.* Rich dark woods, vibrant colors, a chandelier the size of a compact car. Jesus, she liked the good life. He heard a murmur of voices and jerked his head to the left.

Edward and Misty were talking low, somewhere in the bowels of the house. Fine by him. He wasn't going that way. He walked unevenly forward, through the giant archway, into the foyer and through it to the solid double doors at its end. No glass in them. The lady liked her privacy. He gripped the brass handle and turned it.

It wasn't locked.

It struck him as odd, for just a moment, that Sarafina would leave her home unlocked. And that thought sparked another—just where the hell was she right now?

A chill chased a shiver up his spine, and he glanced over his shoulder. No one. He was getting jumpy, that was all. He opened the door and looked outside.

A lopsided moon poured milky light over the wide stone steps, the huge urns of flowers on either side and the flagstone path beyond them. There was a long curving driveway, with a gate at the end. That gate worried him. Tall wrought iron, suspended between twin stone pillars. He stumbled down the steps and started along the path to the driveway, then down the driveway to the gate. On either side of him, rows of carefully pruned hedges lined the way.

When he got to the gate, he stopped worrying. Those hedges, ten feet tall here, made right angles at the gate and marched out in either direction like a wall. Just hedges. No fence. He paused for just a moment to turn and look back at the house. It glared back at him, huge and magnificent, and he almost got the feeling it was saying good riddance.

Shaking off the eerie feeling, he pushed his way between the left side of the gate and the hedge fence. And then he discovered why Sarafina didn't think she needed a fence. The hedges were thorny. Sharp little daggers ripped into him, but he'd come too goddamn far to give up now, so he pushed through.

Thorns tore his skin. One jabbed him in his good foot, making him hop hard on the bad one, and a flash of blinding pain shot through him.

And with the pain came an image, very brief, but just as clear as springwater. Sarafina, sitting on the ground in the middle of a vast garden, with fountains and statuary all around her. Bathed in moonlight, she was leaning on the base of a stone image, head resting on her folded arms, her face hidden. And she was weeping.

Then he was jerked back to reality again as he emerged from the hedge on the far side and fell to the ground, hitting it hard. The impact knocked the wind out of him. Knocked that vision out of him, too, thank God. For a moment he'd felt this insane urge to go to her and make her explain herself. Who the hell was she, anyway? The manipulative, controlling, blood drinker, or the vulnerable, tenderhearted girl he'd known first? He still caught glimpses of that girl when Sarafina let her guard down. He felt her when they made love. He wanted her back, dammit.

It didn't matter. And though his heart ached and every emotion in it told him to go to her, his head and his survival instinct told him to keep moving and to get as far from this place as he could. He was torn for just a moment. Then his sense of duty kicked in to tip the balance. He had promised to protect two young women from harm. His first priority, above anything else, was to find Amber Lily and Alicia, and to make sure they were still safe.

He pulled himself to his feet, continuing to limp along the private driveway until he finally reached a public road. Then he flagged down the first car that passed by standing in front of it and refusing to budge even when it nearly ran him down. He demanded a ride to the nearest place with a telephone.

The driver, once he figured out that Will wasn't a criminal looking to steal his car or his wallet, suggested he take Will to the nearest hospital instead. He must have looked pretty bad. Since the guy was so willing to help, Will had him drive into the city and drop him at his apartment building. He wanted to go straight to the hotel to check on the girls, but he didn't have a room key or any ID—his wallet must have been somewhere back at Sarafina's place—and he sure as hell wasn't going to convince anyone to let him into a four-star hotel looking the way he did.

He pounded on the super's door.

It opened, eventually, and the sleepy-looking, unshaven Señor Del Orto squinted up at him. "Stone? What the hell happened? You get mugged?"

"Yeah, something like that. They got my keys, and I can't get back into my place without 'em."

Del Orto lowered his head, shaking it. "You want me to call the police?" He frowned at Will's face, looked him up and down. "An ambulance, maybe?"

"No, I just want you to let me into my apartment."

"No problem, no problem. Just a minute, okay?" He closed the door, undid the chain, then opened it again, holding a set of keys this time. "You take the key," he said, prying one loose from the hundred or so on the ring. "Slide it under my door when you're finished, all right?"

"Sure. Thanks."

"De nada," he said, and he started to close the door again, then paused. "You sure you don't need a doctor, man?"

"It looks worse than it is."

"If you say so. I'll get your locks changed tomorrow, okay?"

He closed the door, and Will made his way to the elevator and up to his apartment. The key worked. He headed straight for the bathroom and his pain meds. Popped one and washed it down with tap water. He would have preferred to down two, but he knew that would make him too damn drowsy to do much good. He glanced at himself in the mirror as he waited for the pills to kick in. His skin was shockingly pale, and the dark red scratches that road-mapped his face made it seem even paler. Sighing, he ran some water into the basin and made quick work of washing up. Then he located socks and shoes, a jacket, some spare cash and his extra set of car keys. He downed a protein drink and headed right back out.

By the time a taxi dropped him at the hotel, he thought he looked relatively normal, if still deathly white. He was dizzy and weak, but the pain was starting to ebb thanks to the wonders of better living through chemicals.

They gave him a spare key to his room at the front desk, and he went up, itching and eager to see the girls safely asleep in their beds.

But when he got there and slipped their lock, he

found no sign of them at all. In fact, the room looked as if it had been searched. Thoroughly.

Jesus.

He hurried to his own room. While he sensed someone had been there, it wasn't trashed. Things just were not exactly as he thought he had left them. But then again, he wasn't at full capacity, either. He could be mistaken.

He opened the dresser drawer, pawed aside the contents and found what he was looking for. The little electronic tracking device. He flipped it on, nothing happened.

Either the tracker he'd planted in Amber Lily's bag wasn't functioning or it was out of range. Hell. He didn't know what to do next and was sure of only one thing—he couldn't stay awake much longer. Goddamn, the blood drinking had left him weak. Not to mention the lovemaking.

For a moment he was back there, in his mind. Exploring Sarafina's mouth with his own, her body with his own. She'd been delicious and eager and something else. Vulnerable, somehow, in a way that had surprised him. As if he had the power to destroy her with his touches, his kisses, his fevered declarations of undying love.

But that was stupid. She didn't give a damn what he felt. What he said. She couldn't possibly give a damn. She wanted to control him, like a puppet who would dance according to her whim. It hadn't felt that way, during the heights of passion, but he knew it was the truth. She'd certainly tried her damnedest to make it happen.

He pushed thoughts of Sarafina from his mind and realized that he had to phone Jameson Bryant. He was going to have to tell the man that he'd lost track of his precious daughter, fucked up the job, and had no idea where she was.

But the telephone rang and rang. There was no answer.

Will lay down on the bed in his hotel room, just for a moment. Just long enough to clear his head, to think of the smartest next move. But in the wee hours of morning, he fell asleep.

And he dreamed of Sarafina.

17

Amber paced the cagelike room. Eventually the scarred man came to the barred door and peered in at her. "Hello, Amber. Sorry about the accommodations." He shoved her backpack through the bars for her. "We did bring your things along. Minus the phone, of course. We have to be careful with your kind."

"You're damn right you do." She searched the hallway beyond him for something to hurl, spotted a painting on the wall behind him and sent it flying at his head.

He spun around, flinging up his arms, so it hit them instead, but the way he cursed told her it hurt like hell. Good.

"You let me out of here, mister, or you're going to be very sorry."

"You will cooperate with us, my dear, or else you are the one who'll be sorry. Now stick your arm through the bars. We need another little blood sample."

Amber told him to go do something anatomically impossible, in language that would have made her mother cringe, and then she hurled her energy at the light fixture above his head. It crashed to the floor, and the man barely got out of the way in time. They'd done something to her while she'd been unconscious. She didn't know what; she only knew she felt awful. Her head pounded, her muscles ached, and her chest felt odd.

"I'll tear this place apart!" she shouted as things from the room flew against the bars. Lamps, curtains, the bedside clock.

Stiles cowered away for a moment, but then a second man appeared, pulled a gun from his waistband, pointed it even as she dove for cover and pulled the trigger.

The dart jabbed her in the lower back, and once again the drug worked almost instantly.

"Dammit!" Stiles said. "The last dose had her blood pressure so low we can't be certain of the accuracy of the experiments. I told you, no more. We need her alive and in her normal state to learn anything useful."

"This was half as much," the other man said. "What are we gonna do, let her trash the place?"

Amber sank to the floor, fear gripping her mind, panic taking hold. She had no control over what they did to her while she was unconscious. When she woke up the last time, there had been bandages and sore spots on her arms and legs, and she wasn't sure, but she thought they'd cut off some of her hair, as well, and that was only part of it. She was sure there was more. She'd never felt so horrible in her life.

She clung to consciousness as they unlocked the barred door and came in. Stiles bent to scoop her up. She tried to fling things at him with her mind, but the objects only tipped over and fell to the floor. She tried to hit him and found her blows as weak as Alicia's would have been.

He put her on the bed, turned to his cohort. "Bring the equipment in. Let's get this over with before it wears off again."

Her eyes widened. "No, please," she whispered.

Stiles smiled at her. "Now it's 'please,' is it? I thought I was going to be sorry?"

The rattling of a tray drew her gaze. The woman wheeled it in. It was stainless steel and loaded with instruments, including an electronic box with the kind of paddles they used to jump-start heart patients on *ER*. Stiles pulled on a pair of rubber gloves and picked up a tiny, shiny scalpel.

She focused on the blade, fear giving her effort one final burst of power. The blade leaped from the man's hand, spun around and drove into his palm, piercing it straight through.

He howled in pain.

"Sorry yet?" she managed to ask as the others crowded around him.

"What are we going to do with her, Stiles?" the woman asked. "Some of the tests require her to be conscious and cooperative at the same time."

Through grated teeth he spoke to her. "We'll have

her full cooperation soon enough. I expect her parents anytime now.''

And then the drug took over, plunging her into darkness.

Rhiannon drove her Mercedes, Roland in the front seat beside her, sitting stiffly, eyes constantly alert. To this day he had never made peace with moving vehicles. He suffered them, when necessary, or to keep her happy. He did not enjoy them.

Rhiannon loved her cars. Almost as much as she loved her aging cat. A little pang of longing hit her as they passed the exit for the town where Pandora was being boarded. But there was just no time to stop and pick up her pet. Not when precious Amber was in the hands of those bastards.

As they drew nearer, she kept glancing over her shoulder at Angelica in the back seat with Jameson. So far there was no sign the woman sensed her daughter's nearness. It worried Rhiannon.

Eventually she drove the car over winding side roads, through the wooded Connecticut countryside, toward the one-time home of Eric Marquand, Roland's dearest friend. It had been burned, ransacked, vandalized and ravaged by the whims of the sea and her storms, and their enemies, over the years. Eric and his bride Tamara had had to abandon it once the DPI had learned of its existence. Vampires who had been unfortunate enough to attract the notice of that band of vampire hunters never managed to stay in one place for very long. Rhiannon had hoped that would end once the DPI was destroyed. But obviously those hopes had been misplaced.

She pulled the car off the road, into a lot with tall pine trees lining it, the better to keep it from view. The four of them got out and began walking along the needle-cushioned road. Pine scent was strong on the air. In a few more minutes, the house came into view.

The wrought-iron fence around the place, with its patterns of leaves and twisting vines, was still intact. The gate of the same pattern had been sagging the last time Rhiannon had set eyes on it. Now it was straight and level, and looked as strong as ever.

She looked beyond it at the house, three stories of rough-hewn gray stone blocks, each one enormous in size. Its arched windows were sunken deeply into the stone. Rhiannon glanced at Jameson, saw him staring at the place intently.

"Are you all right, Jamey?" Roland asked, slipping into the old habit of calling him by his childish name.

Jameson swallowed. "It brings back memories. Not all of them good."

"You were eleven, I believe," Roland said, "when you squared off against a murderous grown man and saved my life, right here in this house."

"A few days later you returned the favor," Jameson said.

The two men exchanged a long look. They were as

close as father and son, Rhiannon knew that. And even though the younger one sometimes drove her to madness with his impatience and impulsiveness, she loved him all the same.

There were spikes at the top of the fence that surrounded the place, and cliffs at the back that plummeted to the rocky shore far below. Not really a challenge for a vampire. She crouched low, then pushed off hard, clearing the fence easily. The others followed suit, and then they started up the cobblestone path to the front of the house. It had been years. The grounds hadn't been as thoroughly reclaimed as the gate and the house itself. Shrubs, once trimmed, now spread like wild things. The long-dead, thorny stalks of the roses spread over the ground, suffocating the tender new shoots that attempted to spring up in their midst. Scrub brush and weeds had been allowed to run rampant, and only the path itself remained clean and clear of debris.

"I still don't get a sense of Amber," Angelica whispered.

"Maybe she's asleep," Jameson said. *Or unconscious.* He didn't shield the thought fast enough. Rhiannon and the others heard it clearly.

"Or maybe she's not here at all," Rhiannon said quickly, seeing the flush of fear in Angelica's cheeks.

She stopped before they reached the front door, holding her arms out to her sides to halt the others as something tickled at the back of her mind. "What in the world..." And then the knowledge came, with a jolt of alarm. Danger shot through her mind like an electrical current. "It's a trap!" she shouted, even as the brush around them came alive with movement.

They whirled and ran flat out for the fence, even as blinding lights flashed on, glaring down on them from all directions, and men emerged from the shadows, firing automatic weapons.

When she reached the fence, Rhiannon leaped it, hitting the ground on the other side and running for the car. It was only a few steps before she realized that she was alone.

Roland! She shouted his name with her mind.

His reply came to her, weak but clear. *Too late, love. They've got us. Go! Get clear, get help, and come back.*

I won't be long!

Just be safe.

She dove into the car, and pressed the accelerator to the floor, squealing away into the rapidly fading night.

Get help, he'd told her. From where? Eric and Tamara were too far away to be of any use. And the only vampire she knew of who was close enough to be of any help was the one she blamed for causing this mess in the first place; the reclusive vampiress, Sarafina.

Perhaps the mortal, Willem Stone, could be of some help, as well, if he were still alive. Jameson seemed to have placed a great deal of store in the man's abilities. But she had no way to locate Stone—except through Sarafina.

And so, she supposed, that was where she must go.

She could have attempted to contact the woman mentally, but that might only give her enough warning to get away. And Rhiannon had no intention of allowing that. She pushed the car to its limits, but before she ever reached the city, the bloodred curve of the sun began to peer over the distant horizon, blasting through the darkly tinted windshield, searing her eyes, her face.

She jerked down the visor and pushed on, but soon there was smoke rolling from her hair. The delicate skin over her throat and collarbones began to blister. She was out of time. She jerked the wheel, taking the car off the exit ramp, only then realizing it was the same one that led to the ranch where Pandora was currently vacationing.

Heat, light, pain, all combined to make her grate her teeth. The steering wheel was so hot she could barely hold on to it. Her vision was filtered by a red haze. She careened onto a side road, shot down it a few hundred yards, then veered off the side, bouncing the car over a rough, grassy field and toward the woodlot beyond it. She stopped at the line of scraggly trees, then wrenched open the door. Some of the skin from her palm stayed on the door handle when she pulled her hand away and lunged out of the car, and into the trees.

Her strength was ebbing. The day-sleep was irresistibly stealing over her, but if she stopped in the sunlight, she knew she would never wake again. She pushed on, skin sizzling, mind slowly fogging over. Finally she reached a mucky bit of green-water swamp and flung herself into it.

Cool, soothing water, thick with algae and slime, wrapped around her and eased her pain. As her body sank into the soft, blessedly cold mud at the bottom, the murky ooze closed above her, blocking out the killing rays of the sun.

Sarafina remained in the lush, well-tended gardens, out of sight of anyone, until the uncharacteristic emotional thunderstorm had passed. She didn't want to see Willem. She didn't want to see anyone. The garden was her haven, and she remained there for the night, as if it could heal her. She couldn't recall the last time she'd shed tears. Had she cried at Dante's betrayal? If she had, it hadn't been like this. Nothing close to this.

She felt—and this was baffling to her—regret for having conquered Willem Stone's spirit. She'd never experienced any hint of remorse for having made drones of Misty or Edward. But with Willem, everything was different. Even though he had been hunting those two girls, there remained something special about him. Something unique among mortal men. And she had robbed him of that. Taken away his iron will, made him less than he had been before. Less than the man she had loved. She wished to God she hadn't done it, not to a man like him. Better to have killed him outright than to make him live that way. And while it wasn't too late to remedy that mistake, to free his spirit by taking his life, she also knew she couldn't do it. It infuriated her to find herself emotionally hobbled by her ridiculous feelings for a man. And a mortal, at that!

Wrestling with unaccustomed emotions had drained her. She dragged herself up the back steps and into the house through the rear entrance, hoping not to encounter anyone on the way to her bedroom. Dawn was close at hand. Perhaps the day-sleep would restore her to her old self, the woman with the heart encased in impenetrable ice. The woman she had been before Willem Stone.

But her path to rest was interrupted by the voices of Edward and Misty. They were speaking in excited tones somewhere in the house, and her gut told her something was very wrong. She altered her course, bursting in on them in the upstairs hallway.

"What's the matter?" she demanded.

Misty spun, eyes wide and damp. "Oh, my lady, you must forgive us! He fooled us as surely as he fooled you!" She fell to her knees, gripping the hem of Sarafina's robe.

"What are you talking about?" she demanded.

Misty only sobbed harder, so Sarafina looked to Edward, who stood uneasily in front of her. "He's run away, mistress. We left him unbound, the door unlocked, as you told us. We assumed he was as loyal to you as we are. But he fooled us all. He's gone.''

"He's gone...." Sarafina blinked, glancing past Edward at the open door to what had been Willem's room. She wondered briefly why she wasn't flooded with rage at his deception, his escape. Instead she felt an odd sense of relief. She hadn't broken him at all. He'd only been pretending. She wanted to close her eyes and weep with gratitude.

And his declarations of love? His enthusiastic kisses? Those had all been a part of his act. They were no more authentic than they would have been had she succeeded in conquering his mind. But God, she was glad she'd failed. She didn't want Willem Stone broken, she realized. But she did want him, still. Despite his black heart.

"Leave it be," she told her servants. "He was never meant to stay with us." She felt the touch of the dawn working harder than usual on her in her state of mental exhaustion. "His wallet and some of his things are in the desk drawer, in the library. His home address and several telephone numbers are in them. See that they're sent to him today. I'm going to rest. Think no more about Willem Stone."

"Well, good morning, Amber Lily," said the bleached-blond female vampire hunter. Amber hadn't slept. She was sitting up in her bed, watching the sun rise over the ocean, and she refused even to turn and face the woman. Her body felt ravaged, and she didn't know why. This last time, when she woke up, her hair had been wet and her throat sore.

"We've brought you two choices for breakfast. A pint of A-positive, freshly drawn. Still warm, even. And some bacon and eggs. Which would you prefer?"

Narrowing her eyes, Amber turned and glared at the woman. "Your heart on a platter. Lightly roasted."

The woman didn't seem to pick up on the sarcasm. Her eyes widened a little, and she handed the tray to the man who stood beside her, then yanked a notebook from her pocket to jot down a note.

Amber rolled her eyes. "Yes, do write that down, Miz Einstein. 'Patient shows cannibalistic tendencies.' But you'd better get me someone's liver soon, or I'll turn invisible." She nodded toward the man behind her. "His will do. You can use the butter knife there. And I like it with onions. Hurry up, now."

Finally light dawned in the twit's eyes. She stopped writing, looked up slowly from her notebook. "You're playing games again."

"Gee, do you think?"

The woman angrily scratched out what she had written down. "I'll take an honest answer this time, Amber Lily. Which of these two meals represents your normal diet?" She pocketed her notepad and took the jar of blood from the tray. "Do you drink blood like your parents?"

Amber glanced at the jar, sent her anger full throttle. It exploded, spewing blood and glass shards at the woman's chest and face, hands and arms. She shrieked, back-stepping fast, flinging her hands to her face.

"Kelsey!" The man dropped the tray of food to the floor and went to her. "God, are you all right?"

She turned and ran off in search of a towel, with her attentive sidekick right on her heels. Stiles came walking down the hall, clapping his hands very slowly. "Well done, child. Very well done. But I'm afraid we've run out of patience with you and your little tantrums."

"Guess you'd better let me go, then, because you're only going to get more of the same."

"Oh, I don't think so." He stood in front of her cell, arms folded over his chest, a confident smirk on the good side of his face. "You're going to cooperate from here on in. Answer all our questions truthfully and submit to any tests we care to perform."

"Oh, really?" she said. "And why the hell would I do that?"

"Nelson, bring her here," he called to someone, never taking his eyes off Amber.

Footsteps came, slow and measured. And then a man appeared in the hallway, carrying what looked like a body in his arms. It was wrapped in a blanket, head to toe. Amber's heart jumped into her throat.

"Close the curtain," Stiles said. "I wouldn't want a stray sunray to hit her. We've already established that they have no effect on you, contrary to what you led us to believe.''

Blinking rapidly, Amber closed the thick curtains.

Stiles walked up to the man holding the body, peeled away the blanket.

Amber sucked in a gasp and lunged for the bars. "Mom!" She stretched her arm through the bars, touched her mother's face, felt the life in her through that mental bond they had. Not dead. They hadn't killed her. Not yet, anyway. She stroked her mother's hair as tears flooded her eyes.

"Please," she whispered. "Please, don't hurt her. I'll do anything. Anything you want, just don't hurt her."

Stiles nodded. "I thought so. Now, we're going to have a little talk, you and I. You're going to tell me everything about yourself. What you eat. When you sleep. How sunlight affects you, if at all. And anything else I want to know, is that understood?"

She nodded, even as Nelson put the blanket over her mother's face and carried her away down the hall.

"Where is he taking her? Where are you keeping her?"

"Oh, not just her, child. We have your daddy, too. And his pal Roland."

She closed her eyes, weeping. "I'll cooperate, I promise. Just, please, I have to know where you're keeping them."

"In a cell, in a sublevel, underneath the basement

here. It was created by a vampire, I'm told. His safe haven. Ironic, isn't it?''

She swallowed hard. "Is it...is it small?''

He frowned, making the scarred side of his face pucker and pull. "The size of this room, or there-abouts. Why do you ask?''

She tried to control her breath, not to release the sigh of relief she felt at knowing her mother was not confined in some tiny, cramped space. "I just—I want to know they're comfortable. As long as I know they're all right, I'll be the most cooperative subject you could wish for. I promise.''

"Fair enough,'' he said.

Amber nodded and sank onto the bed in the shad-owy room, dimmed now by the drawn curtains. "So what do you want to know?''

18

Sarafina rose at dusk, an empty, hollow feeling in her chest. She kept reliving the touch of Willem's lips on her flesh every time she closed her eyes, and she kept telling herself not to allow such flights of fancy. It was completely unlike her.

She took her time in a deep, hot bath. Then more time as she dressed in her favorite style, that of the old days. A white peasant blouse that left her shoulders bare, full flowing skirts, scarves trailing from her hair and her waist, and so much jewelry she jangled when she moved. Then she went to the kitchen to consult with Misty and Edward about the evening's plans. Part of her was longing to go looking for Willem. Just to see him from a distance and assure herself that he really was all right—untouched by her efforts to control him. She should check on those girls, as well, she thought, though deep down, she knew that Willem was not a threat to them. But before she even began to speak to her servants, there was a crash near the front of the house.

For one insane instant, Sarafina's heart performed giddy acrobatics at the thought that Willem had returned, come back to her—of his own will this time.

But it faded before she could even bother to chide herself for such an idiotic thought, much less that little rush of joy that had accompanied it, because she sensed, very clearly, the new presence in her home. And it wasn't Willem.

It was another vampire, one vibrating with anger, quite possibly murderous with rage.

Sarafina glanced at her pets. "Go. Out the back door—quickly. Get as far from here as you can. Do you understand? Hide yourselves in the woods, and don't come back until I've summoned you."

"But, my lady—"

"Go!" she commanded.

The two obediently scurried through the kitchen and out the back door. Sarafina watched them move out of sight, then swept through the house into the living room.

The woman stood at the base of the staircase, some sort of green weeds clinging to her damp hair and her skintight black velvet dress. The dress was dripping a bit. A tiny green-tinted puddle had formed around her feet. Mud was smeared over her hands and cheeks. Her straight black hair reminded Sarafina of her long-dead sister, Katerina, and a surge of bitter hatred rose up in her belly.

At the woman's side, a black panther sat on its haunches, as the woman's dagger-tipped fingers stroked its head.

"You must be Sarafina," the woman said. "I am Rhiannon."

"I don't really care who you are. I *would* be interested to know, however, why you dare smash a hole through my front door, enter my home without my consent and proceed to drip that sewage all over my floors."

"Oh, you'd be surprised what I *dare*," Rhiannon said. "You have a lot to answer for, vampiress."

"Are you suggesting I should answer to you?"

"It's not a suggestion."

Sarafina laughed, tipping her head back so her many pairs of earrings rang against each other. Rhiannon lunged across the room, gripping her around her nape, her motion little more than a blur of speed. Leaning into Fina's face, the woman whispered, "You attacked and abducted the man who'd been hired to protect Amber Lily Bryant—the person I treasure most in the universe, and the only child ever born to a vampiress."

Sarafina held her temper, but it simmered dangerously near the surface. "You have your facts skewed, woman. I took a man, yes. At Amber Lily's request."

"And because of it, Amber Lily has been taken by the vampire hunters!"

"Take your hand from my neck, bitch."

"Tell me where that man is," Rhiannon demanded.

"I don't know where he is, and I wouldn't tell you if I did."

"Liar!"

Sarafina pressed her palms to the woman's chest and shoved her—hard. Rhiannon flew across the room, hitting the wall so hard she put a hole in the plaster. Paintings crashed to the floor. Rhiannon shook herself and lunged at Sarafina, hitting her like a wrecking ball, and the two fell to the floor, cracking the floorboards, rolling as they pounded and tore at each other.

Sarafina wound up on top. Rhiannon grabbed her by her hair, jerking her head back, then delivered a blow to her face. Sarafina was flung backward again, airborne at first, only to land hard on the floor. She scrambled to her feet, sending a quick glance toward the cat, fully expecting it to pounce and tear her to bits.

But it only stood off to one side, pacing, agitated, its eyes following every move as its tail swished and quivered.

Sarafina attacked again.

She fought for her life, blocking Rhiannon's powerful blows when she could, taking them when she couldn't, and delivering plenty of her own in return. They'd fallen, locked in combat, onto the coffee table, demolishing it, when Sarafina became aware of her servants, just around the corner in the next room.

She'd told them to leave. By God, they'd disobeyed her orders! She pushed Rhiannon off her and spun toward them, saw them huddling over a small black billfold. Willem's. What the hell did they think they were doing, and why had they kept it when she'd told them to send it back?

A chair smashed across her back, knocking her to her knees.

She came up fast, flipping Rhiannon over her shoulder to the floor, kicking her in the head and then in the ribcage, which sent her skidding across the floor. Sarafina followed and went to kick her again, but this time Rhiannon grabbed her by the ankle and hurled her across the room. Her head hit the banister, snapping it in two, and her entire body screamed in pain. Above her, she saw the chandelier swinging dangerously.

"They'll kill each other!" Misty cried. "Here's the number. The phone, Edward, hurry! We have to get help!"

Will woke by noon, picked up his car from the hotel garage and drove almost aimlessly, watching the tracking monitor and praying he would get within range of the girls and the light would come on. He stopped twice to eat, each time making it a high protein meal. He thought it was helping. He was starting to feel more like himself by the time night fell again.

He'd tried Bryant's number several more times, even though he knew the man wouldn't be likely to answer during the day. He figured there might be a housekeeper or an answering service—something. Still, he'd had no luck whatsoever by the time the sun went down again, and he was beginning to wonder if his employer *and* his subjects had vanished from the face of the earth.

And then his car phone bleated softly.

He grabbed it up, pushed the on button and ignored New York State's "no cell phone use while driving" law. For some reason he was almost hoping to hear Sarafina's voice on the other end in reply to his terse "Stone." In fact, every few minutes, it seemed, some longing for her sprang up in his belly. In spite of the job he had to do.

"Willem. You have to come back. Hurry!"

He frowned at the vaguely familiar voice before recognition kicked in. "Edward?"

"Yes. A woman is here. One like the Mistress. They're fighting."

Will dismissed the little skip in his heartbeat. "Right. This is some kind of a trick to get me to come back, right? Where is she? Let me speak to her."

"They're killing each other, Willem. We don't know who else to call!"

There was scuffling, and then Misty's voice came on. "Please, Willem, you have to come!" She was crying into the phone now, and Will could hear the sounds in the background.

Crashes, shattering glass, pounding, thudding—violent sounds. There was a grunt of pain, a yelp, a restrained cry, a string of cuss words. He recognized Sarafina's voice, along with that of another woman, and the bottom fell out of his stomach. "Jesus."

"Please hurry! It's you this stranger wants. It's you! She's killing our lady—because of you! Please—"

"All right, all right. I'm coming." He was spinning the car around and hitting the gas even as he said it. His brain told him it was idiotic. He'd been away from that place for only a day. It was insane to go back. But the rest of him couldn't get there fast enough—and not only because this woman who was asking about him might be a clue to helping him track down the girls. Because Sarafina was in trouble—she was in pain, fighting for her life, maybe—and he couldn't bear the thought of it. Everything in him wanted to be there to help her, to protect her.

Right. That made as much sense as wanting to protect a hungry wolf.

She didn't *need* his protection. And just what the hell he was going to do when he got there, he didn't know. A woman "like the Mistress," Edward had said. Did that mean this visitor, this attacker, was another vampire? What the hell was he going to do with *two of them?*

He veered through traffic, blasting his horn, and when he finally hit a clear stretch, he yanked open the glove compartment, pulled out his handgun, checked the clip. He wasn't going to face them empty-handed, that was for damn sure. And while a bullet might not kill one of them, he figured it would at least slow her down a little bit.

When he arrived at Sarafina's palacelike home, the front gate was open. It needn't have been. The hedge through which he had crawled to escape had been reduced to mulch, apparently because a Mercedes had driven straight through it. The car was currently parked at an angle on the front lawn, the driver's door still open. Will left his own vehicle outside the gate, tucked the keys under the floor mat and got out, sliding the gun into the back of his pants.

He walked at a fast clip, through the flattened hedge, across the lawn, and then along the drive to the wide front steps. The front door was broken, hanging open; light was spilling out.

He slowed his pace then, ready for a trap. Automatically he pulled the gun, holding it in front of him when he moved close enough to see inside.

The room was a shambles, the furniture broken, vases shattered on the floor. Bits of wood from the door and broken glass crunched under his feet as he stepped inside. It didn't look as if a mere fight had happened in this place, it looked as if a hurricane had struck.

Sarafina sat at the foot of the stairs, beside a broken section of the banister. Her upper body was supported by the newel post at the bottom, her head hanging forward, black curls hiding her face. Her blouse was torn, her arms bruised. He took a single step toward her before spotting the cat.

"Holy Christ!" He pivoted left, pointed the gun at the animal, a huge black panther, which looked as if it was about to devour the limp body of the other woman, who sat slumped against the wall.

"Put the gun down, mortal," the strange woman said, her head rising slowly, her voice weak. She had as much long, jet-black hair as Sarafina, but hers was perfectly straight, damp and dirty. "She won't hurt you...unless I tell her to do so." Lifting a hand, she stroked the cat's head.

He lowered the weapon, but only a little, and started across the room toward Sarafina, keeping one eye on the animal. "If it takes a step toward me, lady, it's history."

"Willem?" At the sound of his voice, Sarafina sat up slowly, as if it hurt to move. There was a nasty bruise on one side of her face.

"Jesus, what the hell happened here?" He stuffed the gun into his pants and hurried to her, the cat all but forgotten. God, why did it make his gut lurch to see her hurt this way? Why did he feel like scooping her into his arms, kissing away her pain, and then raining destruction on the person who'd caused it? She was his enemy!

No. She was a part of him, and he knew it. It was stupid to keep denying what he felt for this woman.

He knelt on the lowest step, gathered her to him, helped her to her feet, holding her close as he did. He stroked her hair away from her face. "Are you all right?"

"I'm fine. I think." She leaned against him, stared at him as if not quite believing what she saw. "You came...."

"I had to."

She almost smiled, seemed to stop herself, straightened a little, then shot a glance across the room. The other one was getting to her feet now, as well. Sarafina said, "I *told you* I didn't kill him."

The other one lifted a brow. She, too, was bruised and battered, though it was hard to tell, with the dirt streaks across her face. "You're lucky *I* didn't kill *you.*"

"If you'd wanted me dead, you'd have let the cat have me."

The other one glanced down at the panther. "Pandora's getting old. I don't let her fight anymore. Just feed her the scraps when I've finished."

Will grimaced, then swore softly.

"You're Willem Stone, I take it?" the stranger asked.

He nodded. "And you're...?"

"I am Rhiannon," she said, and she said it as if she were saying "I'm the Queen of the Universe."

"Is that supposed to mean something to me?" He shrugged, glancing at Sarafina and then back at the other one. "Sorry, I'm not up on the whole 'who's who' of the undead, you know?"

Rhiannon scowled at him, but then she went on. "The child you were hired to protect is very dear to me, and thanks to the two of you, she's now in the hands of men more evil than any you've ever encountered."

"Don't be too sure about that, lady. I've encountered a lot of them." Then her words sank in, and Will frowned. "Amber Lily's been taken?"

"Yes. As have her parents and my husband, who went after her." She lowered her head with the words.

She was tough, Will thought, but scared half to death for those she loved and trying really hard to hide it. "What about Alicia?" he asked.

"Safe. Amber hid her from them, protected her. We've sent her to safety with her mother for now."

"And do you have any idea where the others are?"

"I don't know, now. These men are not stupid. They left enough clues to lead us to a small town in Connecticut, right into their trap. I should have known better. They could easily have moved them all by now...if they haven't killed them outright."

Sarafina spoke softly. "Except for the girl. They wouldn't kill her."

"They wouldn't even *have* her, if not for your interference!"

"I *told* you, I was only trying to protect her!"

"From me," Will said. He looked at Sarafina, standing beside him and met her eyes, wondering why she hadn't simply killed him if she'd honestly been convinced he was capable of harming an innocent girl. Then again, he knew why. There was something between them, a bond that vibrated with energy, even now. Maybe now more than ever. She couldn't hurt him, not really. Not any more than he could hurt her. And while he would like to believe it was just the blood, he knew damn well it was more. It had been more even before they'd met. A lot more.

"Can you take me there?" Will asked.

Rhiannon stared at him, her eyes narrow. "Are you volunteering to help me rescue them?"

"Not volunteering. Protecting those girls is what I was hired to do. I've never failed in a mission yet. I intend to see this one through, just like all the others."

Sarafina faced him, her hands clasping his shoulders. "Will, these are powerful men. You could be killed."

"As I said, just like all my other missions. It's part of my job description, Fina. Always was, anyway, until the last one."

She looked down at his leg, the walking cane he held.

"Don't think this is that big a handicap," he told her. "It didn't stop me from getting the best of you, did it?"

She looked away. "Your talent as a liar far outweighed it."

She resented his lying to her, his acting job. That was probably a good sign.

"We need to go now," Rhiannon said. "Already an entire day has passed, and I'm not sure how we'll ever find them if they've moved."

Sarafina looked at her. "You'll want a change of clothes. So will I, before we go."

"We? You think I want help from *you* after what you've done?"

"No," Sarafina said. "You're far too stubborn and arrogant to *want* my help. But you *need* it, otherwise you wouldn't have come here. Come upstairs. It will only take a moment." She turned and limped up the stairs, and Will could almost feel the pain every single step caused her.

Rhiannon moved past Will, holding one arm with the other, as if it hurt to move it. She walked up the stairs behind Sarafina. Halfway up she turned back to Will. "Keep an eye on my cat, mortal."

Beside him, something warm and heavy bumped his leg. He looked down fast, startled, only to see the cat rubbing its head affectionately against his thigh. Were those diamonds on that sparkling collar? He closed his eyes, gave his head a quick shake. He'd entered the Twilight Zone, and he didn't think he'd be leaving it anytime soon.

What the hell, when in Rome...

He patted the cat on its head. It pushed back against his hand, and he could have sworn it purred.

Sarafina jerked a few things out of her closet, tossing them to the bed as Rhiannon walked into the room behind her.

"The bathroom's through there, if you want to wash up. You look as if you spent the day in a mudhole."

"A swamp, actually," Rhiannon said, grabbing one of the dresses from the bed and carrying it with her through to the bathroom.

She didn't close the door. Sarafina heard the water running as she stripped off her torn blouse and pulled on another much like it, then changed the skirt and drew out a few fresh scarves.

Water splashed as Rhiannon quickly washed up. Then she stepped out of the shower, wiping off with a towel and reaching for the clothes. The door was still open, and she wasn't the least bit embarrassed as she pulled the dress over her head.

"So what is between you and the mortal?" she asked as she pulled her long hair free and reached for a brush.

"What do you mean?"

Rhiannon turned, tugging the brush through her hair. "He's not one of us. And he's not one of The Chosen."

"Being neither stupid nor blind, I'm aware of that."

"Then what the hell are you doing with him?"

"I don't know...that it's any of your business, Rhiannon." She'd blurted the answer too quickly, tacked on the last to save face, though she was certain Rhiannon had seen right through it.

"He'll grow old," Rhiannon said. "He'll die. You won't."

"I might. One never knows." She fastened her skirt, stepped into a pair of flat shoes for easy running.

"If I devour him when we finish with him, it would save you a great deal of trouble," Rhiannon said.

Sarafina spun on her. "If you dare to touch him—"

"I knew it! You're in love with a *mortal!* By the

Gods, woman, do you have any idea the kind of pain you're inviting?''

"I am not *in love* with anyone," Sarafina said. She headed for the door.

"Hell, I may not need to tear you limb from limb when this is over," Rhiannon muttered, following her. "He'll hurt you more than I could ever do."

The arrogant bitch was right about that, Sarafina thought. It was exactly the reason she'd vowed long ago never to love again. But she hadn't broken that vow. On that, at least, the vampiress was wrong. She didn't love Willem Stone.

She *didn't.*

19

"I swear, I'm telling you the truth," Amber Lily Bryant said.

She wasn't whining. Stiles hadn't heard the girl whine yet. She was the kind of person he could have admired, in any other circumstances. But she was on the wrong side in this. If his experiments were successful, though, he would soon have the most powerful antivampire weapon in any arsenal known to man.

"How can I believe that you don't know whether you can live eternally or not? Hmm?"

She shrugged. "I grow older. Vampires don't, not from the moment when they're changed. If I grow older, it stands to reason that I'll eventually die."

"One thing doesn't necessarily prove the other."

"Doesn't it?"

He shook his head. "Do you heal like other vampires? All in one day?"

"I've barely had a scratch in my entire life. Though if you want to know that, you've certainly put enough of them on me to check for yourself."

He frowned, glancing at the bandages on her arms and chest, where his team had removed tiny skin samples. She followed his gaze, and her eyes clouded with her true feelings. She hated him. He knew that. But she would cooperate now. He had the ultimate tool to force her. He hadn't bothered to move his captives because he saw no need. His troops were prepared, and since there was only one lone vampiress at large in the area, the one who'd managed to escape his trap, he didn't feel too threatened. "You've never had a scratch, you say. Yet your skin is clearly not impenetrable."

"No. It's just that my parents are somewhat over-protective."

"Ahh. So you've never suffered a major injury, or been in an accident where you should have suffered one but didn't?"

"Right."

"What about illnesses? Colds, the flu?"

"I don't know."

"You've never been sick?"

"Not that I can remember."

"So that's hardly in keeping with your being an ordinary mortal," he told her. She only shrugged. "You know, Miss Bryant, in the end, you might be very glad I helped you find out these things about yourself. You must want to know more about your own nature. Especially something as vital as whether or not you can die."

"Everything alive can die, Mr. Stiles."

"*Dr.* Stiles," he corrected.

She pursed her lips, silently doubting his degree.

She was sharp, he thought. He didn't have one. He was largely self-taught. A lifetime's experience with vampires could teach a man far more that any university could. And he'd had years of research experience at the DPI. He'd worked with some of the greatest scientific minds of their time. He *should* be a doctor, even if he wasn't.

"You have this telekinetic ability—you can move things with your mind. Have you ever tested its limits?"

Meeting his eyes slowly, she shook her head left, then right.

"What's the largest thing you've ever moved?"

Her gaze shifted down and to the right as she tried to remember. "I don't know. A pile of books, maybe. A lamp. I don't know."

"Have you ever tried to move an entire person?"

"No."

"Try. Try to move me." She shot him a look, and he smiled. "Gently," he said. "You want your parents to continue receiving the best of care, after all."

Swallowing hard, she nodded. Then her expression changed. Became very focused, very intense. Her eyes centered somewhere in the area of his chest, and her facial muscles seemed to tighten a little.

And then he felt the blow, dead center of his chest. He flew backward, slammed into the barred door.

She jumped to her feet. "Oh, shit, I'm sorry! I didn't do that on purpose. Honestly!"

He managed to stay upright, lifting up a hand to stop her panic.

"I thought it would take more effort," she told him.

He lifted his brows. Then she was more powerful than even she realized. But it probably wasn't the wisest idea to go to great lengths to make her aware of that. Still, *he* needed to know. He ran a hand over the back of his head, where he'd felt the impact. "What about the thoughts of other people. Can you read them?"

"Only vampires, and only when they're not blocking them. That's how I know my family is okay down there in that cell where you're holding them."

"And can they read yours?"

"Yeah. Same rules apply. They, of course, can read almost any mortal's thoughts, depending on how strong-willed the person is."

"But you can't?"

"No."

"I see." He straightened his lab coat and came back to her side. "Let me see one of those little scrapes, hmm?"

She held out her arm. He peeled off the bandage and noted that she didn't wince. Maybe because it didn't hurt. Stiles frowned, looking closely at the mark in her flesh. "Half-healed already. You may not heal in a day's time like your relatives do, but you do heal far faster than an ordinary mortal. And you're physically stronger, too."

"Look, I've been cooperative. You've taken enough blood and tissue from me to build a whole new model, and I've answered every question. Don't you have all you need yet? Can't you just let us go?"

He ignored her plea, taping the bandage back in place. "What about your menstrual cycles? Are those normal?"

She blinked at him, saying nothing.

"I don't suppose that matters at the moment." He would keep her alive long enough to find that out, anyway. "You can rest now. We're going to see how much weight you can lift a little later on. I'm sure that's something you've always wondered about, isn't it?"

"No, it's really not."

He sighed, still unsure she'd been honest earlier when she'd told him she was a vegetarian. It might have been an attempt at sarcasm, but he had told Kelsey to bring her vegetarian meals from now on, all the same.

"You've been a good girl this morning. We can come back to those other things later on."

He pulled the tranquilizer gun, kept it trained on her while he called for Nelson to come open the door. He never entered the cell with the keys on him. It would be begging for trouble.

Yes, he was going to keep Amber long-term, he'd decided. She would be his personal subject of study for the rest of her life—or his, whichever came first.

He might even breed her, just to see what sort of little monster she would produce.

The others, of course, he would need to kill. He didn't like vampires, and he didn't really believe there was much more to be learned by studying them. The DPI had exhausted every avenue of research, and while he'd once feared most of it was lost in the fire, one of the relics he'd taken from the ashes had turned out to be the massive hard drive from the organization's mainframe.

Everything they'd ever learned was on it.

Her parents and her "uncle" Roland—they were dispensable. But not until he had everything he needed the girl to give him willingly. He went downstairs into the room in the back, which had been Eric Marquand's laboratory once—though why a vampire would have a laboratory in his home, Stiles couldn't begin to guess. It now served as one again. Closing the door and locking it behind him, he made sure he was alone. Then he opened the locked cabinet, made a few notes in the books that were for his eyes only. Closing the cabinet again, he relocked it. Then he went to the tiny cooler and removed a vial of Amber Lily's white cells.

He located a rubber band and tied it around his biceps. Then he filled a syringe with the white blood cells, which he'd extracted from the whole blood in order to ensure that there would be no compatibility issues. He located a bare spot among the needle tracks on his arm, finding a good artery, and then he inserted the needle, depressed the plunger and closed his eyes.

"Two cars will be better than one," Will said. "We'll need every tool at our disposal."

Nodding, Rhiannon marched across the lawn, opened the door of her Mercedes and made a purling sound in the back of her throat. Her cat raced to her side, leaped into the car and made itself comfortable in the passenger seat. "You two follow closely. Don't let me lose sight of you."

"We'll be right behind you," Will promised as he walked down the driveway to the open gate and through it to his car on the other side. He opened Sarafina's door, and she looked surprised by that before getting in. Then he hurried around to his side and got in himself.

He started the engine and backed out of the way, waiting for Rhiannon to drive past him, then pulling into motion behind her.

He glanced at Sarafina. "Are you hurting as much as it feels like you are?" he asked.

She blinked at him. "What is that supposed to mean?"

"I have all these aches I didn't have before. It feels like I'm the one with the lump on my head, the bruised cheekbone and the wrenched ankle, among other things."

"You feel my pain?" she asked.

"I figured it was the blood. Don't Misty and Edward...?"

"No."

"No?" He glanced quickly at her, the bulk of his attention focussed on the road. "They sure sounded as if they were feeling it when they phoned me."

She shook her head. "They crave me like a drug. They think they love me, but it's the blood they love. They don't live inside me the way..."

"The way I do," he finished for her.

She slid her gaze away from his, trying to look out the window. "I was furious with them for disobeying me, and they knew it. They ran off into the woods right after they phoned you, which was what I had told them to do in the first place."

He shrugged. "Then they didn't disobey. Exactly. They just...delayed obeying."

She shot him a glance, brows raised.

He felt her pain when she moved. Her head ached. Her neck was stiff. "What I'm feeling—it's real, isn't it? You're in a lot of pain."

"We tend to feel physical sensations to an exaggerated degree—by mortal standards, at least. Pain, pleasure, they're heightened in my kind, along with every other sense. So yes, injuries cause me significant discomfort. Any real damage will heal with the day-sleep, however."

"But you've got half the night to get through before that." He shook his head. "She really kicked your ass."

Her head snapped toward him, eyes flashing.

"That wasn't a slam. I'm amazed, is all. I mean, *you* kicked *my* ass. I still haven't made peace with that one."

"Why are you doing this?" she asked, still staring at him.

"Doing what?"

"Making conversation. As if—as if you don't hate me with everything in you."

He drew a breath, was silent for a moment. Then he spoke. "I guess it must be because I don't hate you."

She narrowed her eyes as if she didn't quite believe him.

"I probably should, considering what you tried to do to me. God knows I've been trying to. But I don't. Actually, I kind of respect you for taking action to protect two girls you didn't even know. Against a man with whom you felt...connected. Maybe even cared for a little bit. Or am I assuming too much?"

She said nothing, just ripped her gaze away again, aiming it out the side window.

"I'm assuming that's why you didn't just kill me outright. Because of...the bond between us."

"I didn't kill you because I'd never met a man whose will seemed as powerful as yours. Breaking it was a challenge I couldn't resist."

"And that's all it was?"

"That's all it was."

"Sorry, Sarafina. But I don't believe you."

Her back stiffened a little. She didn't ask him why not, but he was on a roll, and he wasn't going to stop now.

"You didn't succeed. And you're still with me. And if the challenge of breaking my will were all you wanted, you'd still be trying. God knows you're strong enough to go a few more rounds with me."

She turned toward him slowly. "In case you haven't noticed, Willem, there are more pressing matters right now. I misread the situation and put the Child of Promise in jeopardy. I have to right this situation. And when it's finished, if we're both still alive, perhaps then I'll consider renewing my efforts with you."

He smiled a little crookedly. "No, you won't."

"And what makes you so certain of that?"

"Because you might win. And then you'd never have the satisfaction of knowing whether I'm so fucking hot for you and out-of-my-head in love with you because of mind control or just because I am."

She looked as if he'd hit her between the eyes with a mallet.

"I am, you know."

She shook her head, short movements left and right, over and over. "You're playing with my mind again."

"I wasn't playing with your mind in the first place. And none of the stuff I did with you back in that room was acting. I wanted every bit of it, and then some. And I can't really blame it on the blood, because I was craving you like a drug before we ever met outside our minds. And I think you know it, because you were craving me, too."

"No."

"Yes. And you want to know why. What the hell it means. And you'll never find out if you zap my brain the way you did those two zombie slaves of yours."

She sat rigidly, as far from him as she could. "You couldn't be more wrong, Willem Stone."

"You wish I was wrong. But we both know I'm not. At least I'm honest enough to admit it, Fina. I loved every minute of being chained to that bed, forced to submit to your will. You'll love it, too, when I return the favor one of these nights."

Her eyes widened, and he saw something he hadn't see before.

"Jesus, you're afraid of me."

She pursed her lips, crossed her arms over her chest. "Don't be ridiculous. I could snap you like a twig, mortal."

"Exactly. So what is it about me that frightens you so much?"

"I do not get 'frightened,'" she told him. "I'm a vampire. I've survived centuries. Monsters. Attacks of all kinds. Vampire hunters from all ages. Nothing frightens me."

"Right."

Will focused on his driving. But as he did, he had the feeling he was on to something. It was niggling in the back of his mind. The key to understanding this woman who so puzzled him. And for some insane reason, understanding Sarafina was as important to him as anything had ever been. Including escaping his captors, surviving his missions, even staying alive.

Sarafina disliked knowing that he thought her somehow afraid of him. She only wanted to see this mission through to the end and get away from him as soon as possible. She didn't want to admit to him that she'd felt remorse when she'd believed she had succeeded in breaking his will. To admit to that would be to admit to weakness, to a lack of confidence in her own judgment.

Nor would she admit how his lies about wanting her still, about loving her in spite of what she was and what she had done to him, had stirred fire in her belly. Much less the longing it stirred in her heart.

It wasn't true. It couldn't be true. And she refused to believe otherwise, or to acknowledge the answering feelings stirring inside her.

She'd given herself, body and soul, to other men— her fiancé, her vampiric sire, her soul brother. All had betrayed her, left her alone in the end, and the pain of it had shattered her, again and again.

With Willem, there was no question that he would follow the same pattern. Even if, by some quirk of creation, he never intended to, he would leave her in the end. Because he was mortal, and she was not.

There was no future with him. None.

A very soft tone, short and repeating at even intervals a second or so apart, drew Sarafina's mind from
her thoughts. She shot him a glance. "What is that?"

He jerked the wheel to the side, stopping the car
and flashing his headlights once to get Rhiannon's
attention ahead of them.

She must have seen, because she, too, slowed to a
stop. Then she reversed her car and pulled it onto the
shoulder just ahead of them. Even as she got out and
walked toward them, Willem was leaning over Sarafina, rummaging in the glove compartment and finally
pulling out the device that was making all the noise.
It had a tiny screen marked into a grid, and a small
light on that grid was flashing in time with the tone.

"Why have you stopped?" Rhiannon asked, leaning over the side of the car.

"This," he said, holding it up. He thumbed a dial
on the side that lowered the volume of the beeps.
"It's a tracking device. I put the other half of it into
Amber Lily's bag. It sends out a signal, which this
part picks up. It tells me where she is."

Rhiannon glanced at the box in his hand. "It tells
you where her bag is."

"Well...yes, that's true. But if her bag is with
her..."

"Yes, I can see where it might be helpful. Is it in
keeping with a mansion about twenty miles ahead?"

He glanced at the box, then at the road. "Are we
moving northeast?"

"Yes."

"Then, yes, that's where she is."

Rhiannon nodded. "Then he hasn't moved her. She's still at the house in Byram. Or her bag is."

"This will pinpoint her for us. We'll even be able to tell what room she's in when we get a little closer. There's an elevation readout on the bottom of the screen."

"That *will* be helpful." She glanced at Sarafina. "We should feed. Neither of us is at full strength after our little...disagreement." She glanced at Willem.

"Not while I draw breath," Sarafina said.

Rhiannon shrugged. "For God's sake, I would only take a little. Just enough to soothe my aching arm. I think you may have broken it."

"You'll have to kill me first, Rhiannon."

She sighed. "I'd be more than happy to, if I didn't need you for the mission ahead."

"Catch a rabbit. Bite your damn cat, if you need it that badly."

"Please." She grimaced. "I'll just drain the first of Stiles's men I happen to encounter when we get there." She glanced at Willem, sent him a wink. "Your loss, pet. I give great jugular." Then she turned and sauntered back to the Mercedes. She started it up, and the taillights flashed on. Then she pulled slowly into motion again.

Will followed, but as he did, he sent Fina a look. "Why didn't you tell me?"

"Tell you what?"

"That...that you could ease your pain by, um... you know...."

"You need to be at full strength, too, Willem. If I drink from you, I'll weaken you."

"Not if you only took a little. I've been downing protein drinks all day."

"What flavor?" she asked. "If they were chocolate, you're history."

He glanced at her, confusion, then surprise, etched on his face. "I don't believe it. Did you just make a joke?"

She averted her eyes, turned her head.

"Come here." He reached out to snag her around the waist with his right arm and pulled her across the seat until she sat so close her side was pressed to his. He tipped his head to the left. "Go ahead."

She eyed his corded neck, licking her lips. She already knew his taste. She wanted it. "When I taste you, Willem, I sometimes...have difficulty knowing when to stop."

"Yeah, and I have trouble wanting you to." He slid his hand up to cup her head, gently pressing it into the crook of his neck. The skin touched her lips, and she darted her tongue over it, tasting its salt, feeling the pulse beat against her tongue.

He shivered. "Do it."

"Perhaps...somewhere a bit less apt to prove deadly." She slid lower down his body, her head brushing across his belly and over his thighs.

"Oh, *shit yeah*," he whispered.

With a fingernail, she sliced open the leg of his jeans, just enough to give her mouth access. She tasted the skin of his thigh, kissed it, and then she sank her teeth in.

He sucked in a breath, his muscle going tight, then slowly relaxing as she nursed at the tiny wounds in his thigh. His hand came to the back of her head, fingers twisting in her hair, caressing her nape, urging her on. She felt his hardness, beneath the jeans, pressing against her cheek.

Power—his power, which had been further enhanced by hers when he'd tasted her blood—coursed through her body. The pain in her eased. She tasted the very essence of Willem Stone, felt his heartbeat joining with hers.

And then the blood flow slowed. She'd punctured only a little, not very deeply, and nowhere near a major blood vessel. She sucked the skin until it gave no more sustenance, and then she lifted her head away.

Her pulled her close to him, and she rested her head on his shoulder as he drove for several minutes.

"Better?" he asked at length, his voice a little coarse but in control. "I'm not feeling the pain like I was before."

"Yes. Much better." She lifted her head. "And you? Did I take too much?"

"Hell, no. Only next time, I think it might be a good idea to stop the car first."

She'd been relaxing against him, almost snuggling.

As if they were a couple in love. But she stiffened, sitting up slowly, smoothing her hair, and putting cold, empty space in between them.

"There...won't be a next time."

"The hell there won't."

She shot him a look. He averted his eyes. "Okay, look," he said, "you had a good point back there— about there being more important things to worry about right now. But when this is over—"

She pressed a finger to his lips. "Don't."

He kissed the finger, nodded. "Okay. I won't. Yet."

She closed her eyes and leaned back against her headrest. Perhaps her relief had been misplaced. Perhaps her efforts to makes him hers to command had worked after all. She hated the idea. But why else would he be acting the way he was?

20
―――――――

Angelica sat on the floor of the cell, awake, but weak. Stiles had been sure to keep them weak. They had been given sustenance, but knowing it to be drugged, they hadn't imbibed. Roland had poured it out onto the floor in case their hunger became strong enough to overwhelm their common sense.

"This used to be part of Eric's safe haven," Roland said softly. He was sitting on the far side of the sublevel room. "It was nicer then. Furniture, lamps. Even music."

Angelica looked around the room, remembering what it had been like before. Sections had been walled off, including the one that led to the secret underground exit. It was nothing but a concrete square now. The only way in or out was a barred doorway that had once consisted of a false wine rack. And none of them were strong enough to break through the barrier. They'd been shot by bullets dipped in a powerful tranquilizer invented decades ago by the DPI. While the day-sleep healed their wounds, only blood would restore their strength. And there was none to be had.

And her daughter, her precious Amber Lily, was in this house. Angelica could feel her. She was frightened and alone, though they hadn't subjected her to torture—not yet, at least. She didn't think Amber had mastered the ability to shield her thoughts to the extent that she could hide intense pain from her own mother. Amber had whispered to her, again and again, that she was all right. That she hadn't been harmed. And Angelica had sent the same reassurances about her own condition back to her daughter, through her mind.

But now she kept her thoughts carefully concealed from her daughter.

Jameson, she whispered with her mind. *There is a way.*

He was pacing the cell, agitated beyond endurance at being trapped, unable to rescue his child. Blaming himself for having let her go on this trip in the first place. He stopped at the bars, his hands curled around them, and he said simply, "No."

It has to be you. I'm not strong enough, even at full power, to take on all of them. But if you drink from me, it will make you strong again. Strong enough to break through the bars. Strong enough to save Amber Lily.

"Don't be ridiculous, Angelica!" Roland said, getting to his feet. "You're far too weak. It would kill you."

She met Roland's eyes. "I'm her mother. If that's what it takes to save her, then that's what it takes. There's no question."

"I won't do it." Then Jameson shot a killing look

at Roland. "Don't even suggest it, because I won't do it to you, either."

Roland frowned in thought. *Jameson, if it would save her from them—*

"I know my daughter," he snapped. Then he caught hold of his temper and spoke silently. *She could never live with knowing that either of you had to die in order to let her go on. She couldn't. I wouldn't ask her to.*

"We have to do something," Angelica whispered. "We can't simply stay here like this, waiting for them to decide our fate—and hers."

"Wait!" Roland stood very still, one hand up. "Listen."

They all went silent, opening their minds.

I'm here. Outside, Rhiannon's mind whispered, and they all heard her clearly. *I've got the vampiress, Sarafina, and the mortal, Willem Stone, with me. Where are you?*

In Eric's old quarters in the basement, Roland replied.

The tunnel…?

Sealed off. Amber Lily is somewhere in the house.

Yes, we know. We think she's on the second floor, in one of the rear-facing bedrooms.

Roland didn't ask how she knew that. He didn't need to know how. And time was short. Dawn was, even now, approaching. *Get her first. Get her to safety and come back for us.*

The moment she's gone, they'll have no further reason to keep you alive. You know that.

Her life is more important, my love. And you *know that.*

Angelica put a hand on Roland's sleeve. *Rhiannon, the guards are sent out onto the grounds just before dusk. They know we can only attack by night, so by day they're lax.*

Good. There was a pause. *The sun is coming up over the horizon. Angelica, before you sleep, tell your daughter to let us know which room she's in—a signal in the window. Perhaps this mortal bodyguard can be of some use to us after all.*

I will.

Roland spoke again. *Find shelter. Be sure you're safe until sunset.*

I love you, Roland. Stay alive or there will be hell to pay.

Roland smiled and told her he loved her, too. Angelica slid into Jameson's arms and let him hold her. "I hope this man is as good as you think he is," she whispered.

"He is. I know he is." He closed his eyes. "God, I *hope* he is."

They'd cased the place, carefully and quietly, but it had been heavily guarded. By the time Rhiannon had finished her "conversation" with her loved ones, the sky was beginning to pale.

"This way," she said, marching off into the woods

across the street from the house, her cat at her side. "There's a shack. I believe it was once used for boiling the sap of maple trees into syrup."

"And the name of the shack is the sugar shack," Willem said. Both women simply looked at him as if he'd started speaking in tongues. "Before your time?"

"More likely after," Sarafina said.

They followed Rhiannon and Pandora along the path into the woods. Rhiannon spoke softly as she walked. "They have Roland, Jameson and Angelica in a hidden room in the basement. It's to the right, at the foot of the stairs. There used to be a large wine rack there that was really hiding the entrance. Now the entrance is barred. There's a tunnel that leads out, underground, but Roland says it's been sealed, possibly at both ends."

"Maybe we should check it out, see just how well sealed it is."

Rhiannon nodded. "You'll have plenty of time to do so while we rest."

He glanced at Sarafina, swallowed hard. "I don't know how comfortable I am with the notion of leaving you two alone, while you're out cold and defenseless."

Rhiannon glanced over her shoulder. "You don't have a choice. Roland says the security is lax by day. They don't expect an attack from a day-walker like you. If there's a way to get into that house and get Amber Lily out by day, do it."

Sarafina shook her head. "But won't they kill the others the moment they find her gone?"

"Probably. Which is why it would be better to wait until an hour before sundown to take her. Any later, though, and the guards will be in position."

Will didn't like that plan.

"She will put something in the window to let you know which room she's in," Rhiannon went on. "There's the building."

They climbed the last hill to a ramshackle shed. Will examined it and shook his head. "The sun will get in through all the cracks."

"There's a crawl space underneath," Sarafina said, examining the shed's construction as she walked around it. "Here, here's a way in." She pulled at a loose board and peered through to the space between the dank, damp earth and the building's floor. It was no more than two feet high, and God only knew what sorts of creatures had made a home of it.

Sarafina straightened. Rhiannon dropped to her knees, then flattened her belly to the ground and slithered inside. Her cat crawled in after her.

"Fina..." Will began.

She met his eyes. "Don't die while I rest." Then she lowered her gaze. "A stupid thing to say. Telling you not to die. It's your inevitable end. You're mortal."

"And you're not." He thought maybe he was finally starting to see himself through her eyes. "I'm not gonna die, Sarafina. Not today. Not for a long time.''

"As if it's in your power to promise something like that.''

He licked his lips. "You're right. I can't promise you that. All the more reason to live every single moment in exactly the way I want to live it.'' He slid his arms around her waist, pulled her body hard against his and kissed her. Her lips trembled, but then they parted, and her hands curled into his hair and she kissed him back, passionately and hungrily.

Will felt the sun on his skin, so he broke the kiss and moved to put her in the shade of his body. When she looked up at him, her cheeks were damp with tears.

"If I die today,'' he told her, "I'll have no regrets.''

"Oh, but I will,'' she whispered. Then she turned away and crawled underneath the building.

Will stood there for a moment. Now he knew he understood. She had loved, and she had lost. Over and over again. If she let herself be with him—care about him at all—she was guaranteeing herself a repeat of that pain. Because he would leave her in the end. He would grow old and feeble, and then he would die.

He bent and replaced the board, blocking out the sunlight. Then he stood there for several minutes, wondering how he would feel if he were the one sure to be left alone.

Something cracked the underbrush, startling him so much that he spun around and pulled his gun before he saw the flash of white tail that told him it was only a deer. Still, it was a wake-up call. He couldn't stand here in the open, because if he were seen by the bad guys, they would know right where to begin searching for the women.

Besides, the queenlike Rhiannon had given him his marching orders, laying them out with more authority than most military commanders under whom he'd served.

He checked the ground, carefully rearranging brush and twigs to erase any sign of human—or vampiric—presence near the shack. Then he made his way back through the woods until he could see the narrow, barely paved road and the massive house beyond it.

The front lawn was littered with trees and scrub brush. He crouched low as the sun rose higher and watched as that brush came alive with movement. Men, garbed in camo and armed with rifles that looked like AKs—military issue—emerged from the bushes and weeds. He counted twenty and kept mental note of the way they were stationed at intervals of six or seven yards. He could see those in the front and around the sides of the house, and wished to Christ he could see if there were any in the back.

Rhiannon's information had been dead-on. They weren't too worried about an attack by day. Even as he watched, they gathered in the driveway, near the front gate. And then he spotted four more, coming from the rear of the house to the front to join their comrades there.

A truck rumbled along the road, stopping at the front gate, and the men, looking tired, climbed into the canvas-enclosed back. A handful of fresh troops got out of the truck and took up positions, two in the front of the house and two others in the rear. Then the truck began maneuvering its oversize bulk in the narrow road, to turn around and return the way it had come.

Glancing back toward where he'd left the women, Will made a snap decision he hoped he wouldn't regret. Then he started toward where they had left the vehicles. His bad leg kept him from moving as fast as he would have liked. By the time he reached the cars, it was throbbing, and the truck had already gone by. But it moved slowly. He could catch it.

He dove into his car, fished for the keys and drove. He didn't have to keep the truck in sight. It was raising enough of a dust cloud so that he managed to follow that instead.

But only until it hit the highway ten miles later.

Once it did, he had no idea how far it would travel, and he didn't want to risk leaving the women that long. But he had another thought. He followed the highway to the nearest town, found a hardware store. He bought a chainsaw, and gas and oil for it. Then he returned and reconcealed the car far enough away that the noise he was about to make wouldn't reach the soldiers posted outside the house.

"Now we're playing my game," he said softly, as he got out of the hidden car and set to work. "And dead or undead, nobody beats me at my game."

When he finished, he opened the trunk of his car to stow the saw—and he remembered the bag he'd stashed there. The stuff good ol' Mike had sold him. Perfect.

He retrieved the package and, with the help of a sturdy limb, limped the two miles back to what he was beginning to consider his base of operations, then made his way toward that tunnel Rhiannon had mentioned.

Sarafina woke and lay still in the tiny, damp crawl space, listening, feeling the vibrations around her, waiting until she was certain no one was about before she even dared to move.

"Are you awake?" Rhiannon whispered.

"Yes. I think it's safe to go out." She belly-crawled to the loose board, but the moment she began to wriggle it free, it moved away on its own.

She nearly sighed in relief that Willem had survived the day. But she didn't feel any other presence with him as she made her way out from under the shack and let him help her to her feet.

She stood up and looked around. Then she spotted two men, unconscious and bound, lying on the ground. One was in military garb, one in his underclothes. Willem was wearing the man's camouflage clothing, carrying his rifle.

"What's this?" she asked, startled. "Willem, what have you done? Where is Amber Lily?"

Rhiannon came out next, brushing impatiently at the dirt on the borrowed dress. Her cat followed her. She glanced at the men. "Don't you get it, Sarafina? Your man has provided us with breakfast." Brushing off her hands, she walked over to where the two men lay, gripped one of them by the front of his shirt and lifted him easily, using only one arm. She drew him close, and sank her teeth into his neck, drinking deeply before dropping him again.

"Eat," she told Sarafina. "We need you at full power."

Will was staring at the man she'd dropped to the ground and looking a little bit shocked. "Is he...?"

"We're vampires, mortal. These men are ruthless killers. If I drained him dry it would be no more than he deserves." She glanced down at the man. "I didn't, however. Life with Roland has its downsides, I'm afraid. One of which is that his bothersome morality tends to rub off on me. I won't kill unless I have no other choice." She nodded at the men on the ground. "Will they be missed?"

"Not for a while. I heard them tell the other two they were going to walk the perimeter. They didn't plan to leave when the shifts changed."

Sarafina moved to the other man, knelt beside him and bent to his throat.

"You failed to rescue Amber Lily?" Rhiannon demanded.

"I didn't try. I didn't see the need of getting the others killed in the process and risking your lives, as well. We'll get her now."

"That wasn't the plan," Rhiannon all but growled.

"I made a new plan. Listen, lady, this is what I do. I'm good at it. Trust me on this. Now, come with me. And we have to be fast, before they realize something's up. Hurry now."

He led them through the woods to the road, found a safe spot to cross, and then skirted the outermost edge of the fence that surrounded the property until they reached the back, where the fence ended at a steep set of cliffs.

Crouching there, Will pointed. "There are two guards under Amber's window. The day shift. You were right, she managed to hang a blouse or something. See it? There'll be a dozen more guards back here soon, but those two will leave their posts when the truck arrives with the night team aboard. That's when we move in."

Sarafina frowned. "But they change shifts before sundown, not after!"

He sent her a wink. "They were delayed. Seems several trees fell across the road today. It won't take long to clear them, but it will be long enough."

They crouched there, waiting for a long time until they finally heard the truck. The guards in the rear yard shouldered their weapons and headed around the house, eager to be relieved of duty. It was nearly ten.

They'd already put in more than an hour's overtime. Sarafina cursed the short nights of summer.

"Let's go."

Will started for the steep drop of the cliffs, and Sarafina knew he intended to swing out around it, to get past the fence. She stopped him by putting her arms around his waist from behind, and Rhiannon rolled her eyes and muttered "mortals." She told her cat to "stay" and "wait." Then the two women bent their knees and pushed off from the ground.

Sarafina leaped the fence easily, carrying Will with her. They hit the ground on the other side hard, but she managed to absorb the worst of the impact. He did wince, and she worried about his bad foot, but there was no time. They raced forward and leaped again, this time landing on the balcony outside Amber's window. Sarafina and Rhiannon each gripped a bar and tugged hard, pulling them apart. The three got inside just as the new guards were getting into place behind the house.

Amber Lily sat up in the bed, startled; then she flew at them, wrapping her arms around Rhiannon and sobbing.

Rhiannon hugged her briefly, then set her away. "Shh. Quiet now."

Footsteps came from the hallway outside. Sarafina turned to pull the curtains tight, hiding the bent bars, and praying the men below wouldn't look up and notice them.

Then Will was pulling her across the room, into the

corner by the doorway. "How many are inside?" he whispered to Amber.

"Four men and a woman, besides Stiles."

Sarafina felt her pulse leap at the name. "Stiles?"

"You know him?" Will asked.

Her eyes narrowed, and she looked more menacing than he'd ever seen her. She only nodded once, then put her finger to her lips.

Amber scurried back to her spot on the bed and sat quietly. In silence, she was focusing, and Sarafina was amazed at her mental abilities to convey her thoughts. She could see clearly what the girl was seeing through the barred door. The woman was coming with a tray of breakfast food on a cart, and one of the men walked beside her, armed with a gun.

Tranquilizer darts, Amber thought at them.

The woman paused outside the bars to insert a key, and then she handed the key to the man. Amber got to her feet as the woman pushed the tray through the door. "Mmm, this looks good," she said, moving closer. "I'm starved."

She reached across the tray as if for one of the muffins on the plate, but instead, she gripped the woman's wrist and jerked her farther inside, kicking the tray out of the way.

The man lifted the gun, but Amber held the woman in front of her, her arm firmly around her upper body, keeping her arms pinned. She kept one hand over the woman's eyes, so she couldn't see the others.

The man outside the door grimaced at her. "Let her go, brat, or I'll dart you right here and now."

"You want her? Come and get her."

Snarling, the man stepped into the room. Rhiannon slid up behind him and gave his neck a powerful twist, even as Sarafina took the gun from his hand. She pointed it at the woman, who was struggling with Amber now.

Will put his hands over hers. "Too noisy," he whispered. He easily removed the dart from the gun, walked over and jabbed the woman in the arm with it.

She stiffened, then went completely limp.

He lifted his eyebrows. "Powerful stuff."

Rhiannon bent to take the keys from the man's lifeless hand.

Amber stood staring at Willem, tears welling in her eyes. "My mother told me... I'm so sorry for what I did to you. I—I thought you were one of them."

"I know. It's okay."

She looked at Sarafina. "I was afraid you'd killed him."

"It wasn't your fault," Sarafina told her.

"Never mind all that," Rhiannon said. "What about you, Amber Lily? What have they done to you, child?"

"They took enough blood to feed an army," she said. "And asked endless questions. And...I don't know what else."

"What do you mean, you don't know?"

She averted her eyes. "I was drugged a lot of the time." She licked her lips, changed the subject. "They've got Mom and Dad. And Roland."

"I know. It's all right. The mortal has a plan." Rhiannon handed him the keys. "Put these in your pocket. One of them is bound to open the room below, where they have the others. Though now that we're in here, I have no idea how you expect to get us out again. There must be twenty armed guards outside this place now."

"Twenty-four." he said. "I counted at the last shift change."

Sarafina closed her eyes. "Stiles has been busy, to have put together an operation of this size. The last time I encountered him, he had only a handful of men working for him."

"The guards look like mercenary types," Will said. "Hired guns. They may not even know what the hell is really going on in here."

"What they know doesn't matter, Willem. We can't take on twenty-four armed men, even if they are mere mortals."

"Let's deal with one issue at a time, shall we?" Will said. "There may be twenty-four out there, but there are only four left to deal with in here."

"One apiece," Amber said, looking dangerous as she clenched her hands into fists. "I can hardly wait."

21

"She should take the girl and go," Sarafina said, gripping Will's wrist, trying to tell him with her eyes how strongly she felt about it.

Rhiannon and Amber huddled in a corner, speaking softly, rapidly and at the same time. Amber wore her own clothes. A backpack with a patch that read 'Stroke 9' on it sat in the corner and had to be hers. *With a dead sound on the final stroke of nine...* The line from T. S. Eliot's *The Waste Land* ran through Fina's mind, and she wondered if Amber had found a literate rock band to admire. It would fit with what she sensed about the girl. Typical teen on the surface—but one with depths beyond knowing. At her age, those depths must be predominantly unexplored. But Sarafina had a feeling this girl had more to her than anyone—even those closest to her—realized.

Sarafina noticed how close the two stood to one another, the way Rhiannon couldn't seem to stop touching the girl, smoothing her hair, touching her forearms, her face. The woman loved the girl fiercely. It was obvious, and it was touching. It shouldn't be quite so *powerfully* touching, though. Not to Sarafina. She'd made it her mission in life never to be that moved by anyone or anything. Her throat shouldn't tighten at the sight of Rhiannon with her precious Amber, and her eyes shouldn't burn, her chest feel hollow and empty.

Will looked at her again, and she got the feeling he could read her thoughts as clearly as any vampire. "You're not as cold as you pretend to be, Sarafina. You might as well stop pretending."

"My coldness or lack thereof has nothing to do with it. The child is important. And it's my fault she's here. She and Rhiannon should leave here. Now."

His eyes moved over her face, and she shivered, certain now that those eyes of his were seeing things deep inside her, things she didn't let people see. She had to avert her own.

"It's a nice thought," he said. "But she couldn't get out of here if she wanted to, not with all the men outside."

"We could do something to divert their attention."

His arctic blue eyes narrowed. "Run out there like targets, get them to come after us? That kind of thing?"

She shrugged. "It might work."

"It might. But I have something else in mind." He glanced toward the other side of the room, at Rhiannon and young Amber Lily. "Rhiannon's husband is one of the prisoners. She'll never leave without him."

"She might. If it meant saving Amber."

Amber lifted her head then, looking Sarafina dead in the eyes from across the room. *He's right. Rhian-*

non might go, but I wouldn't. My parents are captive here, too, don't forget.

Sarafina held the girl's gaze for a moment, finally nodded once, then glanced back at Will again. "Forget it. She won't even consider leaving."

"Rhiannon?"

"Amber."

"Oh."

She bit her lip. "What's the plan?"

"We keep our presence to ourselves. And we wait. There will be a diversion, but not for a while yet. So we stay here in the house, undetected. We take our time, slow and quiet, and we take them out one by one." He looked out through the bars, up and down the hallway. "No one in sight." Then he took Sarafina's hand in his, as if he were big and strong and she was small and weak. It was like a promise that he would protect her, the way he closed his hand around hers. Wordless, but full of meaning.

And utterly ridiculous.

They crossed the room to where the other two stood, and Will began giving instructions as if he were still in the military and they were his troops. "Amber, I want you to act just as if nothing has changed. Stay here in the cage and pretend you're still at their mercy."

"What about them?" She glanced at the two bodies on the floor. One dead, one unconscious.

"We'll get them out of sight."

"And if I need to get out of here in a hurry?"

Will pulled the key ring from his pocket and removed from it the key to her barred door. He gave it
to her. "Hide it somewhere in the room."

"There's a loose floorboard, near the door," she
said. "You could probably reach in and get hold of
it from the outside, if necessary."

"Does anyone else have a key to this room?"

"Stiles, I think. Maybe others. They all manage to
come and go easily enough. I have no way of knowing if they're passing around a key or two, or if they
each have one of their own."

He didn't look as if he liked that idea much, but
he kept his thoughts to himself and turned to Sarafina
and Rhiannon. "The three of us are going to be like
ghosts in this place. We slip through this house like
shadows. We stay out of sight. Patience is the key
here. Don't rush it. When we manage to corner one
of them alone, we take them out, quickly and silently.
Hide the body, so no one's alerted to our presence. If
we do this right, we'll have the house to ourselves
before these amateurs even know anything's up. Got
it?"

Rhiannon's brows rose, and she gave a nod. She
was impressed in spite of herself, and Sarafina's chin
rose in pride she had no business feeling.

"Let's get these bodies out of sight."

"Closet?" Sarafina suggested.

He shook his head. "If someone does find them,
we don't want them blaming Amber."

Rhiannon gripped the two by the backs of their

shirts, pulling their upper bodies off the floor on either side of her as if she were carrying a pair of suitcases. "Where do you want them?"

"Are you going to be all right?" Sarafina asked Amber.

"I'll be fine. Just make sure my parents are okay."

Fina nodded, and then she and Will tiptoed into the corridor. Will went along the hall, listening at doors and opening them, until he found a room that seemed unoccupied. Sarafina peered over his shoulder when he opened the door. It must be a storage room. Dusty boxes, boards, old furniture and books were stacked all over it.

She glanced back at Rhiannon, still waiting in the entrance to Amber's room, and gave her a nod. Rhiannon dragged the two into the hall, and Amber closed the cage door behind her. The vampiress hauled the two limp mortals easily down the hall and then into the storage room, letting them both drop from her hands once inside. She tossed a piece of canvas over the dead man, glanced down at the tranquilized woman. "How long do you think she'll be out?"

Sarafina shrugged. "If that tranquilizer was the same one they used on us in the past, maybe she'll be out for good."

"So much the better."

"Uh, let's take precautions, just in case," Will said. He took a sheet from where it was draped over an old desk and tore a strip from it. Then he stuffed a little ball of it into her mouth and wrapped the rest around her as a gag. He used the drapery cords to bind her hands and feet together and to each other. *Hog-tied* was the term Sarafina thought applied. They stepped out of the room, Will letting the others go first, then turning the lock on the door from the inside and pulling the door closed behind them.

There were voices, muffled and coming from downstairs. Rhiannon and Sarafina both shot Will a worried look, as if he were the natural leader. And Sarafina supposed he was. Will gave a nod, and they crept down the curving staircase, none of them making a sound.

Will had left his walking stick outside the fence when they'd jumped it, Sarafina noticed. It couldn't be easy for him to walk lightly, if unevenly, down the stairs. He was in pain, she knew that. But he had gripped it in that ironfisted will of his, and he wouldn't let go.

She'd honestly never known a man like him.

At the bottom of the stairs there was a large foyer, with two archways leading into other parts of the house. One on the left, one on the right. Rhiannon took the left one. Sarafina locked eyes with Will. "Take the right," he said. "I'm going to find the basement."

She nodded.

He cupped her face, leaned close, brushed her lips with his. "Be careful."

"You're the one who's mortal."

He nodded. "And you're not going to let me forget it, are you?"

"This is no time for joking." She averted her eyes, swallowed hard. "Don't get killed."

"I'll do my best."

Nodding, she linked eyes with him one more time, then finally turned away and glided silently through the archway that led to the right. She didn't look back.

The house was dim. It was equipped with gas lamps, though the mortals using the place hadn't bothered to light them. There were few electric lights on, and only night shone in through the large windows. Fortunately, Sarafina thought, her night vision was better than that of Rhiannon's cat.

She wondered about the cat for just a moment. She hoped the creature was wise enough to stay out of sight out there, away from those men. Those rifles, which would only slow a vampire down, and the tranquilizer darts that would incapacitate one, would certainly kill a panther.

Her thoughts ground to a halt when she heard voices. They grew louder as she made her way through the massive house, from one room to another, closing in bit by bit, until she located them.

Two men, sitting in a library, with a book open on the table between them. Sarafina stood just outside the door, her back pressed to the wall. There was a mirror on the wall to the men's left, and she could see their reflections in it. They couldn't see hers, though.

She stood there for what seemed like an eternity, and it was killing her to stick to Will's instructions— to be patient and wait until one of them was all alone. She didn't sense kills taking place anywhere else in the house, and she wondered if Rhiannon or Will was facing the same problem—too many of them together in one place.

The hours dragged, and she began to wonder if they could complete this mission and make their escape before sunrise at this rate.

But eventually the men's inane conversation turned to subjects of interest, and she paid attention then.

"This is between us, okay? It doesn't go any further." The second man nodded, and the first went on. "Stiles is keeping something from us. Look at these notes." This was the younger of the two, pale complexion, stocky, strongly built, with a crew cut.

The other one had male pattern baldness and looked Italian. He was older, more sure of himself, wiry—a cocky, arrogant man, Rhiannon thought, sizing him up easily. "What's wrong with the notes?"

"Oh, come on. Don't tell me you don't see it."

The arrogant one shook his head.

"Stiles has been questioning the girl for hours at a time," Crewcut said. "So what's she been telling him? It's sure as hell not all here. He could've gotten this much information from her in the course of a half-hour interview."

The other one shrugged. "What are you, blind? Did you not get a look at that girl or what?"

"I don't—"

The dark one smacked the younger one upside the head with the flat of his hand. "He may be spending hours up there, Jughead, but if he's done nothing but question her, then he's no more human than she is." He smiled meaningfully.

"You mean...you think he's been...?"

"Wouldn't you?"

"Jesus, that's sick, Joe."

Sarafina thought "Jughead" might die a bit more mercifully than "Joe." She might even let him live.

"She's an animal," the younger one went on. "That would be like screwing a dog, man. And I don't give a damn how pretty she is, she's a goddamn demon."

Oh well. So much for mercy.

"Yeah," Joe said. "A demon. A little wild thing. And I intend to take her the first time the boss's back is turned."

"She'd kill you."

He reached into his shirt pocket, pulled out a dart. "Not if she's sedated, she won't. Not completely, though. I want her awake enough to know what's going on. Maybe put up enough fight to make it interesting, you know?" He grinned. "Where's the boss now, anyway?"

"Locked in the lab again. We won't see him for a while."

"Mercer and Caine?"

"In the basement, guarding the prisoners."

"Perfect. I guess my opportunity has arrived. You want to join me? You can have sloppy seconds."

"You're a sick son of a bitch."

Joe shrugged, got to his feet and started for the doorway. Sarafina looked left and right, but there was nowhere to go. No cover. She kept her back to the wall, closed her eyes and imagined herself blending into it, becoming a part of it.

"Mists of magic, cloud his sight," she whispered. "Cloak my form as dark cloaks night."

He walked past her, never noticed her there. Didn't turn around, didn't look back. She kept her eyes closed and her mind open. She would have felt him notice her if he had, but he didn't.

When his footsteps faded, she opened her eyes again and saw his back vanishing down the halls. She paused a moment, thought of Rhiannon, felt her mind's vibrations and tuned into them. *Rhiannon, how is your search progressing?*

I've found no one yet. I sense two below, one on this level, but hidden somewhere.

I've had two here with me. They mentioned men named Mercer and Caine. Those would be the two in the basement. Stiles is apparently locked away somewhere. That makes at least five of them.

That's one more than we thought were in the house, Rhiannon's thoughts whispered across the vastness of the mansion. *Not that it matters. We can deal.*

One of mine is on his way up to Amber's room. He intends to drug her and rape her.

Oh, does he now?

Rhiannon didn't need to say more. Sarafina was confident "Joe" was as good as dead. But she was worried. If there were two men in the basement, would Will be able to handle them?

Stop worrying, Rhiannon thought fiercely. *I'll go to the basement the moment I take care of the gnat in Amber's room. You focus on Stiles—having dealt with him in the past, and far more recently than I, you may have better luck honing in on his energies.*

Sarafina agreed. God, it ate at her to care as much as she did. And yet the rage rising up in her belly at the thought of one of these men harming Willem Stone told her that she did care. She would tear them apart if they hurt Will.

She turned her own attention back to Crewcut, who was bending over the notebook now, his back to the door.

She slid slowly inside and thought about closing the door behind her to prevent anyone happening along and seeing, but decided against it. If its hinges creaked, the man would have time to shout, and she couldn't have that.

She glanced once behind her and, seeing no one, glided silently up behind him and positioned her hands on either side of his neck, not quite touching. Just as he sensed her presence and started to turn, she closed her hands all at once, without expending much effort at all. His larynx was crushed in her grip as easily as a paper straw would have been. His bones cracked like tiny, brittle twigs. He died instantly.

"Animal, hmm?" she whispered. Looking around the room, she spotted a closet, lifted the man out of his chair and carried him toward it. She dropped him inside and closed the door. Then she turned and walked quietly back out of the room, taking the note-book with her. It might be of interest to Amber and her guardians to know what Stiles had written there— though if "Jughead's" theory were correct, this was less than the entire story.

"Four left," she whispered. "Three, if Rhiannon and Joe have crossed paths yet." She went to search the house for the lab where Stiles had locked himself away.

She and Frank Stiles went way back. She owed him.

Amber was pacing the room, glancing over and over out the barred window at the guards below, won-dering just how they were all going to get out of this hellhole alive when there were so many of them out there. Footsteps in the hall brought her head around fast, and she jerked the drapes tight, just in case. She hoped to God it was the others, returning with good news. It had been hours since they'd left her alone. Though she doubted it could be true. She'd spoken to her mother mentally, told her what was happening, but up to now, no one in the basement had seen any sign of the rescuers.

Amber recognized the man who stood outside her door as one of those who had brought her here. She hadn't seen him since then. Her meals were always brought by the female, Kelsey, backed up by the big blond man called Nelson.

The look in this man's eyes as he slid a key into her lock told her Stiles might have had a good reason for that policy. This man was slick and slimy. And she knew what he wanted before he opened the barred door, stepped inside and said, "You do me nice and I'll let you out of here. Deal?"

"Oh, I'll do you all right," she told him. She moved closer, wondering why no one had warned him that she was strong enough to tear off his arms and beat him to death with them.

He slid his hands around to cup her buttocks, and she lifted hers to his neck, to break it. But then she felt the sharp jab and realized the bastard had come prepared.

Her head swam, and her knees unhinged. She sank, but he caught her under the arms, hauled her to the bed and dropped her across it. Then he straddled her and fumbled with her jeans, unbuttoning and unzipping them.

He'd left the barred door open. The idiot.

Rhiannon appeared in the doorway. Her form was fuzzy, but Amber didn't need to see her to know she was there. And oh, God, was she pissed.

She strode into the room, gripped the man by the

hair on the back of his head and hauled him off of Amber.

"Wha—? Who?"

She didn't give him time to get any louder. She put her hands on either side of his head and gave such a violent twist that when the body slid to the floor, the head remained in her hands. A length of skinny pinkish cord still connected the one to the other and blood flowed like a waterfall.

"Oh, gee, I think he lost his head." Amber laughed at her own joke. "Shit, Aunt Rhi, look at that mess." Her words slurred together.

"Button your jeans and hand me a blanket."

Amber lowered her eyes in the direction of her jeans, but her hands really didn't want to move. She tried to move them, but they only rose and then dropped lazily onto the bed again, which she found freaking hilarious now that the threat was gone.

"Hell," Rhiannon whispered, dropping the head next to the body on the floor and leaning over the bed. She rolled Amber to one side, then the other, peeling a blanket out from under her.

"He's got the funniest look on his face," Amber said, pointing at the gaping, surprised head. "He's like, 'Hey, where's my body?'"

Rhiannon rolled her eyes, turning with the blanket, intending to wrap the head and body to reduce the mess, but there was already a significant pool of blood on the floor. It would take too long to clean it up, she decided. She kicked the body and head underneath the bed, wiped her hands on the blanket, and then dropped the blanket to the floor to cover the blood-stains. Then she hauled Amber off the bed and dropped her into a nearby chair.

"I'm going to have to take you with me. You can't stay here like this. Any one of them could come for you, and you're defenseless in this condition."

"Yeah, but I gotta tell you, Rhiannon, my head-ache is long gone. So is his, I'll bet."

"Quiet!"

Amber put her finger to her lips, making an exag-gerated *shushing* sound.

Rhiannon quickly arranged the blankets on the bed to look as if someone were lying asleep beneath them, a trick that might fool an army of kindergartners—but only very stupid ones.

Then she fastened Amber's jeans, gathered the girl into her arms and carried her out of the room, closing and locking the door behind them.

"Where are you taking me?" Amber asked.

"To the basement, I suppose. But only if you're very quiet."

Amber nodded and bit her lip to keep from laugh-ing.

Will found the basement entrance right away. It had been his goal all along to get to the prisoners being held down there. It might have been easier to locate the men he suspected were lurking on the mansion's ground floor, but he had every confidence in Sarafina and Rhiannon. They could handle themselves. Maybe not against a tranquilizer-armed militia that knew they were coming, but this was a handful of men who were not expecting them.

They would be fine. And they would see to it that Amber was, as well.

He couldn't be so certain about the trio held in the subterranean levels of the place. Being held in the bowels of the earth was far too familiar to him not to twist his guts into knots. And from what Rhiannon had said about the DPI and the men who had served it, it was as likely as not the prisoners had undergone deprivation of heat, food and light, and possibly more active forms of torture.

He felt sick at the thought but couldn't quite shove it to the back of his mind. He'd lived it. It was too real, too recent, and too much a part of his soul.

He opened several doors as he made his way through the house, until one opened onto a set of stairs, descending into darkness.

He figured there was probably a guard down there...somewhere. Stepping onto the topmost stair, he pulled the door closed behind him, making the darkness complete. His bad foot was aching. He should have brought his damned meds with him, but he hadn't planned on taking an extended trip. It took effort and concentration to step down on the foot, evenly, slowly and soundlessly, despite the pain that shot through it more with every ounce of weight.

A stair creaked, just slightly.

Willem went still, motionless, waiting.

When no sound emerged, he took another step. There was no way to tell where the stairs ended and the floor began, other than to just put his foot out there and feel for it. There were more stairs than he would have expected. The cellar was deep.

His eyes began to adjust to the darkness. He could make out shapes by the time he finally reached the basement floor. Turning right, he moved slowly, arms out in front of him. Somewhere in this direction there was supposed to be an entrance to a secret section of the basement—once a wine rack.

He felt only a wall of crumbling stone.

Inching along it, feeling his way, he wondered if he shouldn't just find a light switch and snap it on.

A flare of light came on the heels of that thought, startling him—and then he realized it was the flame of a match or lighter, only a few yards farther along the wall. He watched the flame move in, saw the end of a cigarette glow and the flame go out. If he'd kept going, he would have walked right into the smoker. Thank God for nicotine addiction.

He shook off the fright and again began moving slowly, steadily, forward. His foot hit something; a pebble or bit of stone skittered across the floor. The glowing tip turned in his direction.

"You there, guards." The voice came from the other side of the wall, though Will realized it must not be a wall where the guard stood. That must be the barred door. But the man had shouted "guards" not "guard."

Hell, there was more than one.

The smoker turned toward the voice, which wasn't a voice Will recognized.

"What the hell do you want, bloodsucker?"

"What I want is to rip your heart out and suck it dry. But that wasn't why I summoned you just now."

Will smiled just a little. The vamp knew he was here. He'd heard the pebble as clearly as the guard had. Maybe he'd heard more than that. Sarafina said their senses were magnified. He guessed the owner of the voice must be Rhiannon's husband—Roland, she'd called him.

"It's Angelica," the vampire went on. "I think she may be near death."

"Right."

"Look for yourself, man!"

"You think I'm an idiot? I come any closer to the bars, you'll have me. I'm not leech food."

Will squinted in the darkness, wishing to God he could see the action.

"I'll stand back from the bars. See?"

The man didn't, apparently, because he flicked his lighter again, holding it in front of his face. Will could see him now, see his face illuminated by the single tongue of flame. As was the dim outline of the man who stood beside him. Will saw only two. He prayed there were not more.

"Mercer, go up and get the boss. See what he wants to do about this."

The second man flicked on a flashlight, and Will ducked behind a support post and watched its beam move quickly across the basement. He heard the man pound up the stairs and close the door behind him after he got up there.

The first one leaned a little closer to the bars, peering in, holding the lighter a bit farther in front of him. He was extremely careful not to put himself within reach of the prisoners.

His back was to Will now, as no doubt, the vampire had intended. Will moved in, swift and silent, right up behind the guard. He cupped the man's mouth and chin with one hand and braced the other at his nape.

"Don't kill him," a woman's voice snapped.

Frowning into the darkness, Will couldn't see, and he didn't ask questions. He changed his grip to a choke hold and squeezed the guard into unconsciousness. When the man went limp, Will dropped him, and his body fell forward. Will bent over to search him. But before he could even begin, the body was jerked roughly forward, smashing against the bars.

Will had no idea what was going on—at least, not until he heard the sucking sounds. He tried his best to ignore the smacking and slurping, along with the guard's position, which soon became apparent—both arms had been yanked through the bars—and finished searching the guy's pockets. He located a set of keys, removed them, then got to his feet, stepping over the guard and running his hands along the barred door, bumping the arms along the way, until he found the lock panel with its keyhole. Then he began trying one key after another, until, finally, one of them fit.

The feeding frenzy had stopped. He rolled the body aside and pulled the cage door open.

"I'm glad to see you, Stone."

That was Bryant's voice. Amber's father, the man who'd hired him. "Wish I could say the same," he replied, blinking in the darkness. "Good move distracting the guard. I'm glad you heard me kick that pebble."

The other male, the one Will assumed was Roland, cleared his throat. "We heard you coming down the stairs, watched you all the way across the basement. Stealth is not your strong suit, Stone."

"Maybe not to you. The guard didn't hear me, though."

"Where's my daughter?" the woman, Angelica, asked.

Will blinked, looking in her general direction. "I thought you two were able to communicate—you know, astrally or whatever."

"Mentally. She's gone silent. Something's wrong."

Will twisted his wrist, squeezed his watch so its face lit green. "Let's get upstairs. We don't have much time."

"Much time before what?" Jameson asked, already heading toward the stairway.

Roland gripped Will's upper arm to guide him across the dark basement to the stairs. Will was grateful; it would have taken him twice as long, blind.

"Before my diversion kicks in—assuming it works."

They were heading up the stairs by now, but before they could make it, the door at the top opened, letting a shaft of light fill the stairway. Rhiannon stood there, carrying Amber in her arms. The girl hung limply, and Willem's heart twisted.

Angelica gave a sharp little cry, and the next thing Will knew she was at the top, taking the girl from Rhiannon's arms.

"She's only unconscious. One of them drugged her again."

"How are you two progressing?" Will asked.

"Sarafina killed one on the ground floor. I haven't seen her, but I saw the kill through her eyes. I killed another, though I'm afraid I didn't do it as neatly as you instructed. You?"

"One dead down here. Another raced upstairs to find Stiles. You didn't see him?"

"No."

They were all on the ground floor now, Roland

closing the basement door behind them, before turning to slide an arm around Rhiannon, pulling her close to him, kissing her hungrily.

"By my count," Will said, "Stiles and the one who ran up here to find him are the only two left in the house."

Jameson nodded. "Then where the hell are they?"

Will frowned. "More importantly, where the hell is Sarafina?"

22

Sarafina opened her mind as she searched the house. She knew that Rhiannon was with Amber, and the slick and slimy Joe was dead. She knew that Willem had gone below to search for the vampires being held there, and that Rhiannon had gone to back him up.

And she knew, from the conversation she had overheard, that Stiles was in a laboratory somewhere in the house. Once assured the others were holding their own—confident they could handle the one mortal thug still unaccounted for—she honed her focus, drew it in until it was as sharp and attuned as a pinprick of light. Within that pinprick, she placed an image of Stiles as she remembered him, with the left half of his face mottled and pink with scars, the left half of his head smooth where no hair could grow. He'd been inside DPI headquarters when the vampires had burned it to the ground all those years ago. He hadn't escaped unscathed.

She wished fervently that he hadn't escaped at all. He'd singlehandedly recreated the DPI, though whether he still used the name, she didn't know. It didn't matter. What he had created was born of the same fear-based hatred. If anything, this new orga-

nization of his was even more despicable than the
original had been. But it would end when he did. And
she intended to see to it that his end found him soon.

She owed the man.

Her instincts led her through the house, her senses
guiding the way, until she found herself in a corridor
lined with doors on either side. Moving through it,
she held her palms to each closed door, *feeling* the
vibrations on the other side—or not feeling them,
since most of the rooms were empty. But then, she
had help from an unexpected source.

Ahead, around a corner, a man—not Stiles—lifted
his hand to pound on a closed door. She moved toward him in a flash of speed, caught the hand before
it could make contact, covered the man's mouth so
he couldn't cry out and held his nose so he couldn't
breathe. It was the quietest method she could think
of, but her patience was stretched to its limits by the
time his oxygen-starved heart finally stopped beating.

She dragged him around the corner and left him
there. Then she returned to the door, put her palm to
its surface and knew that Stiles was inside.

Closing her hand around the doorknob, she tried to
turn it, found it locked. She took two steps back,
turned slightly to one side and kicked. The door burst
open, wood splintering along the locked edge.

Stiles whirled to face her, his eyes wide. He stood
on the far side of the dimly lit room. She took rapid
note of computers, shelves lined with bottles and jars,
microscopes and more sophisticated laboratory equip-

ment and books. There were endless rows of notebooks like the one the two had been perusing in the
library. One such book lay open on the table that
stood between her and Stiles. There was a syringe in
his arm, its plunger fully depressed.

"Funny," she said. "I didn't take you for an addict."

He pulled the needle from his arm, tossed it to the
floor and casually rolled down his sleeve. "And I
didn't take *you* for an idiot—Sarafina, isn't it?"

She nodded, just once. "You remember me, then."

"I never forget an enemy. This is going to be a
supreme pleasure. Of course, you realize you're completely surrounded. Trapped."

"By those soldiers you have stationed outside, you
mean? They didn't stop me from getting in, Stiles. I
doubt they'll give me much trouble when I decide to
make my exit. Not that you'll be alive to see it."

"I think I will." He lunged for the counter behind
him, grabbing a small handheld radio. She shot across
the room, clearing the table easily, landing beside him
and closing her hand over the one that held the device. When she squeezed, Stiles's face contorted and
the radio crumbled into pieces.

He shouted then. "Nelson, Joe, get in here!"

She released his hand, brushing her own as if to rid
it of dirt. "Nelson. That's the big blonde with the
broken neck, isn't it? And I believe Joe has, well, as
someone dear to me put it, he's simply lost his head.

In fact, I'm fairly certain all your household staff have decided to...take the rest of the night off.''

"You killed them. You murderous bitch.'' He was backing across the room as he spoke, toward the right wall. There were numerous items strewn on the counter there, and a small refrigerator, as well.

"I'm not the one who kidnapped a teenage girl, Mr. Stiles,'' she said, picking up the open book from the table as she followed him. She glanced down at the pages.

"*Dr.* Stiles.''

She ignored him, noticing the phrases that stood out on the page.

...tenth injection...noted increase in strength and stamina...no aversion so far to sunlight or solid food...

Frowning, she looked up at him. "What is this? Exactly what were you injecting into what's left of your pathetic body when I walked in here?''

He smiled very slowly. "You'll never live long enough to find out,'' he muttered.

She tossed the book aside, and in a single burst of motion she was on him, had him by the throat, ready to choke the answers from him. Stile drove his fist into her belly with impossible force. Her grip broke, and she flew backward, airborne, until her back hit the table, breaking it in two. She lay on the floor, the jagged wood beneath her, stunned. He couldn't be that strong. He *couldn't be*....

"What have you done?'' she whispered.

He started toward her, and she sprang to her feet, defensive, ready. He made as if to attack, but instead pulled a gun from inside his jacket. An ordinary handgun. He fired it, and the sound was deafening to her sensitive ears as the muzzle flashed blue fire. A redhot brand seared through her midsection. Pain screamed, and blood flowed as she fell to her knees.

She looked down at where her hands clasped her belly, saw the scarlet lifeblood oozing from between her fingers. "You'll die for this...."

"Not likely. You will, though. I guarantee you that."

Even before she lost consciousness, the bastard had hauled her up and thrown her over his shoulder as if she were weightless, and at such close range she smelled him even more acutely than she had before. His scent was off—there was something familiar, something beloved that shouldn't be there. And then it hit her. He smelled like Amber Lily!

He carried her toward the wall. Not the door, but the wall.

Willem heard the gunshot. They all did, and they raced through the house toward its source. Sarafina. Jesus, something had happened to Sarafina. He felt it in his gut—and it burned.

They ran into a hall, down it, the others opening doors as they went. Will didn't bother. He felt pulled, and he followed that feeling, running on his injured foot, completely oblivious to the pain. He nearly tripped over a dead man lying on the floor. Leaping over the corpse, he kept moving and came to a door that was already open. Splintered but open, revealing a laboratory.

"Here!" he shouted, and the others came running.

Silently they took in the surroundings, the equipment, the broken table and the small pool of blood on the floor near it. Amber, rousing now from the mild dose of tranquilizer she'd been given, bent to pick up the notebook on the floor.

"That's Sarafina's blood," Rhiannon said softly. "He's taken her...somewhere."

"But where?" Will looked frantically around the room, his heart racing, his head in chaos. But then he checked himself, fell back on his training, called up every ounce of will and self-control in him. He went still, closed his eyes and let his experience take over.

"Roland, go to the front of the house, where you can see outside through the windows. Check the troops outside, see if they seem to have heard the gunshot."

"It's doubtful, given the thickness of these old stone walls."

"Make sure. And don't be seen."

Roland nodded and left the room.

Will glanced at Jameson. "We left one alive. The woman, in the room upstairs. Get her and bring her down here."

Jameson nodded and left, moving fast.

Angelica said, "We know he didn't carry her out the way we came in or we'd have passed them. I'll check the other way along this hall, see if there are any other exits that he could have used.''

''Look for blood on the floor, as well,'' Will told her. And even as she hurried away, he was looking at the floor, his eyes narrow. There were droplets of blood between the puddle and the wall on his right. Nowhere else.

He shook his head. ''This doesn't make any sense.''

''My God,'' Amber whispered.

Rhiannon and Willem both turned toward her. She was standing in the doorway, her eyes moving rapidly over the pages of the book she held.

She looked up slowly, at each of them in turn. ''He's been—he's been injecting himself with...with my blood. My blood.''

''What?'' Rhiannon took the book from her, reading for herself.

Will understood. ''He says you're animals, evil demons and that he wants to eliminate you all. He uses that rhetoric to draft men to his cause. But what he really wants is what you have.''

Rhiannon looked up. ''He wants to be a vampire?''

''He wants to be immortal,'' Will said softly.

''But why would he think *my* blood would give him that?'' Amber asked.

Will took the book from Rhiannon, flipping backward through the pages, skimming rapidly until he found the section that stopped him. What he read there made him sick to his stomach. They'd been trying to kill the beautiful teenage girl with the piercing eyes ever since they'd had her here. Food laced with poison. Electric shock while she was under sedation. They'd even tried drowning her. Each time, she had revived.

"What?" Amber asked. "What is it, Will?"

He shook his head. "Later. We'll discuss it later."

Jameson arrived, carrying the still-unconscious woman in his arms. He'd removed her bonds and gag. "I'm not sure we can wake her," he said.

"You can. There's an antidote to the tranquilizer. They used it to rouse me when they needed me awake a couple of times," Amber said.

Rhiannon went to the shelves, then to the tiny refrigerator, knocking bottles and jars to the floor in her haste. "Here," she said, picking up a labeled syringe. "This must be it. It seems to be premeasured."

"Premeasured for a vampiric dose," Angelica said from the doorway. "I checked, there are some windows in some of the rooms, but all closed and locked from the inside. No other doors he could get to from that direction. The hall just ends."

Rhiannon brought the syringe to Jameson, glanced at him. He nodded. "Her heart's barely beating. She had a full dose of the tranquilizer, after all."

"Not a full one," Amber said. "They had to dilute it for me. And probably the antidote, as well. If that's premeasured, it was probably meant for me."

"Either way, it will kill her soon enough if we don't try," Will said. "Go ahead, it can't hurt."

Rhiannon injected the woman; then Jameson laid her down on the floor. Roland returned, looked around at them. "The guards outside haven't moved. I don't think they heard anything."

"Good." Will set the notebook on a counter and bent over the woman on the floor. He tapped her cheeks. "Wake up. Wake up now, come on."

She moaned softly, moved her head from side to side. Finally her eyes fluttered, then opened, then opened wider when she saw them all standing around her.

"If you want to live, you'll tell me what I want to know," Will said.

She looked around frantically.

"There's no one left to help you. The others are dead, Stiles has escaped, and the guards outside don't even know we're in here. Now look, see the room you're in? The lab?"

She nodded.

"Stiles escaped from here, but not through any of the exits we can find. How did he do it?"

She blinked, foggy, unfocused, scared as hell. "I don't...I can't..."

"Oh for pity sake, let's just eat her and be done with it!" Rhiannon knelt beside the woman, gripped a handful of her hair and tipped her head back, her eyes blazing and aimed at the tender arch of her neck.

"No!" the woman cried.

"Talk or die, mortal. It's of no consequence to me."

Will had to admit, the vampiress was good. She might have been able to make even him talk.

Nah.

The woman on the floor nodded rapidly. "There's... a hidden panel...in the wall." Her hand rose, gesturing weakly in the direction of the wall where the blood trail ended.

"How does it open?" Will asked.

"The...light switch."

Willem crossed the room and saw the ordinary-looking switch plate hidden in plain sight. He flipped the switch, and a section of the wall slid into itself, revealing a downward staircase.

Roland said, "That wasn't here before."

"Stiles...had it built," the woman said.

Suddenly there was a muffled roar from somewhere in the distance, and the floor seemed to shake beneath them.

"What the hell...?" Roland began.

Willem glanced at his watch. "Shit, it's the diversion. I set explosives on a timer at the far end of the other tunnel—not this one. The one Eric used as an emergency exit from the rooms below. Not enough to blow it open. I only had a small amount of explosive and—"

He was interrupted by a tinny sounding voice emanating from a small box mounted to the wall just inside the door.

"Stiles? There's been some kind of an explosion nearby. How do you want us to proceed?"

Willem glanced at the woman. "Explain. Fast."

"Intercoms," she said quickly. "They're spaced throughout the house so we can communicate with the soldiers."

Will marched across the room to the intercom, depressed the button, spoke into the box. "Someone blew the sealed tunnel. The prisoners are escaping. Take all your men and go after them."

"But the house, sir."

"There are six of us in here, all armed. I think we can handle one little girl. You have your orders, soldier. Go."

"Yes, sir!"

Roland shook his head. "Unbelievable. You sound nothing like Stiles."

"Not to you, maybe," Will said. "But to an ordinary mortal, most deep male voices sound pretty much the same over a cheap intercom. Besides, mercenary or not, a trained soldier doesn't stop to think too much when given a direct order. He just obeys."

A thud drew his gaze, and he turned to see Amber, standing over the book, which she'd just dropped to her feet. While they'd all been involved with the woman on the floor, she had, apparently, been reading about the things Stiles and his monsters had done to her.

"I...I don't understand," she whispered, her eyes welling. "They tried...they tried to *kill me?*"

Angelica gasped and wrapped her daughter in her arms. Jameson said, "What's in that book?"

"Take it with you," Will said. "There's no time now. It's not going to take those troops long to realize the tunnel is still sealed. Get out of here, all of you. Go find the vehicles. Close the door behind you and they'll never know anything happened."

"What about you?" Amber asked.

Jameson smoothed his daughter's hair. "He's going after Sarafina."

"Not alone, he isn't," Rhiannon said. She shot Roland a look. Roland only nodded once.

"There's no time to argue about this," Will began.

"Then don't," Rhiannon told him. "Angelica, Jameson, take Amber and go. Take the car and get out of here. We'll meet you at Eric and Tam's when this is finished. Go."

"No." It was Amber who spoke. "We're wasting time. Sarafina saved my life, and I'm not going to go off safe and sound while she faces Stiles alone." She broke from her mother's embrace, gripped Will's hand and pulled him to the secret passage.

"Stubborn little..." Rhiannon rolled her eyes; then she bent to haul the woman to her feet. "Go on," she told the others. "I'll tuck this one safely in a closet somewhere and catch up."

"Hurry, Rhiannon," Jameson said, even as he and Angelica moved into the dark passageway where Will was still trying to dissuade Amber. "Those troops..."

Roland shook his head. "Not to worry, Jamey, I'll stay with her. Go on. Go with Will and help him save his woman."

Rhiannon turned back to the woman on the floor, "Just a few more questions, and then we'll be on our way."

The others ran down the tunnel, and Roland flipped the switch on the inside to close the entrance.

23

"The tunnel leads where?" Rhiannon repeated, as she stuffed the woman into a closet.

"To the sea. Stiles keeps a boat there in case we need to escape in a hurry."

"A boat. One single boat?" She shook her head. "With room enough for all seven of you?"

The woman frowned as if she'd never considered that.

"Twit." Rhiannon closed the closet door and braced a chair under the outer knob for good measure.

"They're going to be trapped out there," Rhiannon said. "The soldiers will radio the house, and when no one answers, they'll come inside. The twit will tell them about the passage if they don't already know."

Roland raced through the house in a haze of motion, peered out the front window. "They're already in sight on the road, heading back this way. We have to get out of here before they get back into position. Come on, the back way will give us the most time." He gripped Rhiannon's hand, and together they sped through the house and out the back. They made it to the iron fence just as several men came around the house and began retaking their positions. All those soldiers had to do was turn their heads....

Roland and Rhiannon jumped and cleared the fence, landing on the other side and quickly darting for cover. The soldiers heard the impact of their landing, looked toward the sound, and then, frowning, moved closer.

Rhiannon and Roland stayed very still in the brush while a pair of eagle-eyed troops walked up and down the fence, shining flashlight beams through it, searching.

Soft footfalls from behind drew Rhiannon's gaze, and she turned. Pandora padded up to her, almost soundless. Rhiannon wrapped her arms around the cat and nuzzled her face.

After a moment, the soldiers returned to their posts.

Rhiannon rose, cautious and quiet. ''Come on. We have to find a boat.''

They made their way along the road, back to where Will had hidden the Mercedes. Then they got in, Pandora sprawled on the back seat, and drove, as Rhiannon focused her mind on her need and followed the coastline. It wasn't long before they found a small marina, where a dozen or so boats seemed to make themselves at home. Some were dangling from contraptions with straps that held them up out of the water. Some were floating, tied loosely to a dock.

She stopped the car and they got out, walking toward the docks, Pandora close to Rhiannon's side.

The place was dead at this hour. Dawn was just over an hour away.

"I don't know the first thing about boats," Roland told her.

"Then we'll just have to take a driver along with us." She walked ahead of him, out onto the second dock, where a young man was tying off his boat. There wasn't another person within a mile of them.

"Excuse me, but I need you to take me somewhere in your boat," Rhiannon said.

The young man looked at her, and his eyes slid down her body in appreciation. Then they landed on the cat and widened. "Uh, look, lady, I don't know what this is about, but—"

"It's an emergency. A matter of life-and-death."

"Life-and-death?"

"Yes. Yours. Now get in the boat or experience what it feels like to be catnip."

At her cue, Pandora bared her teeth and emitted a dangerous growl.

"Okay, okay." The kid held up his hands and stepped into the boat, starting the motor. Rhiannon got in, and her cat leaped in behind her. Roland untied the rope and climbed aboard last of all.

"Really, Rhiannon, the theatrics," he said. "You needn't have frightened the poor lad like that."

"He wasn't going to cooperate. I didn't have time to convince him."

The kid maneuvered the boat into the open water. Roland took the seat beside him, playing good vamp to Rhiannon's bad vamp, and pointing out the direction to take.

"Look, I'm glad to help you out, okay?" the boy said nervously. And he *was* just a boy. Perhaps twenty. "I wouldn't refuse someone in trouble. I'm not that kind of guy. I just...that panther made me nervous."

"As well she should," Rhiannon said. She watched the coastline with her eyes. She also watched the boy until she understood how to operate the controls. When they got close, she said, "Can you swim to shore from here?"

The kid looked back at her and blinked. "Oh, come on. You're not gonna steal my boat. Come on, please..."

"Young man," Roland said, "there are some soldiers just around this bend. Mercenaries, and they will start shooting at us if they see us. Now, unless you want to join us in ducking bullets..."

He scanned the shoreline as he slowed the boat's speed to a near crawl, then let it float and, finally, sit idle in the water. "I don't see any—"

"Oh, for pity sake." Rhiannon snapped a finger.

Pandora pounced, growling. The boy jumped to his feet, and the cat hit him in the chest with both paws. He went over the side, into the water, sinking out of sight. When his head popped up again, Pandora was looking over the side, and she took a couple of playful swats at him, claws retracted.

"Look, darling. Pandora wants to bob for humans." Rhiannon got into the driver's seat. She'd been watching the young man carefully and thought she had a handle on how to accelerate, decelerate, stop and steer the thing. She hoped she didn't have to attempt to make it reverse at any point. She waved to him. "Go now, swim. I'll try to bring your boat back to you in one piece."

The boy shot a pleading glance at Roland, but Roland only shrugged as Rhiannon coaxed the boat into motion. It was only twenty more yards before the first shots were fired. The shoreline rose steadily, growing into towering cliffs, and the bullets fired from on high plipped into the water around the boat. Rhiannon steered the boat in closer when she saw Eric's former home towering above, with its iron fence marching out to the very edge of the cliffs.

She slowed as the boat drew near. The soldiers above raced toward the edge, because that was the only place from which they would be able to hit them, and even then, they had to aim straight down. It was obvious they were finally aware of what had happened in the house.

"There!" Roland pointed. Rhiannon saw the dark opening in the cliff face and steered toward it, slowing the boat. She spotted Jameson and Angelica in the opening; Amber was with them. Where was the stubborn mortal, Willem Stone?

As the boat slowed, the three jumped from the mouth of the cave, which was some ten feet above the level of the water. They splashed into the water and swam closer, and Roland pulled them aboard one by one, beginning with Amber.

"Where is Will?" he asked.

"There was a rowboat about fifty yards up." Jameson hauled himself over the side and sat on the floor between the front and back seats. "When we got to the mouth, we could still see Stiles—or at least we thought it was him—in a motorboat. Looked like he was heading for that island."

Jameson pointed, and Rhiannon looked ahead. It wasn't so much an island as a jutting pillar of rock.

"Will couldn't see it—there's too much mist for mortal eyes to penetrate. But he did see the rowboat, so he dove in and swam for it. Then he took it and headed straight out there, following Stiles's motorboat.

"We need to go after him."

Amber looked at the sky, then at her parents. "It's going to be dawn soon. You don't want to be trapped out there on that treeless hunk of granite when it comes."

"We have at least another hour," Jameson said. "We can make it."

"Then let's make it quick," Rhiannon said. She raced the boat as fast as she dared, across the waves, toward the nearly perpendicular rock formation in the distance.

Sarafina struggled to remain conscious as the madman—the unnaturally strong madman—carried her

higher and higher, scaling the side of a megalith with
her thrown over his shoulder. He'd grown weary of
her blood soaking into his clothing as he'd run
through the tunnel with her, had cursed her for it,
though she'd reminded him that he was the one who'd
shot her.

When he pitched her from the cave mouth into the
sea, the salt water's sting was nearly unbearable. *Was*
unbearable—yet she bore it. For she was a vampire
and hadn't yet lost every last drop of blood in her.

The water swallowed her down, then belched her
up again, and when her head broke the surface, she
saw him at the bottom of a rope ladder that hung from
the cave. He stepped off the bottom rung, slogging
toward the shore, where a small boat was lying on
the narrow beach, tied to a scrubby tree. He pushed
the craft into the water, leaving it tied, then waded in
until he could reach Sarafina.

She was in too much pain to move away. Pain, in
her kind, was magnified a thousand times, and she
wondered how long it would be before death relieved
her of it. She'd been wrong in her fears of loving
Willem, hadn't she? It wasn't he who would die and
leave her to grieve and mourn. He was the one who
would be left behind to do the grieving.

Stiles grabbed her hair where it floated like sea-
weed on the surface and towed her to shore. All the
way up onto the tiny scrap of beach, he dragged her.
Then he knelt beside her, hooked his fingers into the

jagged bullet hole in her dress and ripped it open. He tore it up to the neckline, ripping that apart, too.

She lay there in the darkness, wondering if he thought this was supposed to make matters worse for her somehow. She had no qualms about nudity. No shyness. Good God, who did he think she was?

But no, that wasn't his objective. He scooped wet, mudlike sand, soaked by saltwater, into his hands and mercilessly packed it into the bullet wound in her belly. He ground it into the hole, and she shrieked in unbridled agony, tears springing into her eyes against her will.

And he laughed. Frank Stiles laughed at her pain.

Then he rolled her over and ground more salty sand into the exit wound at her back.

Red, then white-hot, fire filled her vision. She was quivering in anguish.

He picked her up, dropped her into the boat, then untied it, got in himself and drove it to the island. When he arrived, he threw her over one shoulder and a coiled length of rope over the other. The flow of her blood would no longer trouble him as he began hauling her up to the very precipice of the tall phallic boulder that rose from the sea to impale the sky.

And finally, at the very top, he leaned forward and let her fall onto the angled stone surface.

The impact knocked the breath from her, and her head hit so hard she felt the skin split and blood begin to seep into her hair.

Stiles knelt, bound her wrists together, then got up

and stretched the rope beyond her head, pulling her arms with it. She tipped her head backward, trying to see what he was up to. He was tying the rope around a finger of rock. Then he took out a pocketknife, sawed off the excess rope and bound her ankles to another stone protrusion below her. Ruthlessly he pulled the ankle rope tight, stretching her body, using the boulder as a pulley. As her ribs and stomach muscles pulled taut, the pain screamed.

"There's a monster coming for you soon, Sarafina."

Her mind spun, and she no longer knew if she was alive or dead, or if she'd journeyed backward in time, taken to a dark cave at the hand of her sister, left bound as an offering to a creature she had feared.

"I call it the sun. It's going to rise, and then you're going to lie here helpless as it roasts your skin. It will be a slow burn, until it gets high enough. It will come up this side of the stone, beyond your head, so it won't hit you all at once. You're going to suffer slowly, burn slowly, before you finally burst into full-blown flames."

"Over my dead body, Stiles!"

Fina lifted her head weakly. Willem stood behind Stiles on the top of the pillar, his shirt and his hair dripping wet. He was hot and breathless, and his foot was killing him. How the hell had he ever managed to climb this precipice with that bad foot? she wondered. But then she knew.

Sheer will. Will of Stone.

The two sprang at each other at the same moment, reminding Sarafina of a pair of mountain rams, vying for the ewe.

They clashed, struck, rolled on the ground.

"Will, be careful! He's stronger than a normal man—he's done something!" she cried, though it took every ounce of strength she had to make the words loud enough for him to hear.

Even as she said it, Will took a blow to the chin that launched him through the air, until he landed on his back near the very edge of the boulder.

"Let's end this," Stiles said. His pocketknife in his hand, he advanced on Will.

Will seemed to have been stunned by the impact. He was just lying there on his back, blinking his eyes as if to clear his vision.

"Willem!" Sarafina screamed. She tugged at the ropes binding her, but the pain and blood loss left her too weak to snap them.

Stiles towered over Will, raising the knife.

Will's legs suddenly hooked around Stiles's ankles, while Will reached up to grasp his wrist, jerking him forward. Stiles was falling, even as Willem rolled to the side and gave him an extra push—just enough to send him plummeting over the edge. His horrified wail stopped suddenly at the bottom. Will leaned over, looking down. "Sheesh, he didn't even clear the rocks at the bottom. Too bad."

Wincing, he got himself to his feet and came to Sarafina. He knelt beside her, where she lay. "It'll be daylight soon,'' he said softly. ''Will the bullet wound heal?''

She nodded.

He leaned over her, kissed her mouth. ''But it might not have. I might not have gotten here in time. I could have lost you. You understand that, right?''

''Will, please...just untie me.''

''I'm about to.'' He pursed his lips thoughtfully. ''If you weren't shot full of holes and the sun wasn't about to rise, I wouldn't for several hours yet. Seems to me I owe you.''

She smiled, but weakly. It hurt too much to smile.

He moved toward her ankles, unbound them, rubbed the places where the ropes had been. ''I could've lost you. I could still lose you. At any time, without warning. You're not immortal. You don't age, and you won't die of natural causes, but that's not immortality. You can die, same as I can.''

He ran his hands up her legs, over her hips, then paused, staring at the sand-packed hole in her belly. ''Should I clean this out for you?''

''No. It kept me from bleeding to death.''

He nodded; then he reached up to her wrists to untie them. As he worked the knot loose, he said, ''I love you, Sarafina. You know that, right? It was never a lie. Never a game. Never an act. I love you.''

She closed her eyes. ''Willem...''

''A year of love beats a lifetime alone. Freddy Mercury said something like that, and I'm sure he wouldn't lie.''

"Freddy...who?"

"I'm willing to risk the pain of losing you, of growing old and watching you stay young and vital. I'm willing to risk anything at all, Sarafina, just for the joy of being with you, loving you, for whatever time the universe chooses to let me. Are you willing to take that same risk for me?"

The rope came free. She lowered her hands, and he took them, lifting her wrists to his lips to kiss the rope burns.

"I don't think I have any choice in the matter, Willem. I've tried. I've told myself there's no future for us. That loving you is a guarantee of heartbreak. But it didn't stop me from loving you anyway."

"Thank God," he whispered. He lifted her body from the rock, hugging her gently to his chest.

"I have so many regrets, Willem. Things I can't change. You made me see how wrong I've been."

"About what?"

"For years I've hated my precious Dante for choosing Morgan over me. But now...now I finally understand. I'd have done the same, for you."

He nodded. "Then it's not too late to make amends."

"But there's so much else. Things I can't so easily undo. Misty and Edward, for example."

He stroked her hair. "You told me yourself they were criminals."

"But I took away their will. I never realized what

a valuable thing that was until I saw yours in action, Willem.''

"Isn't there…any way to reverse it?''

She blinked. "There might be. In that laboratory in the house, there were notebooks upon notebooks. Did you see them? And the computer, and all those shiny discs…''

"CD-ROMs.''

"Stiles must have salvaged a lot of DPI research. And no doubt he's added more. Maybe, somewhere in there, they've learned of a way to free a vampire-enslaved mind.''

"Maybe.''

She nodded, snuggled closed to him. "I'm sorry for what I did to you, Will. I'm sorry. I have no excuse.''

"You have the perfect excuse. You loved me. You were afraid to give me the chance to hurt you like everyone else you've ever loved has hurt you. Fortunately I don't have any intention of doing that.''

A motor sounded in the distance.

Will stiffened, went alert and quickly lowered her to the ground. He unbuttoned his shirt and peeled it off, handing it to her. "Put this on.''

He was apparently more concerned about her nudity than she was. She tried to sit up, failed. "Will, I can't—I can't move enough to—''

Turning, his face full of love, he eased her torn dress off her shoulders, slipped his midnight-blue, still-damp shirt on her and buttoned it up the front.

"It's Rhiannon and the others," she said.

Will glanced at the sky. "Not a moment too soon." Rising to his feet, he scooped her gently, carefully, up into his arms and began the long trek down the hill.

"Your foot is killing you," she said, feeling his pain.

"So's your bullet hole, but we still need to get down there to the boat."

He bent to kiss her forehead and continued limping down the path to the bottom.

When they finally got to sea level, the others came running toward them, Rhiannon leading the way. Her eyes shifted to the wound before meeting Sarafina's gaze again.

"You're going to survive?"

"Yes, I think so."

"Good." Rhiannon gave a nod.

Sarafina lifted her brows as Will carried her toward the waiting boat, the "princess" walking close beside her. "Good?"

Rhiannon shot her a look. "You're the first vampiress I've encountered who had the gall to challenge me, much less the power to present a real challenge." She shrugged. "Not a threat, of course, but a challenge."

"I was somewhat handicapped when we locked horns, Rhiannon."

"You were injured?"

"Heartsick."

"Ahh. So then the next time you might even land a few real blows. One never can tell." She didn't *quite* smile, but her eyes did. And she steadied Will by holding his shoulder as he stepped into the boat.

Jameson got into the driver's seat. Angelica squeezed into the center between him and Roland. Will sat in the back with Sarafina across his lap and Rhiannon in the seat beside him. Her cat curled in the small space behind their seats.

Amber stood on the rock.

"Amber? The sun will be up soon, we have to go."

She glanced at the sky, then looked around. "But...where is he? Where is Stiles?"

Fina lifted her head very weakly. "Willem pitched him from the very top. He hit the rocks below, child. You don't have to worry about him anymore."

"Where?" she asked. "I want the bastard dead. I want to see for myself that he's dead."

"Amber—"

Jameson put a calming hand on his wife's shoulder, and she fell silent. He glanced at Will, nodded once.

"Put me down, Will," Sarafina whispered. "Take her. She needs to see."

Will swallowed hard but he did as she asked, easing Sarafina onto the floor of the boat, where she could lie as flat as possible. He climbed out, and walked with Amber.

The two of them stood on the rocks, right where Stiles had fallen. There was blood. Even bits of flesh and hair on the rocks. But no sign of Stiles.

"His boat was still there," Amber said. "Just a few yards from ours, tied to a rock." Then she blinked. "But the rowboat you took wasn't. Did you tie it to the other side, Will?"

He met her eyes, thought about lying to the girl, then decided against it. "No. I left it just over there." He pointed. But of course there was no boat in sight.

"He knows more about me than I do."

"You have his notes," Will told her. "You can find out everything he learned by..."

"By killing me over and over again." She lowered her eyes. "And now maybe he can't be killed, either. Maybe he's even more of a danger to us now."

"Or maybe the waves just washed him out to sea," he said softly. "And maybe I forgot to tie my boat in my hurry to get to Sarafina."

Amber sighed, lowering her head. Her voice breaking, she said, "I don't know what I am, Will."

He slid an arm around her shoulders and turning, began walking her back to the boat and the others. "You think you've got problems? I'm in love with a vampire."

That made her laugh, just a little. He was glad to hear it. She leaned her head on his shoulder. "Sorry about almost getting you killed."

"I've been almost getting killed my entire adult life, kid. Think nothing of it."

The boat came into sight, and he helped her in, let her have the seat, then wedged himself onto the floor with Sarafina.

Fina searched his eyes, a question in hers. He gave his head a slight shake, left, then right.

Then Rhiannon caught his eyes, her own guiding them to follow her gaze to a small speck far out in the water.

He narrowed his. It looked like...a man, in a row-boat.

Rhiannon looked at him again. Her brows furrowed. Will thought he knew what she was thinking.

Sarafina looked from one of them to the other. "You didn't find him?" she asked. "You didn't find Stiles?"

Will said softly, "No."

"But...that means he could have survived the fall. That means..."

"It means we didn't find the body," Will said. "And that's all it means, Fina."

But he could see by the look in her eyes that she thought it might mean more, and he couldn't quite keep himself from wondering if it did.

*   *   *   *   *